THE INCA CON

JC RYAN

BOOKS

By JC Ryan

Dedicated to my good friend Mitch Pender, a military dog trainer, for giving me the idea for this series and guiding me through the intricate and amazing capabilities and psychology of those majestic four-legged soldiers.
Mitch has a lifetime of experience and exceptional depth of knowledge as a military dog handler and trainer.

Vinci Books

vinci-books.com

Published by Vinci Books Ltd in 2025

1

A CIP catalogue record for this book is available from the British Library.

Paperback ISBN: 9781036704698

About The Inca Con

Rex Dalton, and his best friend, Digger, the former military dog, are exploring the remarkable history of Peru when they befriend a retired American couple. The couple invites them to join their expedition to a remote village high up in the Andes Mountains to inspect an archaeological site in which they want to invest.

But on arrival in the village, it doesn't take long for Rex to discover that his new friends are victims of a cleverly designed con. Rex could not stand by idly while the old couple is swindled out of their money.

But when he and Digger get involved, they soon find they have to deal with more than just the conman. A terrorist group also gets involved in the scheme, and if that is not enough, the conman calls in help as well. Not only does Rex have to protect the old couple he also has to protect the villagers.

Chapter One

He'd chosen the high road, which added two hours to his
route, but he was in no hurry. The roundabout route
rewarded him with a lifetime of breathtaking vistas to this
invigorating experience. Walking easterly from Abancay to
Curahuasi, Peru, the higher peaks of the Andes were
usually on his left, while glimpses through river gorges
flanked by lower peaks could be had on the right. Plenty of
switchbacks reversed the views in some places, and at times
they walked toward the north or the south, following the
steep road that would eventually lead downward as steeply
as it had led upward.

Rex Dalton and his constant companion, his Dutch
Shepherd dog, Digger, had arrived in Lima on the day of
the spring equinox. In the intervening weeks, they'd
wandered as the wind took them, exploring the rich history
of the western bulge of Peru. They had just missed the best
traveling weather for one of the most famous of all Peruvian destinations, Machu Picchu. Before the rainy season
started in earnest, it was time.

Approaching the Sacred Valley on foot had been a whim, but after nearly fifteen hours on the road from Abancay, where he turned in his rental vehicle, Rex was committed to the plan. The difference between fifteen hours on foot and four in a car was the opportunity to stop and drink in the spectacular scenery that would have otherwise whizzed by barely noticed.

Digger seemed to enjoy it, too, dashing here and there to inspect some item of interest only to a dog. A bit of a nuisance, but a bit entertaining, was Digger's apparent mission to catch a vizcacha. The peculiar animals, related to chinchillas but looking more like a long-tailed, rather short-eared rabbit, were plentiful along the trail. Their homes, resembling a prairie-dog colony in numbers, interested Digger a great deal, and Rex found it amusing to see him race around after an adult, while the rest of them hurried the babies in among the rocks where he couldn't reach them.

Rex had camped overnight, though he could have walked the entire fifteen hours in one day. He'd elected to break it up because there would be only twelve hours of sunlight. Starting before dawn wouldn't have been an issue but descending the last set of switchbacks after dark wasn't prudent. He planned to get to Curahuasi in time for a midday meal before finding a room for the night, and he was on target when he reached the intersection of Route 116 – the high road – and 3S, the main road. Only a little over a mile to go.

When Rex arrived in the center of the dusty little town, he looked for a café first. He'd have preferred one with tables outside, but the first one he came to had only a wide opening for a door, with tables inside. Oddly enough, it was a pizza restaurant. Digger's nose lifted at the aromas emanating from the open door.

"Really, Digger? You want pizza in Peru?"

Digger's mouth stretched in a dog's broad grin, his tongue lolled out, and if he could have spoken, he'd have said, "Why not?"

Rex could think of several reasons why not, including that garlic, an essential ingredient of pizza in his opinion, was toxic to dogs. And the fact that he had no idea what a Peruvian pizza might have for toppings. But it seemed to be the only option. He'd have to figure out something else for Digger, who had made it clear from the time they became partners that he expected human food. They'd had an ongoing struggle on that subject, and Rex had become an expert on what Digger could or shouldn't eat.

As he stepped inside, and his eyes adjusted to the dim interior from the bright sunlight outside, he realized it wasn't the dingy, dirt-floored establishment he'd expected. The tables were draped with cream-colored cloths, brown runners placed precisely in the middle to bisect the length. A clean tile floor, devoid of animal hair, suggested the place wasn't dog-friendly.

"Digger, you'd better wait outside. Stay."

Digger flopped down on his belly with a sigh that Rex interpreted as dissatisfied acquiescence.

"Hey, you picked the place. I'll bring you a slice, and if you behave, maybe more."

Rex went on in and allowed a young woman with a sleek black bun at the nape of her neck to lead him to a table. The establishment wasn't crowded, but a couple of other tables were occupied, one by two men talking earnestly in stage whispers, and the other by an older couple, tanned and fit for their apparent age, which was betrayed by their graying hair.

The two men could have been American or European, but they spoke English. The whispers didn't convey an accent. Both were blond, though one was older than the other. Rex couldn't see their eyes, and they didn't appear to be much above or below average height.

Rex ordered the house special, wondering if it would resemble an American or an Italian pizza in any way. He didn't particularly care. He wasn't picky about his food. In his thirty-six years, he'd dined on unremarkable but satisfying home cooking from the German-influenced kitchen of his midwestern-raised mother, to the cuisine of countries all over the world in his past life as a field operative of a top-secret black ops paramilitary organization. It was during his time in the latter that he learned that food, as long as it wouldn't make him sick, was fuel, which would keep him going.

Digger might turn up his nose, though. He was a real pain in the ass sometimes when it came to food.

As he waited for his order to arrive, Rex became aware that the two men were discussing a misfortune that had befallen one of them, the younger one. He would have ignored them but couldn't tune them out as the whispers became more strident and the younger man's voice rose. With less than a foot between the tables, which were lined up in military precision, side by side, he and the couple on the other side of the table where the men were seated were witnesses to the narrative, whether they wanted to hear it or not.

"I'm telling you, I don't know what to do," the younger man hissed.

"And I'm telling you, your money is gone, and you might as well accept that fact," the older one said with exaggerated patience. "There's nothing you *can* do. Unless you've left something out. Tell me again."

The younger man sighed heavily. "Telling you again won't change the outcome." His voice raised a few decibels.

"Just humor me."

"Okay. Now please pay attention. I was looking at some curios in the marketplace over in Abancay. They looked old, and I thought I'd buy a statue of Virachocha."

The older man interrupted. "Who's that again?"

"The Inca god of creation. I've told you this. And it isn't important. Just that it looked old." The younger man was becoming more agitated, and his voice was rising in both volume and pitch.

"Okay, go on."

"So, I'm looking at this statue, and this woman comes up to me and takes it out of my hands. She says, 'It's a fake.'"

"Did you believe her?"

"For crap's sake, will you just let me tell the story?"

The older man took a long drink from the brown bottle in front of him and slammed it back on the table. "Fine. Go ahead."

"I asked her, 'How do you know?', and she says she's Ministry. She hands me a card. Ministry of Culture, it says. She tells me there are more fakes being sold than the genuine article, and then, get this, she says, 'Lucky for you. Because it's illegal to buy or sell the genuine antiquities.'

"It freaked me out. It was like she was threatening me, just because I was looking at this old statue, you know? Like she was accusing me of robbing Peru's cultural heritage."

He stopped speaking, shook his head, and took a swig from his bottle of beer.

"And that was the last you saw her?"

"Yeah, that was the last I saw her. But before she left, she told me to call the number on her card if anyone offered me something that could be original. Seems the shop owners have gotten smart. They don't put the real antiquities out for people to see. But when they see an American, like me, they think we all have money."

"You do have money."

"That's beside the point. They'll offer the real deal to Americans or other unsuspecting tourists. So, I was supposed to call this Agent Gonzales if that happened to me, and she'd come and arrest the shop owner."

"And it happened to you," the older man prompted, earning a glare from the raconteur.

"It did. Very next day, I'm looking at stuff in the Mercado Central here, and this creepy old man comes out and whispers he has what I'm looking for in the back. I mean, could have been anything, from drugs to women, whatever. I was curious, right? So, I follow him into the back room, and there's this gorgeous gold medallion, had to be a good four ounces of high-grade gold, right? Carved in the shape of Inti."

"I hesitate to ask."

"The sun god. Jeez, don't you ever listen to anything I tell you?"

The older man made a gesture with his hand, to indicate the other should continue.

"So, I'm thinking, that's gotta be the genuine article. I tell the shop owner, 'Just a minute. I need to get my partner here to talk about this.' I'm gonna call the agent, right?

Gonzales? But the shop owner says, 'You must hurry. Another buyer is coming.'

"I figure he's playing me, but then someone else comes in to look at it. He and the shop owner are jabbering away in Spanish, and he pulls out his wallet. So I figure, I've got seconds to get this, and I'd better do it, or this priceless artifact will be gone forever. You should have seen the guy who entered the shop – he was swarthy."

"Swarthy? Did you just say 'swarthy'? The hell does that mean?"

"You know. Dark. Dark skin, dark hair, dark personality. I figure he's a smuggler."

"Oh, for Pete's sake." The older guy shook his head.

Rex shared his disgust. The young guy was looking more and more like an idiot. He couldn't help but think about the old adage; since light travels faster than sound, some people appear to be bright until you hear them speak. He'd just described every native Peruvian male, except for the personality part. Rex thought Peruvians were unaccountably happy, considering their poverty.

"No, seriously. This guy was not a good guy. So I tell the shop owner I'll take it."

"You bought the statue."

"Yeah, but first it was a bidding war. I had to pay almost a hundred thousand for it."

"Dollars?" The older man's eyebrows levitated to a spot under his shock of blond bangs.

"Soles. But that's still a chunk of change, about thirty K US, right?"

"And you bought it why?"

"To keep it from leaving the country, of course! I figured the shop owner would get busted, I'd get my money back, and this Gonzales chick might be grateful, know what I mean?" The younger man leered as he said it.

"Shit, Junior, how thick are you? So, what's the problem? She's not grateful enough?"

"The *problem* is that the number on the card is fake."

"And…"

"And as soon as I called and found out it was fake, I got worried. I mean, could I get arrested for buying this thing?"

"I have no idea, you might very well find your ass in the slammer."

"Well, *that's* my problem."

"I suggest you pre-empt it all and go to the police and tell *them* this story," the older man said, with a show of indifference.

"Dude, that could get me thrown in jail!" the young man continued.

"I don't know what you want me to do about it. I swear you've got more money than brains. Man up."

"But, Uncle Rich, what if they arrest me?"

Rex looked from the blond older man to the tow-headed youth. He didn't see a resemblance, other than the color of their hair. Maybe the 'uncle' was honorary.

What difference does it make? None. I'm not involved in this.

Rex had to put his hand over his face to hide the grin when Einstein's words popped up in his mind. "Two things are infinite: the universe and human stupidity; and I'm not sure about the universe."

Rex had eaten all the pizza he wanted, and he knew Digger was waiting for his share. Surprisingly, it was a pretty good pizza. Digger would be picky about it. He didn't like green peppers. But he'd eat everything else, including the olives. For some unknown reason, Digger loved black olives.

The pepperoni was a given, but the pepperoni here had garlic in it. He asked the server to have a small pizza made up with no sauce, cheese, or pepperoni. "Just vegetables, please, but no garlic, onions or green pepper. And lots of grilled chicken." Digger would enjoy it, it wouldn't be bad for him, and it would help extend the supply of dog food they could carry while on foot.

Without waiting to hear the uncle's solution to the kid's problem, Rex left the café and gave Digger his 'pizza'. Rex still found it bewildering to watch the dog every time he fed him. A meal which Rex would spend twenty to thirty minutes on to consume, Digger gulped down in less than thirty seconds with three to four bites, and then, most amazing of all, he would sit back, lick his lips, and look accusatory at Rex as if to say, 'when are you going to feed me? I had nothing to eat all day'.

When the dog had finished, Rex rooted in Digger's pannier-style backpack for his collapsible bowl and a bottle of water. Digger lapped the water gratefully.

When Rex had first planned to hike instead of driving in Peru, he'd wondered if Digger would allow the contraption. He needn't have worried. It was like the harness Digger was used to, except that it had a soft cotton canvas bridge over his back with expandable side pockets attached. A sturdy handle allowed him to hold it while Digger stepped out when it was time to take it off, and provided a ring for a leash, which stayed in one of the pockets most of the time.

Rex had put it on him empty at first. When Digger didn't seem to mind that, he started adding weight gradually, until the dog was carrying his own food, water, and toys. At the last minute, Rex had added the coms units and night-vision camera that fit on Digger's regular harness. He didn't anticipate trouble, but experience had taught him trouble seemed to find them anyway. In any case, Rex thought it was only fair for Digger to carry his share, and Digger seemed to agree.

The next order of business was a room, a shower, and a good night's sleep in a real bed. Then he'd replenish their supplies and be on his way to Cuzco.

Chapter Two

The next destination on Rex's agenda was Cusco, jumping off point for tourist attractions throughout the Sacred Valley. Rex wasn't averse to using a guide, and in some cases, it was required. However, walking in a crowd of tourists wasn't his style. Besides, he preferred to acclimate himself to the altitude gradually, by walking from village to village and the historical sites that fascinated him.

Rex had a keen interest in history. Formally trained with double major undergraduate degrees in history and linguistics, he'd further refined his interests with an MA in political science. He had a facility with languages that bordered on the savant. He would have described it, had anyone asked, as a 'knack', but that would have been modesty—it was much more than that. He'd been fluent in German, French and Spanish by the time he'd graduated high school and had a little Italian then, as well. Since then he'd become fluent in Italian and added Mandarin, Arabic, and Hindi to his language repertoire. On this trip, within a couple of months of arriving in Peru, he'd been conversant in

Quechuan, the ancient language spoken by eight to ten million of the indigenous people living in the more isolated rural areas across South America, including Peru.

However, he'd abandoned his plans to enter diplomatic service after his parents and younger siblings, a brother and a sister, were killed in the 2004 bombing of a train station in Madrid, where the family was enjoying a vacation in cele-bration of Rex's newly-minted MA. A short stint in the Marines followed by training as a Delta Force operator, rapidly morphed into his being headhunted as a special field operative for Crisis Response Consultancy, otherwise known as CRC after the fashion of government alphabet-soup agencies. CRC operated where the government, including the CIA, could not.

All that and more was water under the bridge now. Circumstances beyond his control had interrupted that career, and his control of circumstances since then was what had given him the leisure to pursue his first love – the study of history – in the places where it had happened. He had no specific itinerary, no timelines to keep—he went where he wanted when he wanted, and Digger never protested. For now, that was Peru and the Inca civilization.

How he'd come to be traveling with Digger, the former Australian military dog, was part of the career interruption. He'd become a reluctant dog owner with the dying words of a good friend, Digger's handler. In the months since then, Rex had overcome his childhood fear of dogs and learned to trust Digger's instincts, though, especially in the early days of their friendship, he wasn't always fond of the dog's demands. In his field agent days at CRC, Rex preferred to work alone on missions, but since he and Digger were forced to team up, he had to admit, Digger was smarter than many people. The dog had snatched Rex's bacon out of the fire as often as it had been the other way around. They'd wrangled for alpha position in the early days, and Rex had a sneaking suspicion that if he held it, it was only because Digger had conceded out of pity or because Rex had bribed him with peanut butter served in his favorite toy, a now-battered Kong, the peculiar-looking, ribbed, hard-rubber toy dogs loved because of its erratic way of bouncing and the hole in the middle that could hide treats. Digger preferred his filled with peanut butter or lamb jerky. Truth be told, they probably shared the alpha position depending on the circumstances.

On the morning after his arrival in Curahuasi, refreshed by a tepid shower and a night's sleep in a real, though lumpy, bed, Rex was whistling cheerily as he and Digger stopped at a bodega for supplies to last for the three-day trek to Cusco. His map had estimated twenty-eight hours of walking. He'd decided to take it leisurely, making sure he'd be able to see the sights along the way, even if that required a side-trek. Once he reached Cusco, he'd turn north for the Sacred Valley, and take the adventures as they came.

At the bodega, he recognized the older couple who'd been seated on the other side of the men who'd had such a contentious conversation at the pizza restaurant the evening before. He avoided eye contact, unwilling to be delayed by chatting with them, though they seemed pleasant enough.

However, they must have taken note of him as he had of them. The woman greeted him in English. Rex, ever mindful of not standing out, smiled just politely enough to avoid rudeness and returned her greeting with the same careful degree of civility. Then he turned away, intent on his shopping. It didn't work.

"Excuse me, young man, but weren't you in the restaurant last night? We didn't get a chance to introduce ourselves, because of that… oh dear how shall I say it… 'unfortunate' young man."

Rex looked around, pretending he thought she was talking to someone else.

"Yes, I'm sure it was you. Tell me, what did you think of that story we couldn't help but overhear?"

He had to give her credit for her persistence. "I didn't pay much attention," he responded.

"You left before the end of it. But we could see you were paying attention. Oh, I'm sorry, how rude of me. I'm Florence Marks. Barry! Barry, come over here and meet… I'm sorry, what did you say your name was?"

"I didn't say." Rex had several names, as evidenced by his growing collection of passports. He was traveling under the name Raymond Davis for this trip. Resigned to the delay, he answered, "Ray Davis. Nice to meet you."

"And you. So, what did you think of that?" she continued.

Rex glanced at Mr. Marks, who offered him a weak smile in apology for his wife's insistence on engaging Rex in conversation.

Rex decided to be honest, and hope that would help extricate him from the conversation sooner. "I think he was scammed and should go to the police. But honestly, it's none of my business."

"That's exactly what we told him! Isn't it, dear?" She included her silent husband as if it mattered to Rex whether he agreed or not. The man didn't respond.

"Good advice. Hope he took it," Rex muttered.

"Oh, is that your furbaby?" Mrs. Marks exclaimed, spotting Digger's interest from just outside the open-air market's entrance.

Rex suppressed an urge to roll his eyes.

Good thing Digger wouldn't understand that word or Mrs. Marks might have earned herself an indignant growl.

"Well, I call him my buddy," he managed. Digger's tail wagged uncertainly, as if he understood he was being discussed.

"May I pet him?"

"He's a working dog, ma'am. Whether you can pet him depends on him. He'll let you know if it's okay."

Mrs. Marks' face went blank. "Oh, well, then I probably shouldn't."

"Maybe that's best. If you'll excuse me, I meant to get an early start. I just need to finish my shopping. Goodbye." Rex edged away, hoping he hadn't sounded too abrupt, but there was probably not an easy way to make a clean getaway from Mrs. Marks.

"We're going to Cusco. Is that where you're headed?"

Rex would have preferred not to say, but he didn't have a ready lie. "Er, yes."

"Maybe we'll see you there at dinner. Are you taking the Machu Picchu tour that starts day after tomorrow?"

"No, ma'am. I'm hiking. I won't be there until the day after that. To Cusco, I mean." Rex took another step away before Mrs. Marks squealed in dismay.

"I'm so sorry! Maybe we could give you a lift to Cusco? Would that help?"

Before Rex could think of a polite way to say he was walking by choice and wouldn't accept a lift even if she weren't a nosy old biddy, Mr. Marks finally intervened.

"Dear, maybe Mr. Davis is walking because he wants to." To Rex, he said, "I'm sorry. Since our son died, she thinks she needs to mother anyone his age."

Rex felt instant regret about his thoughts on the woman's gregariousness. Having lost his entire family, he understood lingering grief and that it manifested in different ways at different times. "That's all right. I'm sorry for your loss."

"It was a long time ago. But thank you." Mr. Marks stuck out his hand and Rex shook it firmly. "Good luck on your hike."

"Thanks. Good luck on your tour."

Rex finished his shopping, spoke in Quechuan to the proprietor as he paid for his purchases, and waved at the Marks couple as he left. Mrs. Marks gave him a fond smile and waved back.

Before they left, Rex divided his purchases among his backpack and the panniers on Digger's, then hoisted his to his back. "Let's hit the trail, buddy."

Despite it being late spring south of the equator, the air was chilly at nearly nine-thousand feet of altitude. Rex was dressed for the temperature he expected at noon, around fifty-six degrees. At only a couple of hours after sunrise, he'd donned a colorful poncho against the chill. Earlier in his travels, he'd abandoned his light jacket for the poncho. It was much more practical, as it served double duty as a blanket at night and was more efficiently folded for carrying in a roll on his backpack when he was ready to take it off. Otherwise, he wore long denim pants, a Western-style long-sleeved plaid shirt with snaps, and a pair of light-weight hiking boots.

Except for the high-end ultralight backpack he wore, the hiking boots, and his stature, just under six feet but taller than the natives by inches, he might have passed for an urban Peruvian. Weeks in the high altitude of Peru had tanned his naturally olive skin to a shade close to the Mestizo population of the cities, and his dark hair and eyes did nothing to dispel that image. Even his Quechuan, limited though it was, sounded native, an indication of his rare talent for picking up languages and speaking them without a foreign accent. And his vocabulary was growing with every encounter he had with the native population. He'd be fluent before he left, if the past was anything to go by.

Digger showed his appreciation for the cool of the early morning by trotting up to twenty or thirty yards ahead and then racing back to Rex's side. He'd be less eager to run ahead when the sun was directly overhead, beating on his black coat with the intensity found only where the air was thinner. Fortunately, their path crossed streams and lay under trees in many spots, when it wasn't along well-populated areas in the rich farmland of the region. Digger would have plenty of water or shade to stay cool enough, and their trek would gain over two thousand feet of altitude, making it cooler yet. And another reason to hike rather than drive was that they'd get used to the altitude gradually, as they'd been doing since leaving Lima.

Rex let his mind wander, relaxing his guard for the first time since he'd begun to suspect that his old mentor, John Brandt, CEO of CRC, was looking for him. No one would look for him here.

Chapter Three

Flo Marks was seventy-three, but she prided herself on having the health and body of a much younger woman and thought of herself as middle aged. Unlike her husband, she didn't take her identity from the company he'd sold a few years before. She had her own independent persona with a lot of interests, health and fitness among them. She hadn't allowed herself to get soft or fat... *heavy*, she reminded herself. Political correctness was important to her, too. She had to admit, though, she was glad the trail from Cusco to Machu Picchu led mostly downward. More for Barry's sake than hers.

Flo worried about Barry. Before he'd retired, he worked too hard and neglected his health. Afterward, he'd seemed lost, bereft of his beloved company. Their only son, dead too young from a motorcycle accident, had left them without the pleasure of grandchildren in their old age. She missed him, and she missed the grandchildren they'd never have. So, when Barry found a new interest and suggested they spend some of the fortune he'd made from the sale of the company by encouraging responsible archaeology, she'd welcomed it as a worthy cause which would serve a dual purpose—a new interest that would keep her husband's mind occupied and get him out of the house.

They'd set aside an amount that would see them comfortably through the rest of their lives, enough to take trips like this one and stay busy. And the rest, Barry had placed in a foundation for grants to archaeologists. Flo knew he hoped a find of historic significance would come of it before they died. Which, if it depended on her, she intended to be no less than twenty-five or thirty years from now, because she took care of her health and tried to take care of Barry's, though he didn't seem to appreciate it.

She turned to gaze fondly at her tall husband, still handsome, though his red hair had turned white.

"What?" he asked after becoming aware she was staring at him.

"Do you need more sunscreen?" she asked.

"Stop fussing, Flo. I'm fine."

She looked away to hide a smile. He knew she adored him. She knew the feeling was mutual. They'd been married long enough that neither needed to say it every time they thought it.

They'd walked another half a mile when Flo noticed someone was pacing them. She looked to her left, and to her surprise, saw the young man from the restaurant in Curahuisa.

"Oh, hello," she said.

"Hi. I noticed you when we stopped for lunch. Didn't know you were taking this tour," he said.

Flo thought he left unsaid that he'd thought they were too old. She bristled a little.

"I wanted to thank you," he went on. "I took your advice and went to the police."

Flo's motherly instincts kicked in, though this young man was closer to the age a grandchild would have been, had her son lived. "Oh, I'm so glad! It worked out, I guess, since you're here."

"Well, I didn't get arrested. They laughed at me, though. I guess it's one of the oldest scams in the book. The woman who said she was from the Ministry of Culture, the shopkeeper, even the other customer, were probably all in on it."

The boy looked sheepish, Flo thought. She supposed she'd feel the same way, if she'd lost that much money. *Thirty-thousand dollars!*

"I hope that wasn't all you had," she said, inadvertently revealing she'd been eavesdropping on the details of his conversation with the older man.

"Oh, no. I mean, I can afford it, but no one likes to be scammed. And I should know better. By the way, I'm Junior Roper. Short for Walter Henry Roper Jr. You've probably heard of my dad."

Flo couldn't say she had, but she didn't want to embarrass the boy. "I'm sure I must have. But please forgive me, my memory…" She let it trail off. It went against her grain to admit to a failure of middle age, even as a polite fiction. She never, *ever*, thought of herself as elderly. Middle-aged was as far as she was willing to go.

"Anyway, I just wanted to thank you. I won't intrude on your holiday." He started to stride forward.

"Nonsense. We're on the same tour. How could you be intruding. Let me introduce you to my husband. Barry, do you remember this young man?"

She went on to remind him, and to introduce them.

Barry reached over to shake Junior's hand and say something vague and polite about Machu Picchu.

Junior's eyes lit up. "I've wanted all my life to see the ruins," he said. "I'm something of an amateur archaeologist."

Flo knew what would happen next. Before she fully articulated her thought, Barry had switched places with her to walk next to the young man. And before a minute had passed, the two were deep into a conversation about archaeology and the general lack of funding for it. Junior said he'd started to pursue it as a course of study leading to a career, but his father had needed his hand in the family business because of illness.

Hours later, Flo had begun to think of Junior as an orphan in need of a father figure, and her husband as the very man to fill the role. Between the rigors of business and their mutual love of archaeology, Barry and Junior had formed a fast bond.

Flo drifted away from the two to find someone else to talk with as they walked, and then found them still together when the group stopped for the night. As the porters pitched the tents and the cooks began preparing the meal, Junior excused himself.

"Did you enjoy your chat with the young man?" Flo asked Barry.

"I did, and it was more than a chat. You'll never guess what we talked about."

"Archaeology, obviously," she answered.

"Honey, he's done some digging around here…"

"As an archaeologist?" she interrupted.

"No, as in detecting. He's discovered ruins near a village high in the Andes, beyond Machu Picchu. No one knows about them. No tourists, I mean. And the ruins haven't been excavated. He's going there when this tour gets back to Cusco and get this… we're invited!"

Flo saw in Barry's face that he was completely in love with the idea of going. "How high?" she asked.

"Don't worry. Junior said we can take our time getting used to the altitude. And he'll bring oxygen for us, just in case."

"For you, you mean. I'll be fine." Flo patted Barry's protruding belly fondly. "Maybe this hike will help reduce that."

"We can go?" he asked, hopefully.

"My love, we can do anything you want," she answered. She was not going to spike his dreams.

Chapter Four

Rex had been disappointed at first to learn that his original plan to visit one of the most famous sites in Peru on his own would not be permitted. Everyone who visited Machu Picchu was required to have a guide for the privilege. He'd had his pick among several tours, some lasting multiple days, one lasting two days, and the one he chose – which left Ollantaytambo on a train on the old Cusco Machu Picchu railroad to within seven miles of the ancient city.

By the time he'd begun his hiking approach to Cusco, he was resigned to it. The advantage was that he and his guide would be alone as they entered, arriving midafternoon, rather than in the early morning with the rest of the tours. He had sufficient command of the language to ask the guide for silence, and except for necessary directions and a short conversation during the lunch break when they stopped walking to share a meal, the guide had complied.

During the meal, he'd asked Rex to confirm he didn't want any of the patter pointing out sights along the way. Rex had said something about wanting to experience the visit reverently and spiritually. The guide had looked at him with respect and acquiesced. They were walking along the old train tracks, since Digger wasn't allowed on the Inca Trail. Rex considered it a fortunate circumstance rather than an inconvenience. He preferred Digger's company to crowds anyway.

When they got to the edge of the forest near the gate to the ruins, the guide explained that Digger must remain outside the perimeter. Rex had anticipated it, so he'd fitted Digger with the coms units before they'd left the hostel that morning. With his own earbud and mic in place, he'd be able to keep tabs on the dog to be sure he wasn't getting into some sort of trouble. He'd have welcomed a camera view as well, but he didn't want to be burdened with the iPad as he viewed the city.

Rex led Digger a few yards back into the trees and commanded, *Stay*. Digger scratched in the dirt and circled a few times until he was satisfied with the nest he created in the grass beneath the trees and then flopped down with a sigh. Rex placed his backpack nearby and told Digger to guard it. Then he rejoined the guide on the trail and continued to the entrance gate.

It was after entering that Rex realized he was not going to be alone with his silent guide. The place was teeming with tourists who'd arrived on foot or by bus earlier in the day. His guide told him they'd be leaving soon, by five p.m. when the site officially closed. His tour ended at six, so there would be a short window during which he could see the ruins as the city might have looked centuries before, without scores of modern tourists in the way.

In his earbuds, Rex could hear the sounds indicating that Digger was greeting other dogs and presumably people. He counted on the dog's good behavior toward the tourists and his protective instincts for the safety of their gear. Just in case, he spoke to Digger occasionally, praising him for being good, which Digger acknowledged with a soft yap.

Rex noticed that the tourists that were in bigger groups were following their guides closely for the most part. Very few were wandering off marked trails. His own guide had taken him to the western edge of the plateau and showed him the steep drop-off, cautioning him to be careful. After that, he left Rex to his own devices as he wandered among the ruins, recalling in near-perfect detail the maps and guidebooks he'd studied in preparation for the trip.

The afternoon was pleasant, and Rex lost track of the time until he noticed fewer and fewer people around him. When they'd all but disappeared, he soaked up the vistas he'd craved.

Perched some eight-thousand feet above sea level, Machu Picchu is a visual marvel and a technical master-piece ranking among the most iconic and significant archeo-logical sites in the world. Yet its origins remain a mystery to this day.

The Inca who built it and lived there until the early 16th century before suddenly abandoning it didn't leave a record of the reason for its construction.

Archaeologists were still speculating; it was too big to be a local settlement, it was too small and not the right structure to have been an administrative center for the Inca Empire.

Despite its reputation as one of the most important Inca monuments, the citadel holds secrets which will probably never be revealed.

When, why, and for what purpose was it built? Why was it abandoned? And why did the Spanish conquistadors never know anything about Machu Picchu?

After an hour, he judged it was time to meet his guide at the spot they'd agreed on near the tourist entrance and made his way there, unworried that he saw no one else.

Rex waited for about half an hour, idly thinking about the history of this magnificent example of the advanced civilization the Incas had enjoyed. Then he realized it was getting dark because the sun had set, and glanced at his watch. It was nearly six-thirty, well after the time his guide should have met him. Rex had come to understand that in South America, time was mutable. A 'firm' appointment at six p.m. was more of a guideline than a deadline and meant 'about' six p.m., which in turn meant half an hour, give or take, either side of the agreed time meant he was on time. Rex wasn't worried, precisely, but it did give him pause that the main gates were closed and locked. He told himself his guide must have a key.

Rex's voice echoed off the nearby ruin walls and drifted out over the edge of the plateau as he called out his guide's name. He was cognizant of the enormous task ahead of him if he had to search the site. With over eighty-thousand acres to comb, though much of it was free of buildings, searching on his own after dark had fallen was out of the question. He could walk off the edge of a terrace and fall, possibly to his death.

After a few more calls, he became a bit more concerned. If some accident had befallen his guide, it would most likely have happened in the urban section, across the site to the east, past the wall that divided it from the agricultural section, where he said he'd be waiting for Rex. Rex took a moment to choose how to approach the problem, knowing he had virtually no daylight left to conduct an extensive search.

Could Digger somehow get through? If he did, would

he understand to look for the guide without a scent object to tell him who to look for? Rex decided there was only one way to find out – let him try. He reasoned that Digger would be able to better detect the edges of the plateau through subtle cues that he wouldn't have access to as a human. The updraft from the edge, the different smells in it, coupled with dogs' ability to see better at dusk and dawn than humans can would assist him.

He called Digger to come.

Rex stayed where he was. He didn't need to make it any harder for Digger to find him by moving around, though he knew it wouldn't matter. Digger's nose *would* find him. He trusted the dog to find his own way into the site. Rex had seen people carrying small dogs in the site, though the rules said they couldn't come. He assumed the reason was the potential damage to the site from the animals' waste. Digger wouldn't do that, he hoped. He didn't have any plastic bags with him to clean up afterward. But he'd observed that while Digger was working, he seldom stopped for bathroom breaks unless Rex told him to.

While Rex waited, he tried to think of contingencies in case the guide had gone missing or, God forbid, had been seriously injured. Before he'd thought of a way to get a seriously injured man to Agua Calientes, the closest town, he was surprised by Digger greeting him with licks to his hands. It was already so dark that Rex could barely see the black dog.

"Digger, buddy, we've got a problem," he said. He'd been talking to the dog in human sentences since he'd become responsible for him. In the beginning of their partnership, Rex thought it was necessary for him to undergo some dog handler training to be able to manage Digger. However, over time, the two of them somehow surmounted the language barrier to the point that Rex was prepared to swear, under oath, that Digger could read his mind.

"Boy, we've got ourselves a little hiccup here, I think. Our guide is missing. Remember him?" Rex held out his right hand, palm up, for Digger to sniff. He'd shaken the guard's hand hours before, as they parted ways after agreeing to meet here. It was a long shot. "Scout," he commanded.

Digger hesitated, his head tilted.

"Hey buddy, don't look at me like that. You know what I want. Go find him, Digger. Scout." Rex repeated.

Digger wheeled and ran out into the flat, grassy area of the center of the Agricultural district. He ran here and there, sniffing at the ground. Rex hoped he wasn't investigating where llamas and alpacas had been, or where other tourists had set down their lapdogs. Then Digger's head came up, and he headed purposefully toward the path that led to the City Gate, the ancient structure that allowed limited access to the Urban section.

Rex followed.

He took it to mean that his assumption about the guide's whereabouts was correct, and that Digger had picked up the scent. "Take it slow, buddy," he called. "Wait for me." His reason for slowing Digger down was primarily to give the dog time to sense an edge if he came close to one, but a close second was because it was getting darker by the minute. Until a moon made its appearance above the distant peaks, he wouldn't be able to see Digger if he were more than a couple of yards out. Without his iPad and Digger's night-vision camera, he was blind.

From the time they crossed into the Urban section, Rex was calling out, hoping the guide would answer. What it would mean if he couldn't, Rex didn't want to think about.

First order of business – find him. Then see what has to be done, if anything.

"Digger, to me, buddy. Come."

Digger's wet nose found Rex's hand, and Rex grabbed the handle of his back pack to keep him there. "Sorry, buddy. I'm going to have to put the leash on you. This is for me, this time. I need you to guide me."

As if he'd understood, Digger stood patiently while Rex pawed through the panniers, finding the leash by feel. He hooked it to one of the D-rings and stood. "Okay, boy. Find him. Scout."

Digger took off rapidly, almost jerking Rex off his feet. "Whoa, slow down!" Rex said to Digger. In a louder voice, he called the guide's name again. This time, he was rewarded with a faint reply. He felt Digger tense against the end of the leash. Rex also tensed as he saw Digger sensed something was wrong and was anxious to get to his target. It wasn't looking good.

He called out again, in Spanish, "We're coming!" Then he repeated it in Quechuan. The voice answered, this time closer. Now Rex could hear him well enough to make out what he was saying. He knew then he'd found the guide, and it was he who was injured or stranded – Rex couldn't quite tell which.

A few minutes later, the leash went slack at the same time as the guide began uttering thanks to God, mixed with sobs. Rex felt his way down the leash and sank to his knees when he felt the guide's body beneath his hands.

"What happened, *amigo*?" he asked.

As the guide told his story, Rex felt his arms and legs, finding the compound fracture of the guide's femur just as he got to the part where he was accidentally pushed off the terrace above by a rambunctious child, he thought. Though he cried out, no one came to check on him. It had happened minutes before five, he thought. Perhaps the child was running because frantic parents were calling. He didn't know. All he knew was he couldn't move without agony.

Rex felt equally helpless. He had nothing with which to splint the leg. Without splinting it, even if he could move confidently in the dark, he doubted he could carry the guard through the narrow streets and up and down the terraces and steps without hurting him. It looked like they were there for the night, which wasn't ideal.

They wouldn't die of the cold, though they wouldn't be very comfortable. The average night temperature was about forty-five Fahrenheit, Rex remembered. Fortunately, the rainy season, though close, had not started, so he thought they could count on it being dry. His biggest challenge would be keeping the guide from going into shock, if he hadn't already.

Rex felt for the guide's wrist and took his pulse, the weak illumination of his watch allowing an accurate count. It was elevated, but not by much, a natural reaction to pain. He hadn't felt a large pool of blood under the fracture, and the pulse seemed strong, so he assumed that shock hadn't set in. All he could do anyway was try to keep the guide warm and address any fear he might have.

The other concern was food. Neither he nor the guide had eaten since lunch, right before they entered the ruins. Food wasn't allowed in, but he had water, and Digger had water and his food in his pack.

Rex gave some thought to sending Digger to go and fetch his backpack from the spot where he'd been guarding it but quickly gave up on the idea. The first problem was that the bag was too heavy for Digger to carry and second, it was also too dangerous to try and navigate this terrain without a light.

Rex loosened the cinches of Digger's pack and had him step out of it while he held it up by the handle. He got out the collapsible bowl and gave Digger a drink and handed the rest of the bottle to the guide. Digger had probably drunk from a trickle of a mountain spring near where he'd waited earlier, too. He turned away from the water before it was gone. The guide finished what was left in the bottle.

Meanwhile, Rex rooted in the panniers for Digger's food and some alpaca jerky he'd purchased in Ollantaytambo that morning. He didn't suppose the guide would appreciate being offered dog kibble to eat, though it would provide needed nutrients. The jerky, though, was sold for human food. It would do for all three of them, and yes, he'd save some for Digger, who deserved a treat for finding the guide.

"It's going to get cold," he said. "I'm sorry, but I think it's best we stay here until someone comes in the morning. Then we can send for a litter and get some people to help me carry you out."

"I agree. Thank you for staying to find me. I thought…"

"Don't worry. The dog and I will stay with you. We'll do our best to keep you warm, and you will be fine."

It had been a long day, more than twelve hours since they'd set out that morning for a seven-mile hike, a few hours amid Inca ruins, and a seven-mile hike back. A few hours sleep, if he could get them, didn't sound like a bad idea. He only wished he could get to his back pack. Those few hours would be a lot more comfortable for the guide on a ground cover and inflatable bed, but it was not worth the risk.

Rex reckoned the first visitors would begin arriving at sunup, but they'd be more likely to be at the Sun Gate or the Sacred Rock. In the morning, he'd decide what would be the best way to get the guide and themselves off the mountain.

The next morning came much quicker than Rex had expected, probably because he'd slept better than he'd thought he would, spooning the guide from behind while Digger curled up in front of him. The ground was cold for all, but at least the guide had enjoyed the shared warmth. The man was in good spirits when the sun woke them, though he complained of pain.

He asked the guide what he thought about Digger's safety. Clearly, he wasn't a lap dog. His presence in the ruins wouldn't be welcomed by guards, but were they armed? Would they shoot first and ask questions later, or would the guide have time to explain if Rex went looking for help and someone else found the injured man before he got back?

The guide thought Digger would be safe. Rex may have to pay a fine for calling the dog into the site, but most Peruvians loved dogs. The guide didn't think anyone would shoot him.

Rex thought the guide was disingenuous for suggesting that he'd have to pay a fine, since Digger was only there because the guide needed finding. He was sure he could afford the fine, it was just the principal of saving a man's life and then getting penalised for it. He decided it was best to say nothing for now and plead his case when it came to it. One perk of being a freelancing 'cleaner' ridding the world of bad guy trash almost everywhere he went was that they invariably had stashes of ill-gotten money or other valuables. Since changing from salaried work to freelancing, Rex had made a good living by liberating the bad guys of their dirty money and turning it to better use. He had enough to live comfortably even after distributing the bulk of the spoils of his one-man war to the victims and their families of the villains he eliminated.

Rex got out another bottle of water, gave some to Digger and the rest to the guide, and watched until Digger had emptied the bowl. Then he put in some kibble and another small piece of alpaca jerky.

"Stay, guard," he said, setting Digger to protect the guide and stay with him while Rex went looking for help. His stomach growled as he walked away, and Digger gave a sympathizing *woof*.

Rex wasn't surprised to find a large group of tourists as soon as he exited the Urban district. They were grouped around a couple of guides who appeared to be dividing them into two groups, so they could go in opposite directions. What surprised him was who he saw in the front of one of the groups. He broke into a jog and beelined for that group.

"Mr. and Mrs. Marks! Good to see you!" he called.

Mrs. Marks heard him first and looked his way. She immediately turned, tugged on her husband's hand, and pointed at him. Mr. Marks broke from the crowd and started walking as fast as he could toward him.

He'd started to explain his dilemma when the tour guide arrived, explaining that Mrs. Marks had told him Rex was an acquaintance. "How may I help? Are you lost?"

Rex told him he wasn't lost, but his guide was hurt and needed help. The tour guide immediately lifted a walkie-talkie from its holster on his belt and radioed someone at the entrance gate. While they waited for an EMT team to arrive, Rex explained his dilemma about Digger.

"I meant no disrespect. I needed my dog's help to find the guide, since it was dark when I realized he was missing."

The tour guide assured Rex he'd done the right thing and told him he'd help if there was trouble. He didn't expect any, though.

"How are you going to get back to Ollantaytambo?" he asked.

"I'll be okay to get back if you could help to take care of my guide," Rex said.

"Why don't you join us? I am grateful for my colleague's sake that you helped him survive the night."

Just then, Rex's stomach growled noisily again.

"We have food," the guide added with a knowing grin.

That cinched the deal. "I'd be happy to, and thanks," Rex said. He'd had enough of being solitary in the Andes. Food and company sounded like a great idea. Especially when the tour guide added that Digger would be welcome.

When the group left around noon, Rex and Digger were with them. His guide had been splinted and taken by litter to Agua Calientes. His new group stopped not far outside the entrance for a picnic lunch that tasted to Rex like a feast. Digger didn't have to argue his case for human food this time. His kibble was gone, and Rex couldn't deny him something to eat.

I'm getting soft. Time was, twenty-four hours without food wouldn't have bothered me at all.

Rex and Digger were sitting a little outside the circle of the people who'd been on the tour all along. Rex had asked for a few minutes to retrieve his back pack from where Digger had stayed the previous day, and when they got back, the rest of the group was sleeping off their lunch or chatting among themselves, having made friends on the trek. Rex was about to take a siesta himself when he heard

Mrs. Marks admonishing her husband that he should be more social.

They were heading his way, and they weren't alone. To his surprise, the young man from the restaurant was with them. He hadn't expected to ever see the kid again and wasn't particularly pleased to see him now.

Mrs. Marks led her husband and the kid to where Rex was sitting and looked down at him. She glanced around, apparently for somewhere to sit. Not finding what she was looking for, she began talking to him while she was standing.

Rex felt forced to stand up.

"I'd like to introduce you to Junior Roper," she said. "We've been traveling together since just after we saw you last, Mr. Davis."

"Call me Ray," Rex said automatically. "Nice to meet you, Mr. Roper."

The kid grinned and mimicked Rex's answer. "Call me Junior," he said.

Rex started to extend his hand, when Digger interrupted with a growl. Rex looked down at him. "It's okay, buddy. These are friends. You've seen them before." He extended his hand again, and Roper shook it despite Digger's continued protests in the form of soft growling.

"Nice doggy," Mrs. Marks tried. She held her hand out, palm down, toward Digger to allow him to sniff it. He complied, then wagged his tail and licked her hand.

"He likes me," she said, almost ecstatically.

"Yes, ma'am. He's a good judge of character," Rex said. "Where are you headed next?" he asked. "When you get back to Cusco, I mean."

Mrs. Marks became animated. "Oh, we're not going back to Cusco. We're…"

Mr. Marks interrupted. "Remember what we agreed, dear."

"I'm sure Mr. Davis won't tell anyone, will you, Mr. Davis?"

Rex was about to ask 'tell anyone what?'

Roper looked as if he might interrupt, too, but Mrs. Marks beat him to it. "Junior has discovered some unexcavated ruins. Tell him, son," she urged in a whisper.

Roper squirmed, earning another growl from Digger. "What's that dog's problem?" he asked.

Rex didn't answer. He figured he'd already told them Digger was a good judge of character, and that should be explanation enough. Maybe Digger shared Rex's first impressions of the young man. But when Roper reluctantly began telling him about the remote village he'd stumbled into on a previous trip and the oral history the villagers had shared with him, Rex forgot about Digger's animosity.

"Oral history?" he asked.

"Yes, sir. It's remarkable. You know Quechuan has no written tradition, right? These guys, they're brought up to remember all their tales and history. So, when a visitor comes, they have a feast and they'll spend all night telling you this stuff."

Rex wasn't happy about this kid thinking he was old enough to be called 'sir'. But he was intrigued enough to listen and suppress the irritation.

"Fascinating," he said.

"For sure! It *was* fascinating, and the most fascinating thing about it is they told me about this old place. They called it 'village of the old ones' or ancients or something like that. My Quechuan isn't perfect. Anyway, I asked to see it, and man, it's something! Not as big as Machu Picchu, but according to the villagers, it's never been studied by outsiders. I mean, there are artifacts just laying there. Mr. and Mrs. Marks are going to fund a dig, and I'm going to run it!"

Junior Roper had apparently forgotten his initial reluctance to talk about it.

Rex could hardly keep up with the stream of words as the enthused Junior barely took a breath. He was cynical about the 'village of the old ones or ancients' of whatever, but the oral history of the village intrigued him.

"Mhh. I see. Interesting. My Quechuan is pretty good," he heard himself saying. "What do you say we, my dog and I, tag along? I'd like to meet the villagers. I'm interested in the oral history of the natives around here."

Chapter Five

It didn't take long for Rex to remember why he hadn't joined this tour from Cusco in the first place. Two guides, a handful of porters, a cook and his assistant, and about fifty contentious, complaining tourists was too much of a crowd for Rex. They'd hiked three days to get to Machu Picchu, spent five hours in the site, and then turned back to spend another three days covering the same route back.

Fortunately, Rex and his new traveling companions didn't stay very long with them. At lunch, Rex had questioned Junior more closely about the location of the village he'd told them about. Flo and Barry Marks listened as the younger men discussed the best way to get there.

To Rex's disappointment, it was nowhere near the Sacred Valley, where he knew many ruins had been found and villages seemed to be situated at every bend of the river. That had been his next destination.

However, the prospect of meeting villagers untainted by tourist influence and hearing their version of Inca history was a strong pull, and he didn't regret joining the impromptu expedition. As the tour group loaded up to head out, Rex and Junior continued to discuss the best way to get their group to the village near the Hidroelectrica power plant, the nearest place where they might find supplies for a long trek into the higher reaches of the Andes, where their target village lay. From there, it was a five-hour hike to the town of Santa Teresa, where Junior said they could definitely get supplies and porters if they wished, for the final approach to the village of *Hatun Rumi*, literally translated from Quechuan as High Stone.

There was no direct route hiking, though Hidroelectrica was only a little over a mile as the crow flies from where they sat. Unfortunately, that mile included a sheer nine-hundred-foot drop through uncharted jungle and bush-whacking along the east bank of the Urubamba River until they could cross where the highway from Aguas Calientes to Hidroelectrica bridged it.

Rex knew he and Digger could have made it on their own. It was possible Junior could have made it, though Rex had his doubts. But there was no way either Flo or Barry Marks would have made it.

The only choice was to retrace Rex and Digger's route back to Ollantaytambo and try to rent a car there. From there, they could take Highway 28B all the way around Machu Picchu Mountain, a distance of about eighty-three miles. But it would take seven hours to hike to Ollantay-tambo. With dwindling water supplies, Rex was the only one who was prepared for it. Before they went there, they'd have to go to Aguas Calientes, where they might as well spend the night, since it was already well past noon, and the round trip to the tourist trap town would take five hours.

Rex pondered ruefully what it meant to be on foot or even have a car in a country where twenty-thousand-foot peaks might mean a drive of hours to gain a few miles. Previously on this trip, he hadn't cared. He'd taken weeks to get from Lima to Cusco, unable to fly even if he'd wanted to skip the sights of the coast, because Peruvian airlines didn't pressurize their cargo holds, and none would take a dog Digger's size in the passenger cabins. Now he was anxious to get to the remote village in the shortest time possible. But the irony was it might take hours of walking before they could hitch a ride to bring them closer, which might still leave them with another day or more of hiking to get there.

There was no help for it, though. Rex had learned the best way to tackle the inevitable was to put your head down and just do it.

"Let's go, then. I have three bottles of water left. Two for Mr. and Mrs. Marks and you, Junior. One's for Digger and me. I suggest you all pace yourselves, because it's going to be a muggy walk to Aguas Calientes."

Flo giggled. "That's apropos, don't you think?"

Rex didn't get it. Which part was apropos? He frowned and tilted his head just like Digger would when he was puzzled.

She took the hint and explained. "Aguas Calientes. That means hot water, doesn't it?"

So it did. Rex hadn't been there. He wondered if there were hot springs there.

As he'd expected, the hikes between the rest stop where they started and Santa Teresa were long, hot, and uncomfortable. Digger continued to growl at Junior whenever he got within a few paces of Rex. Junior ignored him but kept his distance when he could. Rex was surprised that Junior didn't complain about the heat or the walking. He seemed to be in better physical shape than Rex would have expected after his first impressions of the young man. However, it didn't seem to give him a pass on whatever Digger had against him.

He was also surprised that the older couple held up as well as they did. Of course, they'd been conditioned to the long hours of hiking on the first part of their tour, but Barry was overweight. Rex had to adjust his assessment of the couple's hardiness for the adventure. Maybe they wouldn't need to hire porters for the final leg of the journey, after all.

Two days after their impromptu joint venture began, they stopped for the night in Santa Teresa. It was there that the first three-way disagreement came up.

Rex had noted the descent from the seven to eight thousand feet of altitude where they'd begun. It worried him, since as far as he could tell, the others hadn't stayed in Cusco long enough to really acclimate to the higher altitude. They'd descended steadily, and Santa Teresa was at the lowest point of any place they'd been since then. It wouldn't take long to decondition, and they were going to have to climb now. But they'd need at least a day to outfit themselves for a long trek.

The Markses wanted to stay for about a week to rest, they said. They dismissed Rex's concerns about altitude, saying Cusco hadn't bothered them much. Despite his caution that Junior couldn't tell them the altitude, and it could well be three thousand feet higher than Cusco or more, they were adamant they'd be okay.

Junior agreed they needed to stay a few days. He didn't give a reason other than it might be difficult to get the expedition gear together in only a day. He wouldn't say on what he was basing that estimate. Rex didn't want to argue, since he'd never been to Santa Teresa before. Junior didn't say outright that he had been, but he seemed confident that he knew the way from there to Hatun Rumi, so Rex had to assume he knew what he was talking about. Even three or four days delay could be an issue for the altitude conditioning, though. Rex didn't like it.

At the end of the discussion, they had to compromise. The old couple grumbled but agreed to set out in four days. Rex suppressed his impatience and concern, knowing they'd pay for the delay later.

Junior seemed more pleased than he should have been at the minor victory.

Digger, of course, sided with Rex.

Rex did win a concession from the couple. If they were going to rest, he reasoned, maybe they'd trust him and Junior to acquire the gear they needed. With that agreed, he and the younger man went about outfitting the group with little contention. Junior said he agreed the delay wouldn't help the older couple with their conditioning, but he suggested a llama or two rather than human porters.

"I've never been a llama handler," Rex replied. "Have you?"

"How hard can it be? They're just little camels, aren't they?"

Rex raised his eyebrows. "Have you ever handled a camel?"

Junior grinned. "Nope. But it can't be that hard."

Oh, no? Camels are more stubborn than mules when they want to be. But you don't need to know I've been in the Middle East.

After discussing the issue with a local who agreed to sell them two llamas and assured them the animals wouldn't give them any trouble, neither man was willing to admit he had any qualms. They paid the man a deposit and told him they'd come by to get the animals and their pack saddles in three days' time.

They acquired dried food, bottled water, and a bigger camp stove for the journey. Rex had a small one in his gear that they would use to heat water. They got ground covers, sleeping bags and extra blankets, ponchos and plastic sheets to cover them against the coming rains. Everyone already had hiking boots, which was good. Rex wouldn't have wanted to deal with breaking in new ones on a trek he already suspected would be arduous.

Rex made it a private errand to acquire something he hadn't thought he'd need on this trip before – a replacement for his beloved Sig Sauer P226, which he couldn't bring into the country. Peru was generally regarded as a safe country to visit and travel in, but Rex always felt naked without a gun on his body. Besides that, he had other good reasons to arm himself as they were going into remote areas off the popular tourist routes with long stretches of wilderness, wild animals, and not much or any in the way of law enforcement.

Gun ownership in Peru had to be licensed, but once a license was acquired, it was a de facto concealed carry permit. He found a shop owner who, for a consideration, 'rushed' the licensing process and sold Rex a used Sig the day after he inquired about one. The serial number was intact, so he didn't worry about it having been used in a crime previously.

Rex also bought a hunting rifle. Some of the wildlife in Peru could be dangerous, after all. Buying the rifle was also his cover for picking up the Sig, so he didn't have two unexplained errands to account for if anyone asked.

He would have liked a more modern rifle, but in this remote part of Peru, there was only one dealer, and the choices were second-hand ancient and second-hand old. So, he settled on a second-hand old, Winchester Model 70, known as 'The Rifleman's Rifle', a favorite of hunters and sport shooters since it was first produced in 1936. Rex got one that had left the factory in 2005, had a walnut stock, and was overall in good condition. The merchant gave him a half-price deal on the box of fifty .308 cartridges.

By then, the group had been together for nearly a week, and Rex had formed opinions on each member except Junior. The jury was still out for him, mostly because of Digger's animosity. Rex still couldn't account for it, but he'd trusted the dog for more than a year by then, and he saw no reason to change his mind about that. Nevertheless, Junior's behavior hadn't raised any red flags since that day in the restaurant. He seemed to have taken the loss of his money in that scam in stride.

During his quiet musings about Junior, Rex couldn't help but recall his stormy relationship with Digger in the beginning. And that had all to do with Rex's fear or rather, phobia of dogs, originating from being mauled by a dog when he was a little boy. Rex still didn't know why Digger terrorised him like that. Since the death of Trevor Mulligan, Digger's previous owner in an ambush in Afghanistan, Rex and Digger had their squabbles, but Digger had stopped intimidating him. Maybe it was a similar situation with Junior. Rex decided not to ask because he knew how embarrassing it was for him to admit that he was terrified of dogs.

Regarding the Marks couple, to Rex it was clear Flo was the tougher half. She appeared to keep her mind on maintaining her physical strength, which he found impressive for a woman her age. She had also been the deciding factor in the compromise, and she'd done it in a way that Rex felt didn't make Barry feel undermined.

Barry was a peculiar mixture. He'd showed strength of character in building a business he'd been able to sell for enough money to live in luxury and have enough left to indulge in a charitable activity. Rex had no quarrel with the activity he'd chosen, either. Archaeology and history traveled hand-in-hand, as far as he was concerned. He could get behind a foundation that sought to uncover more of human history. He wholeheartedly agreed with philosopher George Santayana's statement that those who cannot remember the past are doomed to repeat it.

On the other hand, Barry didn't take care of himself. He relied on Flo to do it. To Rex, that was a bit of a strange concept. He was trained to take care of himself and live with the consequences of his decisions and actions. Admittedly, he and Digger had fostered some interdependence, so maybe the relationship between Flo and Barry was similar to him making Digger eat healthy food. A little smile played on his face when that thought crossed his mind.

"Penny for your thoughts."

Rex was startled to find Flo at his side. He'd been woolgathering as they walked from the hotel to a restaurant, the fourth they'd tried in as many days. He took a beat to center himself and glance quickly at Digger, who paced by his side.

"I'm afraid they aren't worth that much," he said, putting an easy grin on his face. "Just daydreaming."

"About the treasures we'll find?" she prompted.

"About collecting some rare tales from the Quechua people," he answered. It wasn't a lie, exactly. He did dream of making important discoveries. If he really did make discoveries, he owed it to the world to make them known, but he was still contemplating how he would publish any findings without breaking his cover.

"What is it you do, Mr. Davis?" Flo asked.

"I'm not going to answer until you agree to call me Ray," he teased.

"Okay, Ray-of-sunshine, what do you do? Or are you independently wealthy?"

He laughed. "No, nothing like that. I'm a journalist of sorts."

"What do you mean by 'of sorts'?" she persisted.

"Mrs. Marks, are you computer literate?"

"Now who's standing on ceremony? I won't talk to you again unless you call me Flo," she giggled. "Yes, as a matter of fact, I am. Why?"

"Then you know about blogs, yes?" Rex was winging it, and he'd have to put some evidence in place soon to support his cover. "I am in the process of assembling material to write a travel blog which might make me a bit of money, hopefully enough to sustain my traveling. In the meantime, I have a small inheritance that I'm using to support myself until it does."

"Well, good for you! We like entrepreneurs, don't we, Barry?"

Barry, deep in conversation with Junior, didn't hear or respond.

Chapter Six

By the morning of the fifth day, the Markses declared themselves sufficiently rested to go on. Everyone made sure they had a nutritious breakfast without overeating. The climb from here would be steep, and no one needed to be slowed down by an over-full stomach. Flo joked that Barry would be in much better shape after this, maybe even the handsome rake with the slim build that she'd fallen in love with. Barry only shook his head and blushed at that.

Somehow, without Rex and Junior's knowledge, the couple had gone out and acquired a lot more gear than was necessary. In addition to what the younger men had provided for them, they had several extra sets of clothing, laundry detergent, an outdoor shower contraption, a double blow-up mattress and pump, more bags of food, and a large bag of trinkets – for the natives, they said. They'd hired a taxi to bring it from the hotel to the llama trader's establishment.

Rex and Junior exchanged incredulous glances. Would it

all fit on the llamas' packs, or would the poor beasts revolt before they set foot on the trail? There was only one way to find out, so the two men set about rearranging the packs to accommodate it all.

Digger sat a few yards away and watched with interest. His own backpack lay on the ground near Rex's. He watched Rex load bag after bag and secure them with ropes and bungee cords. When there were no more bags by the llamas, Digger went over and grabbed his in his jaws, by the handle. He had to hold his head high to keep it from dragging on the ground, and walking with it was awkward, but he managed to get it over to Rex and set it down. He pawed Rex's leg to get his attention.

Rex looked down and saw Digger's pack and started laughing. Every time he managed to stop laughing to take a breath, he was overcome by another bout, until he was bent over, his hands on his knees, gasping for breath. Flo Marks had seen the exchange, figured out what Digger was up to and was laughing, too. When Barry and Junior came over to see what was so funny. Rex had to explain to them, between gasps, that Digger had decided the llamas made better pack animals than him.

That started another round of laughter, while Digger looked from human to human with an expression that said, "What's the big deal?"

Rex said to Digger, "The llamas are to help carry everything else. Your big bag of chow is on their backs, but you must carry your daily ration." He picked up the pack and set it on Digger's back. The dog didn't balk. If he could, Rex thought, he might have shrugged and said, "It was worth a try."

The comical interlude had put everyone in a good mood. Though the sun was higher in the sky than Rex would have preferred when he fell in line behind Junior, he was in great spirits. The air was crisp for now, though it would probably be muggy later in the day when the rains came. Digger was by his side, and they were finally on their way to an unplanned adventure. This was the life he'd been wanting ever since he left Afghanistan after the tragedy that had brought him and Digger together.

Junior set a pace that would give them respectable progress for the day, even if they had to stop when the rain started. Rex thought it would be too fast for Barry and maybe for Flo, but he didn't want to start an argument. If they found it too fast, they'd slow down by themselves and Junior would know to slow down as well. Rex had no doubt Flo would speak up if she needed to.

Junior was a couple hundred yards ahead, leading one of the llamas by its bridle. Rex had hung back to let the Markses go next, so he could keep an eye on them. He was only about ten yards behind them, and he had to keep slowing down as the trail turned steeper. He'd schooled himself to patience – they'd get to the village when they got there. Digger was at heel position as usual, though if they'd been alone Rex would have sent him a few dozen yards ahead. The second llama trailed them on the lead.

To Rex, the benefit of Junior's pace was that it made conversation difficult and he could do what he had done for many days and miles before he'd met them. He whistled, thought, and closely observed his surroundings, sometimes remarking on them to Digger. He'd discovered great contentment in such circumstances. Now and then, Digger left his side briefly to investigate the abundant wildlife or leave his mark on the area they were passing through. Rex saw no point in picking up after him out in the jungle. Packs of wild dogs roamed in there, after all. Digger's contributions most likely wouldn't destroy the environment any more than theirs would.

Though Rex had been on missions in the jungles of south and central America and Africa before, he didn't think he'd ever seen any as beautiful as the one through which he walked now. Part of his contentment was the fact there weren't any terrorists bent on killing him. Another part of it was his absolute freedom to do whatever he wished. And part of it, to his continuous astonishment, was the companionship of Digger and his obvious delight in the new sights and smells.

Despite all that, it was second nature for Rex to keep his eyes and ears open for trouble. Even though he didn't expect it, trouble had a habit of finding him on a regular basis.

He'd spent hours trying to figure out why Digger disliked Junior Roper so much when he himself couldn't detect any threat from him. If Junior was a real bad guy, Digger would have attacked him. He didn't. The only logical explanation was the one he thought of before—for some unknown reason, Junior was afraid of Digger, and the dog could sense it. Why he would then torment the guy for it was inexplicable. But after spending so much time with Digger, Rex knew better than to interfere with the dog's intuition—the reason for it would reveal itself in due time.

He didn't think the locals were hostile to outside visitors, but they were going deep into the interior where westerners didn't often venture. Tales of vicious primitive tribes in the Amazon were plentiful, so it wasn't beyond his imagination to believe others could inhabit the high backcountry of the Andes. Their party was following a well-used trail, so there must be some contact between the inhabitants along the trail and the small city of Santa Teresa. Probably his caution was for nothing. That didn't mean he'd drop it.

After a couple of hours, he and the Markses caught up with Junior, who had stopped to wait for them.

"Anyone hungry? We've covered about five miles, and from here the trail gets steeper. I thought we might be able to use a rest and some food before we push through."

Rex liked the kid's diplomatic manner and consideration of the older couple. "I could. And Digger's always up for a snack."

Flo chuckled and agreed. Barry just sat heavily on a nearby downed tree trunk and sighed. Rex took note of it. They'd all need to keep a close watch on Barry.

Junior had told him it was about thirty miles to the village. They hoped to make ten miles per day, but Junior said they'd better count on half that when they planned the food. Some stretches of the trail were very steep, and they were going to gain over ten thousand feet in altitude. Not to mention the days would be shortened when the rains came, which could be soon. After that, he wasn't sure how far it was to the ruins. Maybe another two days' hike.

However, today's progress was ahead of schedule, largely because the trail had been relatively flat so far. Rex reckoned they were only about two hundred feet higher than they'd been when they started. They'd covered five miles of the thirty, which meant during the twenty-five left they'd be gaining an average of four-hundred feet in altitude per mile. About one-thousand feet in altitude per hour at their current pace. Barry would never be able to keep up with that pace, and Rex doubted Flo could, either. Especially not as the air became thinner and thinner.

Before they started again, Rex had a quiet word with

Junior. "I'm sure you understand they can't keep up the pace you set if we start climbing."

"No worries, man. We won't go any faster than they can. That's why we planned for twice as much time as you or I would need, right?"

Rex nodded. As he walked back to the spot where the llamas and Barry waited, he turned Junior's remark over in his mind. It wasn't lost on him that his physique announced to anyone who saw him that he was fitter than average.

Junior's doesn't, so how is it that the kid equates what I can do with what he can? Is it just the natural arrogance of youth, or is there more to the kid than meets the eye? Is that what Digger knows about and doesn't like?

In the absence of other evidence, Rex decided he was being unnaturally distrustful. The kid was probably just a bit competitive by comparing their ages, which were relatively close compared to the gap between either of them and the Markses. He forgot about it as he got to Barry and noticed Flo wasn't around.

"Where's Flo?" he asked.

Barry waved nonchalantly away from the path and into the jungle. "Call of nature," he said.

Rex felt a thrill of alarm. "By herself? How long has she been gone?"

Barry shrugged. "A few minutes. She'll be okay."

Rex suppressed his annoyance. Barry was probably right, and he certainly wasn't going to go crashing through the brush and disturb her. She'd probably take his head off if he caught her in an embarrassing position. Still, he was uneasy. She could get into all sorts of trouble, from run-ins with wildlife to unexpected drop offs disguised by dense foliage. He wouldn't be happy until he saw or heard her coming back.

Junior had waited a few minutes before rejoining them, at Rex's suggestion. He'd rather the Markses didn't become concerned that he and Junior were conspiring behind their backs, and he didn't want to embarrass them by discussing their fitness in their presence. Now Junior walked up and asked if everyone was ready to go.

Rex told him they were waiting for Flo. There wasn't much to do, but while they waited, they made sure no scrap of food or other evidence of their stop remained, and still Flo wasn't back. Barry didn't seem concerned, but Rex was.

Finally, he had an idea. Digger had learned the names of their companions by now. He liked Flo as much as he disliked Junior. Rex had no doubt he could find either of them on command. Barry, he wasn't sure about. Digger didn't seem to have any issues with him, ignoring him most of the time.

"Digger, find Flo," he commanded and pointed in the direction of the bushes where Barry had pointed before.

Digger looked up and got to his feet. He looked at Rex and then at the jungle in the direction Barry had waved.

Rex nodded and said, "Go on, boy, find Flo."

Digger opened his mouth in a wide grin and let his tongue hang out as he trotted into the bush. Rex was reassured by Digger's casual body language. The dog hadn't detected anything amiss. Most likely he was just fretting about nothing.

A few minutes later a cacophony of barking erupted from somewhere in the direction Digger and Flo had gone. Everyone, even Barry, jumped to their feet.

"What the…" Barry started.

No sooner than he'd said it, the barking stopped. Rex started forward. "You guys stay here." He ignored Barry's protest as he moved swiftly into the jungle.

He'd gone only a few yards, looking for evidence of either Flo's or Digger's passing through, when both appeared about six feet in front of him. Flo was smiling. Rex unconsciously relaxed.

"What was that all about?" he asked.

"Well, I had a little encounter with some wild dogs," she said. "Did you know about them? The Peruvian dogs? They're so funny-looking. No hair except at the very top of their heads, and it's kind of orange and straggly. Their bodies are almost purple."

Rex relaxed more at her evident lack of distress. "What do you mean, encounter?"

"Well, if you must know, five or six of them came along while I was, um… They seemed a bit fascinated. Embarrassing, really. But when I was done and tried to pet them, they ran away."

"You tried to what?" Rex was horrified. She could have lost a hand, or worse.

"Well, they didn't seem unfriendly. Then your big boy came along and started barking at them, and they barked back, and he ran at them and they scattered."

She seemed disappointed.

"He was protecting you," Rex said. She was fine, and he didn't want to fight with her. She was his favorite of the three humans on the trail with him.

"He's sweet. But I didn't need protecting." She turned and rubbed Digger's ears with both hands, bending down to look him in the face. "Good boy! Thank you for protecting me."

Rex told her not to try and pet or approach wild animals again and explained the dangers of it to her.

Initially, she was a bit taken aback by Rex's admonishment but in the end she took it graciously and gave her word that she wouldn't do it again.

The silly grin on Digger's face almost made Rex laugh. So much for sparing his feelings. Flo was a natural with dogs.

They returned to the others, and they fell into line again, walking more slowly now as the trail was growing steeper.

Chapter Seven

That afternoon, about another two hours into the hike, Junior hung back. They'd all noticed heavy clouds darkening the day. It looked like the anticipated rains were about to descend. He suggested Rex and the Markses continue at their previous pace while he went ahead to find a spot to camp for the night. He'd stop at the first spot that looked like it would give them shelter.

Rex thought a spot providing shelter might still be miles away, but he couldn't think of a better idea. Even if he could find one faster than Junior could, he didn't know the way, and he doubted Junior's ability to protect the older couple as well as he and Digger could.

Junior told them he'd leave a trail marker if he had to get off the trail to get to shelter. Rex suggested Junior leave his llama behind unless he knew how they'd react to rain. He agreed and headed up the trail at a jog. Rex gave the llama's lead to Barry and closed the distance between them, so they were bunched on the trail, three humans, two llamas, and Digger.

Before long, the first fat spatters of raindrops began to fall, and Rex halted the procession to get the ponchos out of their packs. Hopefully the kid had found shelter and was waiting for them high and dry.

Before many minutes had passed, they were slogging through a running stream that had found the trail they were walking to be the path of least resistance. The three humans were huddled under their plastic ponchos, beginning to shiver as the temperature dropped rapidly. Digger had his head down, the picture of misery. His only protection was his canvas back pack.

He didn't have any idea what the llamas thought about the rain, but they weren't balking or otherwise misbehaving, for which he was grateful. When the downpour got heavy enough, they couldn't see more than two feet ahead, he called a halt. Everything he knew about tropical rainstorms suggested this would pass soon. There was no place to hide, and it was dangerous to continue as long as they couldn't see in front of them. Also, if they missed Junior's trail marker, he'd be stranded without the supplies. It was best to stop and wait it out.

About ten minutes later, the downpour slowed, and visibility improved. Rex urged the bedraggled group to continue up the trail. It was harder now, as the muddy ground was slippery and caused them to slow down to an almost shuffling pace. That proved to be a blessing in disguise when Flo exclaimed in surprise. Just as she'd caught herself from landing flat on her face in the mud, she'd noticed a small cairn of rocks beside the trail, and an even smaller trail leading off it.

"Would this be Junior?" she asked Rex.

"Yes, I'm sure it is. You stay here, and I'll check." Rex told Digger to stay and headed out quickly on the smaller trail. He'd gone just far enough that he couldn't see the others when Junior hailed him.

"*Hola!* You made it!" He was sitting dry and cozy in the mouth of a shallow cave. "It looks like there's room for all of us and the llamas in here. I don't see any wildlife spoor. I think this is a good place to stop for the night.'

Rex agreed. "Next time, it's my turn to find shelter. If you don't mind, I'm just going to send Digger in to make sure this isn't some unfriendly wildlife's home. His nose is better than ours."

Junior shrugged. "Be my guest. Shall I go get the olds?"

Rex didn't like the phrase, but he didn't detect any derision in Junior's tone. So, Rex left it at that without comment. Maybe it was some new slang he wasn't familiar with.

"Sure, go ahead. We should have it all clear by the time you get back." He shouted for Digger to come as he watched Junior crash down the trail to the Markses. Digger arrived moments later, and Rex commanded him to scout. If there was any wildlife around, it would probably be scattering now.

It's lucky we don't have to rely on hunting for our food.

———

Flo stopped outside the cave entrance and called out, "Halloooo?"

Digger ran out to greet her, with Rex right behind. "Looks like Junior found the perfect spot to spend the night."

Flo suspected the younger men had stopped early on her and Barry's account, and she was grateful. The last bit of trudging through the mud in the sudden downpour had taxed her, and she could see Barry was done in as he plodded, yards behind her.

"So, we're not going any farther today?"

"Nope. Time to circle the wagons, get some grub, and turn in for the night," Rex said.

"Did you suddenly become a cowboy, Mr. Davis?" She smiled mischievously as he wagged his finger at her and grinned. "Shall we try to start a fire while we wait for the others? Though I doubt there's any dry fuel," she added.

"I'll try to rustle some up," he answered, his sly smile making her laugh out loud.

She went inside the cave to wait, and in a few minutes, Barry came lumbering up to the entrance. "Come inside, love. There are some dry rocks to sit on in here. Ray has gone to find some dry wood for a fire. Where's Junior?"

"Right behind him," Junior called out. "These llamas are giving me grief. You'd think they'd *want* to get under shelter. They're soaked."

"Oh, dear. Are our sleeping bags dry?" she asked.

"Yes, ma'am. We covered the packs with waterproof tarps. We planned for the rains."

"I thought it was summer here," she complained. "Why is it so chilly and wet?"

Junior explained that the temperatures were basically uniform, with the weather more defined by the dry and rainy seasons than temperature. "It's only chilly because it's just rained. Remember, we're south of the equator, so we're headed into summer, not winter. The rains are a little early, but not completely unexpected. They'll happen every afternoon, probably. It won't get much hotter, though. The higher you go, the cooler it is."

She thought about it, then looked over at Barry, resting

on the flattest rock she'd been able to find for him inside the cave. She lowered her voice.

"Just how high are we going?"

Junior caught her concern and answered in a lower voice as well. "The village is around thirteen or fourteen thousand feet. The ruins, maybe eighteen thousand. Is he going to be okay?"

Flo sighed. "I hope so. We may have to take it slowly for him."

"That's all right. We planned for extra time to rest, too, even if it's for a day or two. I knew you weren't used to this altitude."

"Thank you, dear." Flo saw Rex outside, clearing a spot to put down an armful of twigs and small branches. "Did you find anything dry?" she called. She got up to watch him start the fire and offer her cooking expertise.

"Would you like help with the meal?" she asked.

"If you'd like," Rex answered. "That's if you're okay to cook over a campfire."

"Young man, you'll be surprised to know Barry and I camped out for every vacation we took when we were younger. We couldn't afford anything else, and we thought it would be good for our son to learn to love nature from a young age."

Rex remembered lessons of that sort from when he was a kid. His family had enjoyed nature together – hiking, fishing, hunting, camping, and skiing. Since then, he'd honed his skills in the wilderness to a fine point.

"Indeed, I underestimated you," he said. "In that case, please help me. I'll bet you can make a tastier stew than I can from what I have here. I'll just get the fire started, and then I'll get the supplies out."

Soon Flo was stirring the meat into boiling water and

cutting up an onion to go in next, while Rex scrubbed *mashua* and *olluco* for her to cut up after that.

"Are you sure those are edible?" she asked, looking with doubt on the tubers Rex was preparing. What he'd called *mashua* looked like orange, purple, and white carrots. He answered her by popping one into his mouth.

"It's a little peppery raw, but it becomes milder when cooked," he answered. "And the other one, the *olluco*, is basically a potato." As he cut into one of the latter, he uttered a surprised, "Oh!"

Flo noticed Digger looking closely at what Rex had in his hands, his nose almost buried in it.

"Get off," Rex complained, pushing Digger gently away with his forearm. What he had in his hands was bright orange, but with green skin.

"What's the problem?" Flo asked.

"It's *olluco*. I didn't know it was orange inside."

"How did you learn about these, and what makes you sure they're edible?" Flo demanded.

"I asked in the market back in Santa Teresa," he admitted. "I figured there'd be plenty of edible stuff we could harvest in the forests we're going to travel through, which means we wouldn't have to carry so much. A woman told me these things grow wild all over the mountains and are the basis for a lot of native dishes." He opened his cell phone and showed her the pictures he'd taken in the market and some he'd collected from the internet. "I made sure I'd know what they looked like."

"Oh. Well, that was very sensible, Ray," Flo said. "So why didn't you know it was orange?"

"What was in the market was yellow," he answered. "Must be a cultivated variety."

"You're sure it's the same thing?"

"Yes. But I don't know if this variety is sweet. It might not taste good in stew."

"Of course it will," she said. Truthfully, she wasn't sure. But he'd been proud of his foraging, and she didn't want to discourage him. Besides, she'd tasted many new dishes since she and Barry had arrived in Peru, and they were all delicious. She loved the purple corn pudding they'd had in Cuzco, especially.

Soon the delicious aroma emanating from the stew pot, lured Junior and Barry out of the cave.

They didn't need the ground covers inside the cave, where the ground was dry and there were patches of soft, powdery soil, free of plant life. So, they arranged them around the fire to sit on, cross-legged for Rex and Junior, and on a couple of logs from downed trees that Rex and Junior dragged over for Barry and Flo. When the stew was finally ready, they ate every last morsel.

"I nominate Flo to be the chief cook every day. Couldn't have done it without her," Rex said.

Barry and Junior supported Rex's proposal, and Flo basked in the praise. Even Digger had enjoyed some of the stew, which Rex had picked free of onion pieces before mixing it with his kibble. It was one of the few occasions when Digger had no complaints about eating his own food.

They sat by the fire until darkness fell, and then doused it and went to bed, cozy inside the cave. Barry and Junior had done well, situating the sleeping bags of the younger men near the front of the cave and partially across the opening. One or the other of them would keep watch through the night, taking turns. Digger would, as always, insist on remaining close to Rex, and with his keen sense of smelling and hearing, it was highly unlikely that anyone or anything could surprise them.

Flo and Barry lay in their zipped-together sleeping bags, the inflatable mattress shielding them from the ground. No matter how soft the dirt underneath, their aged joints didn't appreciate sleeping on the ground.

As she lay her head on Barry's shoulder and his arm came around her, she asked if he thought he'd be able to walk to the elevation Junior had told them.

"Of course. I'm all right, Flo. Stop fussing."

She whispered, "I'm your wife, and it's my privilege to fuss over you. And dear, please note the use of the word privilege, not duty." She kissed him and closed her eyes. Barry smiled, let out a soft sigh of satisfaction, turned on his side, and fell asleep almost instantly.

———

When it was his turn for the watch, Rex went outside the cave, and Digger followed. He sat down against a rock about twenty yards away from the cave and switched on his smartphone. Surprisingly, he had a signal. Counting it as good luck, he spent the rest of his watch with his ears attuned to the jungle noises and his eyes and hands on the smartphone, creating the rudimentary blog he'd claimed to have when Flo had asked what he did.

Before he woke Junior to take another turn, he got curious about how he could possibly have a signal in this remote area. Taking advantage of it, he used his smartphone to find the reason and learned that before the turn of the century, most of the cell phone coverage in Peru had been on the coast, along the Pan-American Highway, where more than half the population of Peru lived. It was in 2000 that a third provider was licensed, and coverage in the highlands began to spread, and by 2007, the positive effects on household income had proven the experiment valuable. Rex was reaping the benefits.

He also realized he may have found the way to make his findings known for real, while maintaining his cover. The Ray Davis persona hadn't been used anywhere except here in Peru, and bloggers enjoyed a certain amount of legitimate anonymity if they wanted to. It was something to think about. If he decided to do it, there'd be a lot of work to do on the blog, but it could be worth the effort.

He woke Junior and slept lightly for another two hours before taking the second half of the third watch as he'd agreed with Junior the night before. Neither thought it was a good idea for either Marks to keep watch.

In the morning, though everyone would have enjoyed a hot breakfast, they made do with fruit and some sweet buns they'd brought from Santa Teresa. Now that the rains were starting, they wanted as early a start as possible to make the hoped-for progress before they'd have to find shelter again. This time, they'd start looking for it before the clouds got so dark.

With Junior in the lead again and the rest of the procession arranged as it had been the day before, they went back to the main trail and started up the mountain again. Just before they stepped onto it, Mrs. Marks waited for Rex to catch up.

"Barry didn't have a good night. Will we make it to the village before we run out of food?" she asked. "And by the way, how is it you can keep up with Junior as well as you do? He must be ten years younger than you."

Nonplussed, Rex reflected for a moment on the bluntness of the elderly while he decided how to answer her.

He wouldn't tell her the whole truth. His former work as a black ops assassin for CRC was beyond top-secret, so compartmentalized the President didn't even know about them. He'd been trained to the most rigorous standards in military and espionage techniques, which included missions in mountains, jungle, and desert, on almost every continent and under every condition. Staying fit meant staying alive.

And then it had all come crashing down in the ambush where all his team members, including Digger's former handler, were killed. That ambush was orchestrated by powerful people out of America, and its sole purpose was to kill him. That much he knew, and that was the reason he'd disappeared off the radar. In the back of his mind he was slowly but surely working on a plan to go back to America when the time was right and avenge the death of his team. But for now and the foreseeable future, his take on it was, to stay alive he had to remain dead. He and Digger had been wandering as they pleased since then, with occasional forays into personal missions they'd taken on to help people in need of his and Digger's skills and expertise.

"Well," he began, "you know, I told you yesterday I love history and wanted to write about my travels to the historical sites across the world. I've spent a lot of time in primitive conditions and at altitude. Only just recently realized I could maybe make a living with my observations."

She fixed him with a gimlet eye. "Ray Davis, my gray hair is not a sign that I've gone stupid. What is it you're trying not to tell me?"

Rex didn't know whether to laugh at her persistence or be alarmed at her insight. With a grin he knew would charm her, he dissembled. "I'm not hiding anything, ma'am. Not really. I find that people don't really want to hear about my military experience, and, well, I don't really like to talk about it myself. But you've probably heard the saying, 'once a Marine, always a Marine'. We tend to keep ourselves healthy like we were taught."

It seemed to satisfy her for now, but Rex realized he needed to be careful not to underestimate her intelligence and powers of observation. As she went on ahead and he hung back to keep the same distance as the previous day, he muttered to Digger, "She's pretty sharp for her age, isn't she?"

Digger grinned.

Chapter Eight

The second day and night passed uneventfully except for Flo's continued obvious concern for her husband's physical condition. They covered only half the ten-mile goal, and Rex paid as much attention to Flo's condition as to Barry's. She seemed to be adapting to the altitude well, though.

By the middle of the third day, they'd passed the eleven-thousand-foot mark and were now at the highest elevation the Markses had been exposed to on their trip to Peru. Junior was evidently used to it, as he only kept his pace slow to accommodate the others. Rex had no problems either, for him this was like a relaxing stroll in the park. He stayed behind the Markses at a leisurely pace and made sure they got frequent rest stops. Digger seemed to be totally unaffected by the altitude, since he periodically ran forward on the trail and then back as if he was deliberately trying to get rid of some surplus energy.

Rex didn't know what was in Digger's mind at those times, but he assumed the dog was checking on Junior's whereabouts. He'd stopped growling at him every time he got near, though he still acted leery of the kid and did let out the occasional growl just to let him know, "Don't push your luck, I still don't like you."

They'd had a long lunch break, well over an hour, and Barry stood to indicate he was ready to go. That signaled Junior to move out while Rex tidied up and saw Flo and Barry well started on the trail again. As usual, Flo waited a minute until Barry was out of earshot.

"I wish I'd thought to have you bring some oxygen along. Do his lips look blue to you?"

Rex thought about it. "I don't think so. But you know him better than I do. Do they look blue to you?"

"Only sometimes. Should we turn back?"

It was a good question, and Rex thought they probably should have turned back the previous day. He also thought Barry would have nothing of it. He'd been increasingly vocal about how excited he was to see the unexcavated ruins. Neither his wife's concern or the advice of a man he'd known for less than two weeks would be enough to turn him back. Only if he began to have acute problems breathing or walking would he do so, in Rex's opinion.

He said as much to Flo.

"That's what worries me. Why didn't I think to ask how high this village was before we started? We could have brought oxygen. Another llama could have carried several bottles."

"Even so," Rex said, "it wouldn't have been likely to be enough. And what would Barry have thought or said?"

"He'd probably think it was for me. He's never thought I was as strong as he was. And of course, I never was... Maybe I'm worrying for nothing."

Rex hoped it was so but began thinking of ways to get Barry to a lower elevation in a hurry if a crisis arose. He wondered how one of the llamas would react to being ridden.

Digger came flying around a bend in the trail, excited to be back on the trail. He skidded to a stop beside Flo, licked her hand, and gave Rex a look that clearly said, "What are you waiting for? Let's go!"

Flo laughed. "Well, at least *he* isn't having any trouble." She turned away from Rex and hurried up the trail to catch up with her husband.

"Everything okay up there, buddy?" Rex asked.

Digger *woofed.* Then he wheeled and tore back up the trail in Flo's wake.

Rex picked up the llama's lead and clicked his tongue indicating to the animal it was time to get moving again.

Two hours later, the clouds were beginning to form, and it was time to make camp. They hadn't found a cave again, but the tents were weatherproof, and with the groundcovers under their sleeping bags, everyone but the llamas stayed dry, and they didn't seem to care. Rex suspected their thick coats kept their skin dry in even the worst of the rain.

Today, however, though the clouds were thick and almost black, the rains held off. Once they'd made camp and stashed MREs in the tents for their dinners, Flo headed across the trail and started to step into the jungle under-growth on the other side, when Junior suddenly yelled, "Don't move!"

Everyone froze, unsure who he was talking to. Rex turned his head toward Junior and noticed the gun in his hand at the same time Digger did.

Digger moved first. In a flash, Digger sprinted toward Junior, whose gun was pointed in Flo's direction.

Rex had just enough time to think, *what the…* before his own gun was out and pointed at Junior. He didn't have a clear shot because Digger was in the way. The dog took a flying leap and grabbed Junior's forearm, dragging it down a split-second after the shot rang out.

Flo shrieked.

Junior was flat on his back, screaming at Digger to let go as blood began dripping from where the dog had his jaws locked around his arm.

Rex kept his Sig pointed at Junior and called to Digger, "Leave it!" He couldn't spare a glance at Flo, but he called to her, asking if she was all right. A shaky affirmation came from her direction.

"Yes, I'm okay. Just startled."

Startled. After being shot at. This girl's one cool cucumber.

Aloud, he called to Barry, who he hadn't seen or heard since the shot. "Mr. Marks, are you okay?"

"A little rattled," he wheezed. "I'll be all right. Is Flo okay?"

Rex yelled at Junior. "What the hell was that?"

Junior was still nursing his bleeding arm. Shakily, he pointed toward Flo as Rex disarmed him and told Digger to guard him. It wasn't an answer. Rex was livid and didn't look. Instead he went to Barry. The man was clutching his chest and gasping for breath, pawing at a pocket in his cargo shorts.

"What do you need, Barry?" Rex asked.

Within a couple of seconds, Flo was at his side, a look of love and despair on her face. "Honey?"

"Pills," Barry gasped, letting his left arm fall to his side as he pushed on his chest with the palm of his right hand.

Rex dug in the pocket Barry had been trying to reach and came out with a small amber bottle. He read the label and turned to Barry.

"Nitroglycerin? Mr. Marks, with all due respect, what the hell are you doing on this trek?"

Flo gasped. "Honey, why didn't you tell me? I would never have agreed..."

"And that's why," Marks interrupted. "Is it too much to ask to take advantage of an opportunity of a lifetime before I die? And I'm not going to die any time soon, its only angina, not a heart attack."

Rex's medical training in the Special Forces and CRC taught him that angina is a short-term discomfort or pain in the chest caused by the narrowing of arteries leading to the heart and which was brought on by physical exertion or intense emotion and would go away after a few minutes of rest. The nitroglycerin would help to open up the arteries and relieve the condition quickly.

Flo gasped again and started crying.

"Just give me a damn pill and find out what Roper was thinking, damn him." Barry's color had started to come back, and he was now turning red in the face with anger.

Rex recognized it as a reaction to the adrenaline spike from the fright. Maybe it was a good thing. But one thing was sure, they were going to have a sit-down talk about whether to continue this journey.

"Is anyone going to ask me *why* I fired the gun?" Junior lamented.

Digger growled in response. That was enough to make Junior turn even paler and shut his mouth.

Rex left the Markses murmuring quietly to each other and assuring each other they were both okay. He walked over to Junior, who'd sat on the ground, still holding his bleeding arm.

"All right, asshole. Why did you fire the gun?"

"Because of that," Junior answered, pointing again.

This time Rex looked. Near where Flo had been standing, a yard-long black object lay on the ground. Without calling Digger off, he walked closer until he made out more detail in the gray gloom of the cloudy afternoon. A shiny black snake with a beautiful yellow-gold band of color wrapped around the middle of its face lay in the dust of the trail. Its head was neatly separated from its body by Junior's slug. Flo's footprints were less than six inches from it.

Rex knew snakes. Identifying every venomous snake known to man was part of his training. This one was an Andean coral snake, *Leptomicrurus narduccii*. He'd never seen one in the flesh before, but he knew its venom was among the most potent neurotoxin found in snakes, causing respiratory paralysis and suffocation. In Mexico, its cousin was called the twenty-minute snake, because that's how long you had to live after being bitten.

Junior had probably saved Flo's life.

A flood of relief and remorse flowed through Rex. He turned around and called Digger off.

"Sorry, man," he called out. He started across the trail to the clearing where they'd set up camp and handed Junior's pistol back to him. "The thing is, Digger doesn't like guns."

Junior bristled. "If I'd stopped to explain, Flo would have stepped on the snake and been bitten."

Rex nodded. "You're right. No problem with that. You did the right thing, and I'm sorry about Digger's and my reaction. Let's get over it."

Junior's hands curled into fists. "Next time, I'll shoot the damn dog first."

Rex, who was a yard or so away back on his way to the Markses, stopped and turned slowly. He looked Junior straight in the eyes and spoke softly. "No you won't. You'll be dead before you can pull the trigger."

Rex held Junior's gaze until he dropped his eyes.

Junior squirmed, and Rex knew he'd come close to voiding his bladder.

Good – he got the message.

Rex turned his back on Junior and started walking toward the Markses. He knew Digger would keep the kid from attacking him from behind, and so did Junior, probably.

He had a very important question for Junior, which was, why are *you* carrying a gun? It was a catch-22 situation. He couldn't ask without explaining why he himself was carrying. In his case, he knew why. In Junior's case, he'd have to find out without asking. There was more to Junior than met the eye, and it troubled Rex that he didn't know more about the guy and had begun to trust him so easily.

You're getting sloppy, Dalton.

Flo watched him closely as he approached.

Rex noticed her stare. Great. Now she doesn't trust me.

He forced himself to slow down, look less intimidating, and speak softly. "Are you two all right? Barry?"

Barry nodded wearily. Rex assumed Flo had given him a piece of her mind about the danger he'd put himself in. He glanced at her and repeated the question.

"I'm fine. But I'm wondering why either one of you is carrying a pistol. And I saw how fast you pulled yours. You both owe us an explanation."

Before he responded to her demand, he made sure she knew it was damn lucky for her that someone had been armed.

"I'm sorry I overreacted to Junior pulling his gun. Did

you happen to look down before you moved from where you were when he did?"

"No, why would I?"

"No reason. But if you had, you'd have seen the snake he killed. You were in mortal danger, and he acted to save you. I can't speak for why he has a gun, but I can say that if I'd seen the snake, I'd have done the same thing."

Rex knew he had to give credit where it was due. But if he'd thought it would distract Flo from her original question, he was mistaken.

"Good. I will thank Junior for that, and he can speak for himself about his gun. My question to you remains the same. Why are *you* carrying a gun?"

"Simply put, Flo, I carry a gun for protection. As you have seen, there are wild animals out here, and some can be unfriendly. Snakes, packs of feral dogs, and who knows what else? That's why I carry my pistol, and why it's always on me. There could be bad people out here, too.

"Just so you know, in case you didn't see it when we loaded up, there's also a rifle in one of the packs. That's for bigger wild animals and other threats in whatever form they present themselves.

"And finally, my take on carrying a gun is that I'd rather be judged by twelve than carried by six."

Flo nodded. "All right, I'll grant you those are valid reasons. I still think we should have known. Concealed weapons are dangerous."

Rex didn't reply. He crossed his arms. That was his last word on the subject.

Flo got the hint and turned to Junior, who had managed to get himself up and join the group. "Thank you for saving me," she said.

"You're welcome." Junior cast an injured glance at Rex and Digger but said nothing else.

"Now I'd like to know why you were carrying a weapon without telling us," Flo persisted.

Junior's expression took on the spoiled-brat look Rex had first seen in the restaurant days ago. "To shoot snakes with," he answered condescendingly.

Flo softened her voice. "Do you know of bandits or other human hazards out here?"

"No," Junior snapped and turned away abruptly, leaving the Markses and Rex staring after him.

"Junior, come back. I would like to look at the wounds on your arm and treat them properly. You don't want to get an infection."

Junior ignored her and kept on walking.

"What's got into him?" Barry asked.

Rex wondered the same thing. Of course, being attacked by Digger and having a gun pointed at him would have put anyone in a sour mood, but something was off about Junior's exchange with Flo. Rex intended to find out what it was.

Digger was growling and muttering at Rex's feet. Rex took him a few yards away from the Markses to calm him down.

"It's okay, boy, really. You need to lighten up on him. I've got this."

Digger turned his head away. Rex took his face in both hands to look him in the eye while he repeated his assurances, but Digger twisted out of his grasp, got up, turned so his back was to Rex, and sat down again.

"Well, I guess we know how you feel about it. But seriously, stop growling at him, and don't bite him again unless he attacks one of us."

Rex leaned around to see Digger's face. He was yawning.

Chapter Nine

The next morning, Junior approached Rex despite Digger's continued animosity. He looked nervously at the dog and then appeared to gather his courage.

"Hey, man, I'm sorry I lost my shit yesterday. Even though your dog doesn't like me, I'd never do that. I was just upset about the snake and the misunderstanding. And the bite," he added, looking again at Digger.

Rex wanted it behind them. They still had to decide what to do about Barry's angina and increasing distress in the higher altitude. He accepted Junior's apology with as much grace as he could, and then changed the subject.

"How much farther to the village do you think?" he asked Junior.

"We should get there today. Maybe three to four miles."

Rex addressed everyone when he asked, "Is it really a good idea to continue? Barry, wouldn't it be safer for you to return to a lower altitude? I know Flo has been worried about you."

Barry took on a stubborn look, and Flo spoke up quickly. "We talked about it last night after we went to bed. Barry says he feels fine, and that he hasn't needed the nitroglycerin on the hike before. If anything, his condition has improved since we got to Peru. He feels the exercise and fresh air is good for him. He just got a shock from the... incident."

Rex nodded. "Okay let's hope we don't have more incidents then." Rex asked Junior if the day's hike to the village would be as steep as the day before.

"Yeah, I'm afraid so. But Barry said it was just chest pain, not a heart attack. What difference does a steep trail make?"

You can't be that stupid.

Rex stared at Junior for several seconds.

The younger man stared back.

Flo stepped in.

"Rex, you're welcome to turn back if you don't want to continue. But Barry wants to go on, and I'm going with him, if Junior is still willing to take us."

Rex couldn't see any advantage to turn back four miles from where he wanted to be. He could tell he wasn't going to change Barry's mind, and that Flo was determined to stay with and support her husband. And above all, he had a gut feeling that no good would come of him leaving the Markses in the hands of the not so capable Junior. Although he couldn't put his finger on the reason, the kid's demeanor remained a source of concern for Rex.

"I guess it's settled, then. Junior, how long will it take to get there if we keep it very slow, say a mile an hour?"

"We'd still get there long before dark," Junior answered.

"Then let's load up. Barry, take it slow. As you've heard,

we're not far away from the village, don't push yourself. We've got a lot of time to get there."

"Will do," Barry mumbled.

While they were strapping the tents and other gear back onto the llamas' pack saddles, Rex found a moment to speak to Junior alone.

"Please keep it to that pace," he said. "I don't think Barry should be going any higher at all, even though he says it's okay. But at least let him do it slowly, all right?"

"All right, man. Whatever you say." Junior's insouciant grin was back. Rex felt like wiping it off his face, but he refrained. They didn't need any more discord on this trip.

Hours later, a gaggle of children met them on the outskirts of the village. Flo was all smiles as she handed out candy and little gifts. They were carried to the center of the village in a tidal wave of smiling, laughing villagers who came out of their homes to greet them.

A man of about Rex's age came out of the adobe structure where the crowd stopped pressing them and greeted Junior. They had a hurried conversation, and Rex saw a note pass between them. He moved forward to hear what was being said, and heard Junior ask when the note had arrived.

"Seven days, I think," the man answered.

Junior frowned. He crumpled the note in his hand and turned to the Markses.

"I'm sorry, but I have to go. My uncle has been in an accident, and I need to move fast. I suggest you stay here. Alexandro knows the site, and he will take you there tomorrow or anytime when you're ready. I apologize again, but I have no choice, I need to leave urgently. I'll be back as soon as I've seen to my uncle."

Before they could discuss it, Junior had hoisted his back pack and hurried back the way they'd come. Rex and the Markses stared after him, open-mouthed.

Barry said, "What just happened?"

"I think we've just been ditched," Rex answered. "But don't worry. If he's not back by the time you want to go back, I'll accompany you, we know the way now. What do you want to do?"

Flo spoke firmly. "We've gone to the trouble of getting here for a reason. That reason hasn't changed. My husband and I want to see those ruins, and if you're willing to stay until we've done so and accompany us back, we'll appreciate it very much."

"I'm not in a hurry to return. I'll be happy to stay here for a few days or longer, if the villagers are okay with it."

Barry and Flo both sighed in relief and smiled.

Rex looked closely at Barry. He didn't seem to be in any respiratory distress. If the ruins were another four-thousand feet up the mountainside as Junior had indicated, that might change. But he didn't expect it to change tonight or in the next few days. Flo was already trying to communicate with some women who had circled them, apparently to thank her for what she'd given their children.

He stepped over to translate the Quechuan and told Barry and Flo that the villagers were inviting them to some kind of feast. He wasn't sure if it was in honor of their arrival or another reason. When he'd finished that, he sought out the man who'd handed Junior the note and who seemed to be a kind of leader in the village.

"We'd like to pitch our tents nearby. Where would you like us to do that?" he asked.

The man wouldn't hear of it, though. He insisted that Rex and his companions take an empty house for their shelter. Rex accepted and led the llamas to the hut, where he unloaded them with the help of several village boys, whom Flo rewarded with more candy. The villagers were so excited to see them and interested in them that Rex could only conclude that having visitors not related to their tribe was not something that happened often.

He wondered how the note Junior was handed on their arrival had gotten here, and why they hadn't encountered the messenger on the way. As soon as he'd arranged their possessions for their stay, he went to question the man more closely. The man, Alexandro, claimed to be the village leader. He used the term *Inka Mallku*, which Rex understood to be a high priest in Inca spiritual practice.

Rex soon learned the probable source of Alexandro's stature in the community. Inside his hut, where he invited Rex to sit and speak with him, was an ancient CB radio.

Rex's bullshit gauge was flashing red lights. So, that note hadn't been delivered by messenger, it came in on the radio. Interesting. Very interesting. Why didn't Junior use the radio to contact his uncle then? And if the message came in seven days ago and was so urgent, why didn't Alexandro send someone from the village to meet them on the trail? Why let them walk all the way there just to let Junior go back all the way?

Alexandro must have been educated elsewhere, or by missionaries. He could speak and write Spanish, though he seemed to prefer speaking Quechuan. Rex lost track of the time as Alexandro revealed a wider knowledge of the world than he would have expected. While Alexandro talked, Rex improved his own grasp of Quechuan by asking in Spanish about words or concepts he didn't quite get. Alexandro seemed enchanted by Rex's interest. If he could've stayed here for four to six weeks, he'd become near fluent.

Rex heard Flo calling him from outside and excused himself to see what she wanted. His first thought was that Barry might have taken a turn for the worse, but seeing Flo's smiling face dispelled that quickly.

"What is it?" he asked.

"It's time for the feast, I think," she said. "The women want me to go with them, but I can't understand what they're saying."

Rex waved at Alexandro, who'd followed him out, and called, "Excuse me, I must help this woman."

Alexandro waved back, smiling.

Rex and Flo approached a group of women who were dressed in traditional, colorful woven serapes and short skirts, with the peculiar flat hats of the region set in rakish tilts on their heads. When he'd first seen the hats, he'd assumed they were shaped that way to allow the women to carry large burdens on their heads, as he'd seen in Africa and elsewhere. However, he soon learned that any burden placed on these women's heads would have immediately fallen off, as the colorful hats were as angled as the most proper of British royalty would have worn them.

A short conversation with them revealed that they wanted Flo to accompany them so that she could be dressed in similar traditional clothing. It was their thank-you to her for the gifts she'd handed out so generously. The practice, *ayni*, had to do with sacred reciprocity, or 'if you give, you will receive, and if you receive, you must give back'. In bringing gifts, Flo had made it imperative for the women to reciprocate.

When Rex explained it, Flo started protesting, but Rex told her gently it would be a grave insult not to accept the reciprocal gifts, not to mention putting their hosts in bad standing with their gods.

Flo sighed, but agreed to comply.

Later, when she reappeared, she was wearing a glassy-eyed smile and clasping her hands together. She wore a red wool skirt with designs of blue, orange, green, yellow, and black zig-zag embellishment woven in, a long-sleeved shirt, and a striped shawl of the same colors, plus pink knotted at her throat. Atop her head was the shallow bowl shape of the traditional hat, covered in wool and flat on top, with more geometrical designs. It stayed on her head only because of a strap that was tied under her chin.

When Barry saw her, he burst into laughter, and the women surrounding Flo laughed with him. Rex gathered from the women's chatter that they thought Barry's laughter was because of his delight in his wife's beauty in her new finery. Rex asked her why her hands were clasped so tightly.

"Because this get-up itches like hell!" she stage-whispered.

Rex couldn't help but laugh, too, and be glad he hadn't given the villagers anything. But he thought he'd need to give them something for their hospitality in providing food and shelter. He just hoped they wouldn't insist he wear an itchy wool hat.

The feast turned out to be both delicious and educational. Alexandro sat beside Rex and explained the meanings attached to some of the happenings. Rex found it interesting that as *Inka Mallku*, Alexandro was called upon to heal several children with minor sniffles and other ailments by laying hands on them before the feast started.

He then started a ritual offering, which he called *haywarisqa*, to the deities of the Andes mountains. The villagers all faced the mountains during the ceremony and spoke in a series of ritual gestures acknowledging the power of the mountains and asking for kindness and provision of rain and abundant streams to water their fields, so that they would have overflowing harvests.

Rex knew that he and the Markses were privileged to have been invited to this event, which was usually closed to outsiders.

After that, the villagers began passing dishes around, offering them first to the Markses and Rex, and then to others. It seemed no one ate the food they'd brought themselves, but shared it generously with other families, while they in turn partook of what others had brought.

Rex asked Alexandro about the spiritual practices and listened carefully as the priest lifted the veil on a simple but lovely religion. It seemed enlightenment and a deep appreciation for nature and one's place in the cosmos was at the heart of it. He also talked of female and male energies, attributing gender even to mountains and other natural elements. Rex was intrigued by the difference in his cultural perception of opposites such as male and female being considered complements in the Inca view of things. Alexandro called it *yanantin*, meaning the harmonious relationship of different things.

One of the most striking aspects he learned about the gentle Quechua people was their acceptance of nature, all of it, including animals as part of their family. They admired and petted the llamas and were fascinated with Digger. Their experience of dogs was limited to the Inca orchid dog, the same breed that Flo had tried to befriend in the wild. Digger's heavier build and his black hair were objects of much comment and affection as all of them wanted to touch and pet him. To Rex, this was a welcome change from parts of the world where he and Digger had been where dogs were feared, and in some even viewed with disgust.

That night, he wrote down everything Alexandro had told him before going to sleep. The Markses were both snoring in another room in the tiny house. Digger was already asleep in the middle of the sleeping bag.

Chapter Ten

Rex had only a passing interest in the ruins the Markses were interested in. His true interest was in the history of the people he hoped to gather from the older residents of the village. Peruvian history was more ancient than the Inca civilization for which it was so well-known. He hoped to hear some pre-Inca history from the oral traditions of the villagers.

The next day, the Markses were determined to see the ruins, but no one knew when Junior would return. On their way to the village, they'd passed the tree line at around twelve-thousand feet and entered the environmental realm that Spanish-speaking Peruvians called *tierra helada* – the frozen zone. Arriving in summer as they had, the daytime temperatures were in the mid-fifties – chilly but livable, even without the warm clothing the locals wore.

Rex spoke with Alexandro at length about any dangers that might be lurking for the old couple on a trip to the ruins. Alexandro assured him that there were no large predators here or higher, and that included bad men.

Rex concluded that the Markses would be safe in Alexandro's company, and he was free to gather the tales he'd been anticipating ever since Junior had told him about the village. He saw them off after a hearty breakfast, and then he wandered about the village, speaking to anyone he saw.

He couldn't help but be enthralled by the villagers' friendly, warm, and personable manner wherever he encountered them. Before long, he'd been introduced to a handful of very old men who sat sunning themselves on the east side of the adobe and stone walls that soaked up the sun and reflected the heat back to them. He heard a few folktales, mostly gruesome stories of monsters and gargantuan snakes that guarded lakes and high peaks from human predation.

Especially intriguing was the tale of El Jarjacha, which they pronounced *har-ha-cha*. They explained that people who committed the sin of incest were turned into Jarjachas, the demon of incest; werewolf of the Andes, terrifying creatures, half man, half llama, condemned to stalk around at night.

Rex had always been interested in how such folktales originated, even though it wasn't exactly history. He felt there were hints about conditions in the past that caused the first person to make up such a tale and then caused it to persist. His take on this one was that as higher civilizations made inroads into the remote regions of the Andes, the indigenous people were warned in this way, through fear rather than reason.

As he wandered the village that day, he also observed there were few young men present. He'd seen plenty the evening before, so he eventually asked where they had gone, assuming it was to work in the fields. But to his surprise, someone told him many were at work in the mines.

It was the first he'd heard of mines in these mountains and learned there were, according to them, still rich veins of gold, silver, zinc, copper, and other minerals. The men trekked to the mines early in the morning, and usually returned late at night.

And that led to another tale Rex recognized as one of miners' superstitions around the world. He knew them from his mother's knee as kobolds, tiny human-like imps, hunched and ugly from working in mine shafts. The Quechuan equivalent was Muki, a small humanoid, less than half the size of an adult human. Muki was said to have long blonde hair, a white beard, and piercing eyes, and to waddle like a duck. And it made a bargain with the miners. Bring it the sacred coca leaves, and it would allow the miner who brought it to find rich ore. There was however one condition to this bargain—the miner was not allowed to speak of it. If he did, he ran the risk of dying in a shaft cave-in.

One old man sent Rex a sidelong glance. "Muki has been known to inhabit the places of the old ones," he intoned.

Rex was amused at the tale, but disappointed in the age of it. It had to have originated no earlier than the Inca civilization, which made extensive use of precious metals in its art and ceremonial observations. Not pre-historical at all, maybe not even pre-Columbian.

"Do you know any older tales?" he asked. "Something about the people who were here before the Incas came?"

The old man's demeanour suddenly changed, and he muttered something in a language Rex didn't recognize. It was neither Spanish nor Quechuan. He asked the old man to say it again, in Quechuan.

"Young people are all alike," the old man replied tersely. "They cannot see what is laid before them. You must pay more attention to the Muki."

Confused, Rex asked him to explain. "Do you mean there is more to the story, and I don't yet understand?"

The old man rose and walked away without answering. When Rex asked those who remained if he'd said something to offend the man, they all looked away. He decided not to prod them further and rather ask Alexandro when he and the Markses returned.

When the conversation with the men dried up, Rex left them thinking he might be able to talk to the old women, but they only stared at him as if they didn't understand. A few of the younger women, some with babies carried on their hips or backs in a sling made of the colorful shawls, only giggled when he tried to talk to them.

When he'd exhausted his options for talking with the villagers, he retreated into the house and wrote up what he'd learned on his laptop. As he typed the story of the Muki, he searched each phrase for some deeper meaning. Of course, the meaning of the tale as a whole was that those who work for it will be rewarded, while those who take shortcuts will be punished by losing their riches. He understood that, but had he missed something more profound? It was puzzling.

Digger was showing signs of restlessness, so Rex took him outside for a walk and a play. He took out the kong and stuffed it with dried meat while Digger watched with ecstatic anticipation. It was an oddly-shaped item, made from tough rubber, part cylinder, part cone, with indentations that made it look like a hard-plastic snowman, with a hole running through it from top to bottom. The kong was a special treat, reserved for times when Digger had done especially well, and given sparingly. Digger worked for praise, not treats.

It had been a while since they'd had the leisure to practice his commands. They started with voice commands. Rex commanded, "Scout", and Digger dutifully trotted silently through the nearby area, stopping and lying down on his haunches when he saw anyone. Rex had been trying to teach him a hand signal for the same command, but he was having a hard time coming up with one that would make sense and wouldn't confuse Digger, who knew the circling finger as the command "Circle and return". The difference was vague even to Rex, except for the 'return' part. Digger didn't return when he scouted – he lay down.

Before they'd been at it very long, the children had noticed the activity and correctly deduced what Digger was doing. So, they began to make a game of hide and seek of it. It probably wasn't good for discipline, but Rex was amused when the same child would sneak away after Digger had signaled on him and appear in another place just before Digger got there. At first, Digger seemed confused by it. But after it had happened a few times, the dog let his wide grin tell Rex he was enjoying the game.

Rex teased the children by changing the command. This time he called out, "Run and hide." Digger shot out from between two small stone structures and away from the kids, who all ran after him. In a few minutes, the children ran back toward Rex, all shouting in piping, excited voices that the dog had disappeared.

"Where is he? Where is he?" they called to each other and to Rex. To make it even more fun, Rex yelled, "Up!" The challenge to Digger was, there were no trees. They were above the tree line, and they hadn't seen a tree in two days. Digger would have to find something else to climb to get on top of a house. When he appeared, and Rex pointed at him, the children all screamed with joy and pointed too, laughing. Digger sat down at the edge of the roof and offered his doggy smile. The kids clapped and called to their mothers to come and see the clever dog.

Rex and Digger were still entertaining the village children with Digger's tricks when the Markses and Alexandro returned. The kids immediately abandoned Rex and surrounded Flo, hands out, faces smiling. She smiled back and reached into her pockets.

Barry and Alexandro continued through the street until they met up with Rex, who'd started walking their way as well. Barry was as animated as Rex had ever seen him.

Chapter Eleven

They met in the center of the village, in the small square where the feast had been held the night before. Barry's enthusiasm was infectious, and Rex found himself smiling broadly before he even knew about the reason.

"You won't believe it!" Barry exclaimed. "There are priceless artifacts lying in plain view! No wonder Junior didn't think the site had been excavated. If it had, those artifacts would be long gone."

"Isn't that what's supposed to happen now? Archaeologists are supposed to leave things where they find them, right?" Rex asked.

"Not exactly. Well, it depends on the country. If they'll be damaged by exposure or are in a place where looters can get at them, the scientists will map them to a grid, for provenance, and then remove them for protection. They wind up in the country's museums now. Or that's what's supposed to happen. Previously, they'd wind up in some other country's museums, usually a first-world country like the US or UK, somewhere in Europe."

"So, now that the site is known, is it in danger of being looted?"

"That depends on who knows about it. Therefore, we'll have to ask you to not write about it."

Flo must have told him about my travel blog idea.

"No worries. I won't, if it endangers the site. So, are you going to fund the kid's dig?"

"We have to work out the details, but I think so. We more or less promised him we would if the site turned out to be what he told us. Now that I've seen it, I'm happy that he didn't exaggerate. However, I'm thinking it's going to take more funding than we can swing on our own, but I do have some contacts." Barry looked pleased with himself.

"What else has to happen? Permits? Importing workers?"

"There will be a permit process to go through. For that we'll have to go to Cuzco when Junior returns. As for workers, I think we'll be able to use the locals. It will improve their economy."

That last statement made Rex look around. What he had observed so far didn't convince him that these people wanted or needed to improve the economy. The children he could see trying to tease Digger into playing some more looked healthy and well-fed. He hadn't seen anyone in the village who looked like they didn't get enough to eat, for that matter.

What he'd learned from Alexandro about their spiritual beliefs struck him as nearly ideal. It was basically the Golden Rule, and since they didn't have much to do with outsiders, they had no personal experience of war, except perhaps the oral histories of tribal strife. That had come to an end as far as he could tell. This was a peaceful and contented community working together for their food, shelter, and clothing. No one had more than the other, therefore materialism was not really a factor for them, unless he counted the ancient CB equipment in Alexandro's home. And the village was small enough for self-enforcement of community mores. No one could step out of line and get away with it. What about any of that needed improvement?

These people seem happy to me as they are.

But he withheld his opinion. Being independent, with no fixed address and no specific end destination in mind, having the world as his home, he probably had a very different view of the things that matter in life than most people, including the villagers and the Markses.

Flo joined them, her pockets now empty of candy and whatever other trinkets she'd stowed there. Rex could see she was now mother or grandmother to the entire village, a saint bearing sweets and gifts. And their goodwill extended to Barry as well.

"You've spoiled those children," Rex teased her. "What will they do for candy when you're gone?"

"To be honest, they shouldn't have it, but who can resist those beautiful little joyful faces? But I think they'll be okay when I leave. It's like when your grandmother came to visit when you were a child. Didn't she bring treats that you didn't normally get?"

Rex continued to smile, though he didn't want to discuss his childhood, including the lack of grandparents who'd died before he was born. He nodded, content to let Flo think her point was something familiar to him. He knew very little about children, so he had to trust her judgement.

"I was just telling Ray about how rich a find that site is," Barry said to her.

"Oh, yes! Ray, it's incredible! Some of those pieces are gold, I'm sure."

Rex didn't even try to conceal his disbelief. "Gold, just lying around on the ground?"

"Well, sculptures and masks, funerary objects, that sort of thing. Not solid gold, probably, but at least decorated with gold and precious gems."

"Lying on the ground." Rex's tone swooped downward with his last word, again conveying his skepticism.

"Not precisely. Half-buried, or inside structures that have partially collapsed, so we could see very little inside, but enough to get a peek."

Still aware of his lack of expertise on the subject, Rex nevertheless couldn't help but think there was something very wrong with the picture he was getting. Why would the locals trust someone like Junior enough to show him such treasures?

"We'd like to ask you a favor," Flo was continuing. Barry nodded his head.

Rex turned his attention back to her. "What's that?" he asked.

"We'd like you to come and see for yourself. It would be good to have an unbiased opinion."

"I don't know anything about archaeology," Rex demurred.

"Neither do we. We're only amateurs, but we just want you to see it and give us your opinion. Maybe you'll know if what we think is gold *is* really gold."

Rex didn't know what he'd done to make her believe he was an expert on gold, but now that he considered it, he *would* like to get a look at the artifacts they'd seen. Adding to his curiosity was his protective instincts raised by the continuing niggling feeling that all of this, including Junior's behavior, just seemed off somehow, though he couldn't put his finger on why.

Maybe it was none of his business, and maybe he was too cynical. But the Markses had invited him along, and they were now seeking his reassurance. He'd reached a dead end for now in his historical research. What could it hurt to indulge them? And if he could piece together the reasons or hints that were making him uneasy about the whole trip, then maybe he could do some good here. Protect the old couple, if nothing else. From what, he wasn't sure.

"All right. Tomorrow?"

"Yes, of course. There's no time to waste. Junior should be back in a day or two. We'd like to be prepared to give him a firm answer."

"Okay it's agreed then. But I just want to make it clear that you can't base your decision on any opinions that I might have. My advice is that you get the opinion of an expert before taking any steps." Flo and Barry just nodded and went to their shared shelter to rest from the exertions of the day, so Rex took the opportunity to talk with Alexandro again.

"Forgive me for intruding. But I have more questions for you, if you'll indulge me."

"Of course. Anything for a friend of Junior's."

That was exactly where Rex wanted to start the questioning. "Junior seems to be a good friend to your people?" Rex didn't elaborate, he didn't want to come across as too inquisitive and raise Alexandro's hackles.

Alexandro paused his steps and looked in the direction he and the Markses had traveled when they left the village that morning. "Yes, he is indeed a good friend of ours. He's the one who made me aware of the value of the place of the old ones," he said. "My village is apart from the world. My people know nothing of the luxuries and comfort that your people enjoy. Junior has told us with the money he gives us, it will improve our lives, we can also have a doctor to attend to our very young and very old. Children will no longer die of diseases we can't cure with traditional medicine. Our elders don't need to suffer pain in their final days." He began walking again.

Rex heard the pathos in what Alexandro was saying, but underlying that was something that piqued his sense of something not right.

"Junior has given you money?"

"Oh yes. He told us that the land here, including the site of the ancients, belongs to us. He asked to buy the site, so he could study the ancients and preserve their art and heritage. He gave us money, and we gave him that land."

Rex's senses were on full alert now. He'd have to verify his theory, but he was pretty sure the government of Peru owned all the land that wasn't already occupied by indigenous people when the country was organized in its modern form. Even if this village owned a vast amount of land around it, the government would probably have some rules and regulations in place about foreign land ownership. And he was darn sure they would have very strict rules surrounding archaeological sites and the artifacts unearthed there, let alone selling such sites to a foreigner.

However, he wasn't certain of his facts. He needed to do some research.

Rex had been focused on Alexandro and on his footing as they walked. He paused now to look further afield, and noticed they'd climbed a good bit higher on the slope. The village looked like a toy from here. It was arranged in neat rows around the central square, maybe thirty or forty small stone and adobe houses.

"Do you know how many people live in your village?" he asked.

Standing next to Rex, Alexandro looked downhill at the village. "I haven't counted lately. Babies are born, old ones die. My guess would be around one hundred adults and maybe twenty or so children."

Reflecting on the crowd at the feast, Rex thought that was probably about right. "And some of the men work in the mines? What use do your people have for money? Don't they just barter?"

When Alexandro's answer came, it wasn't responsive to Rex's question. "What do you know about the mines?"

Rex turned to look at him and wondered why he was frowning.

"I was talking with the old men today about what they remember of your history. The history of your people, that is. They told me about the mines and some folk-tales about Muki."

"You mustn't listen to foolish old men," Alexandro said. Abruptly, he turned and started back toward the village.

The next day, Rex, the Markses, and Alexandro set out early in the morning for the archaeological site. Barry was full of energy, in better shape and spirits than Rex'd seen him in all the time since they'd met. Rex could only conclude that the excitement of the find had rejuvenated him. He wouldn't have imagined Barry would be up for a second four-thousand-foot ascent in as many days. Maybe Flo had been right, and the fresh air, thin as it was, and exercise had done him good.

The hike was strenuous, because the site was less than

three miles from the village by Rex's estimate once they got there. The trail was as steep as any part of it had been since Santa Teresa, if not more so. The chill morning air was refreshing, though. Digger must have agreed, as he raced back and forth between Alexandro and Rex bringing up the rear several times until they arrived.

"Should I make Digger stay outside the ruins?" he asked, when they came to a low stone wall that surrounded the old site.

"That isn't necessary," Alexandro answered. "He is a good dog."

"Let's go inside. Don't make a mess inside," Rex said to Digger, who responded by drawing closer to Rex's leg as they entered by an opening that must once have held a gate of some sort.

Barry had become even more animated once they were inside the wall. He led Rex to a crumbling structure. It had no roof, and Rex was prepared to believe it could be centuries old, especially when Barry indicated he should look inside.

Through a slot no wider than six inches, but tall enough that the missing upper walls and roofs interrupted it, Rex could see a room that appeared to be laid out for a ceremonial purpose. In the center of the room was a low stone table, and surrounding it were paving stones pierced with holes about a foot in diameter. In one of the holes, a rotted stump still stood, ten inches high and appearing broken.

Rex's eyes roamed from there to the far walls, and he sucked in a breath. He could see three niches, each about a foot from the next, and sitting inside them were intricately wrought statues that looked somehow familiar. As he stared through the alternating shadow and light trickling in from the missing roof, he recognized the statues as resembling the fantastic figures of what he knew as the Mayan calendar.

What the hell?

And as his eyes adjusted to seeing through the rays of sunlight into the shadows, he realized also that the statues had eyes made of what looked like precious or semi-precious gemstones or turquoise, and decorative touches that looked like what Flo and Barry believed them to be – gold.

Not being an expert, he couldn't tell, especially from a distance, if the artifacts were genuine. His thoughts were divided on the subject. If they were genuine, and the people of Alexandro's village had known about the site all this time, why hadn't they previously made it known to outsiders, or put a different way, why had they now? If the artifacts weren't genuine, of what value were they in such a remote location? Could it be…

Barry's voice interrupted his pondering.

"Well? What do you think?"

Rex answered honestly. "I don't know what to think. If this is genuine, then you're right, it *is* incredible." He turned to Alexandro. "Why are your young men toiling in mines, when all this treasure is here for the taking?"

Alexandro smiled and shook his head. "These objects are sacred to us. We won't touch them. Our ancestors showed artifacts like these to the Europeans when they came to our lands a long time ago. Those foreigners took our beautiful art and melted it into lifeless bricks of gold. We didn't understand, then, because to us, the metal is just metal. The real value is in the art because our gods inhabit the artworks."

Rex nodded. He'd read about that before. Nonetheless,

Alexandro's answer raised more questions. "So why now? Why show this to Junior and Mr. and Mrs. Marks?"

"Junior has made a sacred vow to us that these pieces will be treated with respect, not melted for their gold and jewels. He has paid us for them in money, which we will use to improve the lives of everyone in our village."

Alexandro's smooth, seemingly ready-made answers only served to raise more alerts with Rex. One minute, he seemed to understand the modern world, and the next, he seemed to be immersed in the ancient one his village still inhabited.

"Do you understand that to find all the treasures in this site, Junior must bring many men and women to dig and brush away the soil and stones, layer by layer? It will no longer look as it does now when he's done. And he will carry the artifacts away. Your people will never see them again."

Alexandro shrugged. "We do not visit this place now. It doesn't matter."

Oh, I thought you just told me your gods live in these objects. I would've thought for that reason this place would be important to you. You should make up your mind. One minute, the objects are sacred, and the next, it doesn't matter.

Rex was more and more alarmed by Alexandro's inconsistent elucidations.

When the time came to return to the village, he still hadn't decided what he would say to the Markses to caution them that something wasn't right. They'd asked him if he thought the artifacts were made of real gold. He told them he had no clue but mentioned that it didn't really matter, because if they were genuine, it was as Alexandro had mentioned—the value was in the art. After all, the gods lived within.

He hated to think that these nice people were really artifact looters, but he couldn't rule it out and decided to keep an open mind until he could get his head around what was really going on here. If it turned out the Markses were there for nefarious purposes, a word to the Ministry of Culture would take care of that quickly.

Chapter Twelve

When they got back to the village, Rex was surprised to find Junior had returned already.

He'd made good time on the trail. Too good, in fact. To descend, get to Cuzco, and return in less time than the five of us had taken getting up here is not plausible.

"Hey Speedy Gonzales, how'd you get back so fast? How's your uncle doing?" he asked.

Junior ran a hand through his blond hair, which was already mussed. "I hired a helicopter in Santa Teresa to take me to Cuzco. That was some flying, let me tell you. As soon as I found out what was going on with my uncle, I raced back here. I haven't slept since I left."

Rex was doing the math in his head. It still didn't add up, but he waited for the rest of the story.

"My uncle is sicker than I realized. He needs major surgery, and he can't get it in Cuzco. I need to fly him to the States."

Before he could hear any more, Rex felt a tug at his elbow. Looking down, he recognized the wizened face of one of the elders, known as Pidro, he'd talked to the previous day. Judging by the expression on Pidro's face, it seemed urgent. Rex apologized as he left Junior and the Markses to follow the man.

The elderly Quechua stopped when they were near the edge of the village, out of earshot of everyone. He looked around fearfully, and then pulled Rex's arm until he stooped to the man's shorter stature.

"This man is evil," he whispered.

Rex found he wasn't very surprised. He only needed to know which man was evil—Alexandro, or Junior, or Barry.

"Who is evil?"

"This white man who comes today. He makes pact with our leader. Our leader knows he is evil, but he tells us this promise must be done, for the doctor."

This was the third time Rex had heard about a doctor – twice from Alexandro, and now from this man.

"Your village needs a doctor?" he asked.

"Yes. Doctor drives evil spirits from this place, children and old people like me no longer sick."

"This man, Junior, is evil, and Alexandro is not evil?"

"Alexandro makes bad judgement. First the mines, now this. We must return to old ways."

There was too much information here to sort out while Junior Roper was alone with the Markses, Rex decided.

"We will speak more of this," he told Pidro. "I will keep your secret."

Pidro nodded vigorously. "Yes, keep secret. I am forbidden to tell you. Not tell anyone, please."

Rex wasn't sure of his Quechuan pronouns yet, but he understood what the man had said was the villagers knew of a plot that outsiders shouldn't know about. Why Pidro had chosen to tell him anyway was something he might never know. But for now, he had to leave the mystery behind and get to the Markses, before they committed to something foolish.

Junior didn't mind that Ray Davis had left the conversation, in fact, it suited him very well. Davis was too curious. And way too quick with his gun. The dog, too. Damn mutt nearly took his arm off before. He looked around uneasily. Seeing that Digger had gone with Davis, he continued his story.

"I want to apologize again. I didn't feel good about abandoning you up here, but it was lucky I got to my uncle when I did. I have to go back immediately, but I only came to let you know what was going on."

Flo was looking at him like he thought a mother or grandma would have, her face full of concern for him and his 'uncle'.

I have her in the palm of my hand. Now I only have to convince Barry. They'd be up here gloating over their prize while I make my getaway.

Right on cue, Barry asked, "What *is* going on, son?"

Son. That's good. He'll buy it.

"Ahh... mhh... I can't burden you with my problems. I'll work it out."

"Come on, son. What's the problem? Maybe we can help."

"Well, the thing is, in a nutshell, we, my uncle and I, are out of money. I don't have anything left after losing that thirty-thou on that artifact scam. But that's not your worry. Somehow, I've got to get my uncle back to the States, and to do that, I've got to go back to Cuzco right now. Don't even have the time to eat something. But I have to know you two will be all right. Do you want to go back with me?"

He was skilled at reading faces, and he could tell they were not ready to leave the village yet. Alexandro must have done a good job when he'd shown them the fake site, or rather, the real site with fake artifacts. They'd bought it, hook, line and sinker.

Time to set the hook.

Barry was responding as if he'd memorized his role. "Can we help you with money, son?"

"No, no, of course not! It was my foolishness that lost all that money. I'll figure something out. Sell my body, maybe." He grinned at the tired old joke.

Flo put her hand on his arm. "As handsome as you are, Junior, I don't think that's going to help. What if we buy the site from you? That way, you're not taking charity."

Junior mentally pumped a fist. Schooling his face, he answered, "It's not mine to sell, Flo. But thank you for the thought. I'm glad you understand."

"But Alexandro told us you bought it from the villagers."

"Well, that's what I told him. I wanted to help them get a doctor here, but they're too proud for charity…"

"Like someone else I know," Flo interrupted, smiling sadly.

"Well, anyway, it was just a polite fiction to get them to take the money, and I guess to buy their goodwill, to allow me the right to find someone to fund an archaeological dig."

Junior was well aware that Barry had been watching the exchange between them. He'd seen Barry's eyes move back and forth as he and Flo talked. Now he looked like he had something to say.

"In that case, we insist," Barry stated. "It sounds like we can do two good deeds in one. When your uncle recovers, get in touch with us, and we'll talk about funding the dig. Agreed? Now, what did you pay these people for their site."

Junior knew not to protest anymore. The hook was set, all that remained was how much he could reel in. Barry was about to negotiate the price, pretending to want a bargain when he really meant to include some charity for Junior and his 'uncle'.

And that's just fine with me.

"I gave them fifty-thousand. But it isn't your responsibility."

"Nonsense. Would you take a check, or would you prefer we arrange to wire you the funds?"

Hell, this is going much better than I'd thought.

If he had a check, he'd be able to cash it and disappear before they were even back to civilization. But he was cautious about the amount.

"Well, to be honest, a check would be more convenient for both of us, I reckon, but I don't know how we'd cash such a large one without having to go back to a town with a bigger bank."

"We'll give you five smaller ones. Will that work?"

"Perfect. And I'll only cash what I need to get my uncle to the States and into good care."

"I insist you take it all. After all, we'll be partners in this excavation, soon. That's what partners do for each other."

Junior started fidgeting. Flo took the hint. "Wait here. I'll be back in a jiffy."

When she returned, she was holding six checks. "I wanted them to be less than ten-thousand each, so it wouldn't raise any red flags with the bank. Cash them over several days, and you should be fine. Now, get back to your uncle and get him the care he needs."

Junior hugged her, shook Barry's hand, and started back down the trail at a jog. By the time Davis got back to them, he wanted to be out of sight with a good head start. Just in case.

Rex was troubled to find Junior gone again without saying goodbye to him. The Markses made excuses for him, saying he'd only come out of duty to them, to let them know he had to get his uncle back to the States urgently. Rex just nodded and pretended he understood Junior's haste. Until he had his ducks in a row, he was not going to tell them about his misgivings.

But the weirdness of it all was no longer speculation. If Junior had only meant to inform the Markses that he had to go back to the US with no delay, why would he have taken the time to hike to the village again, when Alexandro had a working CB radio?

What was wrong with the children in the village, that both Pidro, whom Rex judged to be honest if naïve, and Alexandro, whom Rex didn't trust anymore, would mention it in conjunction with the need for a doctor? These people had existed for centuries with no need for medicine other than their own, natural remedies. And all the children Rex had seen were healthy. Were they hiding the sick ones? If so, why?

The Markses' umming and ahhing as they made excuses for Junior made it obvious they were withholding something from him. Since Rex had already seen the archaeological site, he assumed it had something to do with Junior. He just didn't know what. But they were smiling secretively at each other. Something was up. He'd get it out of Flo, later.

When the Markses left for their hut, Rex mumbled softly, "Digger, who's lying around here? Besides Junior. I'm almost certain he's lying – I just don't know about what."

Rex knew if he could talk, Digger probably would have said, "I told you so." He'd been following Rex around dutifully, not even giving him trouble about food. Rex wondered if he was sick, affected by the altitude, or had just given up trying to save him from his own stubbornness. The only times he'd seemed animated for the past couple of days was when he was playing with the children.

Since Rex was too late to hear what Junior told the Markses, he sought out Pidro again when Flo went to see about something for dinner and Barry followed her. He found the old man skulking around outside Alexandro's house.

"Can we talk?" he asked, not realizing Pidro hadn't seen or heard him approach.

The old man gave a squeak of alarm and whirled to face Rex. His eyes were round as saucers, the whites showing all around his pupils. He grabbed Rex with a gnarled old hand and pulled him away from Alexandro's house. When Rex followed willingly, he let go.

Pidro led him away, remaining silent until they reached another house on the other side of the village. Digger padded softly beside him. All over the village, smoke arose from crude chimneys as the women were cooking the evening meal.

At the house, Rex waited for Pidro to say something. He seemed to be having some kind of difficulty finding words, though.

Finally, he did speak. "My daughter," he said. Then he

walked in through the woven wool covering that served as a door. Rex followed.

Inside, a woman toiled over a stone stove. It was a clever contraption, like the barbecue pits Rex knew from his childhood. Mostly square, though not precise, it had an opening to feed in wood and a crude chimney leading from the back to a hole in the roof of the house. This one had a flat piece of metal laid precariously on the stone walls of the stove, and on the metal rested a cast iron pot. Both the metal and the pot were items Rex hadn't observed elsewhere in the village before.

The man spoke to the woman, his daughter, in the language Rex had heard from the old men the day before. He'd like to know the name of it, but now was not the time to ask.

When the daughter replied and pointed, Rex turned to look into the corner she'd indicated. To his shock, a small child lay there, his skin covered in painful-looking sores. Rex mentally reviewed his own inoculations. This child had a dreadful disease, though Rex couldn't guess which one. Hopefully, his own shots were current for whatever this was.

Then he realized that if the child was that sick and the adults weren't, it must not be that communicable.

"What's wrong with him?" he asked. He winced at the bluntness of it, but he didn't have the Quechuan vocabulary yet to be more diplomatic.

"It is the wasting sickness. We do not know what to do to help him. Our medicines do not work. Like the others, he will die."

Wow. And I thought I was blunt.

"The others?" he prompted.

"This is why we need a doctor. Many children have died."

"Only children?"

"Yes. Our future."

Rex nodded. He wanted to look more closely at the child, but he knew it would do little good. He knew emergency field medicine, but illness wasn't part of that, except for what all US soldiers called Montezuma's Revenge – intestinal upset due to unaccustomed food and water sources. Although he wished he could, he knew he was unlikely to be able to diagnose the illness.

"I will speak with Alexandro and find out why the doctor hasn't arrived."

"Please, do not tell him you have seen my grandchild," Pidro pleaded.

Rex put his hand on Pidro's shoulder and felt it shaking. He was either grief-stricken or terrified – perhaps both.

"I won't," he promised.

Digger didn't have the same qualms about approaching the child, Rex discovered. When he turned his attention back to the pitiful pallet in the corner, he saw Digger had lain down beside the child, his head on the little one's chest. The boy had one frail hand tangled in Digger's coat, and a wan smile on his face. Rex hadn't even realized the dog had followed them into the house.

He started to apologize, but the man's daughter spoke in the unfamiliar language, and the man translated. "This is the first time my grandson has smiled since he became ill. She thanks you for bringing the good spirit into the house. Maybe he will recover now."

If only it were that simple. And how different this is from Afghanistan, where they viewed Digger as a djinn, or evil spirit.

Rex realized he had found his latest crusade. On this trip, he'd been nothing more than a tourist, and while he welcomed the lack of stress on this adventure, he'd felt something missing. In every other place he'd wandered, there had been drug or weapons dealers, terrorists, or other of his sworn enemies to deal with. Justice to be served, injustice to be righted. Maybe he was destined to always turn up in places where people were in need of help. There seemed to be a ceaseless stream of new bad guys to take the place of any that Rex had brought to justice in the past. He couldn't help but think of Sisyphus, a figure of Greek mythology who was condemned to forever be pushing a boulder up a mountain, only to see it roll down again and have to push it up all over again.

He left the little house with a new sense of purpose. Sometimes, clusters of things that didn't make sense individually were somehow related. He and Digger had a new mission – to find out how these were related and get to whatever nasty business was at the bottom of it. Then take care of that.

Chapter Thirteen

On his way to Alexandro's house, Rex passed the guest house, as he'd come to think of it. Barry was sitting outside on a stone bench he'd laid some blankets across. He hailed Rex and told him Flo would have dinner ready in a few minutes.

"Where have you been, anyway?" Barry asked.

"Talking to one of the elders," Rex answered. It was true, but Barry would assume it was about history, not about conspiracies in the village. He wasn't ready to talk about that yet. But he did have a question. "I thought you'd be upset about Junior going off again."

"Of course, we want him here, but he has to attend to his uncle's needs first."

"True. I just wondered, because you and Flo seem pretty happy about something."

Barry looked over his shoulder toward the door of the house. "Well, we weren't going to say anything. Didn't want to toot our own horn. But since you ask…"

Rex tried to conceal his eagerness to hear what was coming next. Barry winked.

"We bought the site from Junior." He made air quotes with two fingers on each hand as he said 'bought'.

"What does that mean?" Rex asked, a feeling of dread creeping through his solar plexus. Digger, who had flopped to his belly at Barry's feet, raised his head to look at Rex. The stress must have come through in his tone. Fortunately, Barry hadn't noticed Digger's reaction, and even if he did, he probably wouldn't understand it.

"Well, you know Alexandro thinks he sold that land to Junior. Junior said he just gave them the money to get a doctor and to buy the villagers' goodwill to allow him to setup a dig on the site. Anyway, it turns out Junior's broke. Remember, he lost that thirty-thousand dollars to that scam he was talking about when we first met him?"

Rex nodded. Technically speaking, it wasn't correct that they'd first met him at that restaurant. They'd been unwilling witnesses to the sad story. The Markses hadn't made his acquaintance until the next day, and Rex even later, at Machu Picchu. But he encouraged Barry to go on.

"Well, now he needs the money to get his uncle back to the States, like we told you. And they're tapped out. So, we insisted he take some money to help out, and he wouldn't hear of it, until Flo thought to offer to 'buy' the site. That's when he told us it was all a sham, he just wanted to help the village. And we insisted he let us help."

All sorts of alarms were going off in Rex's mind. The first of them was how could the kid have chartered a helicopter in Santa Teresa to get him to Cuzco faster, if he had no money? Added to the rest of his doubts about that journey, how it had taken much less time than it should have, and the strangeness about the site and its value or no value to the villagers, and the sum that Rex reached spelled 'scam'.

"If you don't mind my asking, how much did you pay?"

Barry looked down. "Aw, it doesn't matter. We've got plenty."

"How much," Rex insisted.

From the door, Flo's voice answered. "Fifty-thousand, if you *must* know. And by the way, dinner's ready."

"Thanks for the dinner, Flo. Sorry, I didn't want to stick my nose in your business. I'm just trying to figure out what a doctor costs in these parts. Did Junior say whether that was for a year, or what?" It was thin, he knew. The question was impertinent, even for that reason. He could see Flo wasn't happy. She'd raised her eyebrows at him and then glanced at Barry before she answered.

"Oh. Well, that's what Junior told us. We didn't ask when the doctor would arrive and how long he or she would stay. Come and eat, before Digger decides it's all his."

Rex looked down. Digger was no longer at their feet. "Digger! Leave it!" he shouted, running into the house to save their dinner. Back in the days when Trevor was Digger's owner, the dog was trained to not help himself to food unless Trevor told him he could. But that kind of discipline had gone out the window since Rex became his owner, and he'd been unable to reinstate it. Fortunately, their dinner was on the stove, out of Digger's reach.

That night, Rex couldn't sleep. He debated telling the Markses his suspicions, but he still had no evidence, and he still didn't know how it all tied together. Had Alexandro made the deal with Junior because of the sick children? It seemed probable he had. But was he scamming Junior, or were both of them scamming the Markses? Were the artifacts genuine, or not? And what the heck was wrong with the kids? Rex had only seen one so far. How many sick children were there really?

He resolved to answer one of the questions tomorrow. He was going back to the site and risk contaminating it by getting his hands on one of those artifacts. If he still couldn't tell, he'd have to make another plan. If it turned out they were genuine, then the Ministry of Culture should be interested, and if they were fake, then the police should be.

It all needed to happen quickly, before the Markses' money was gone, although he had a feeling that their fifty-thousand was already down the drain. He wanted to know how they'd paid it, but any more questions would destroy every bit of trust the Markses had in him. He'd have to investigate on his own, at least until he had enough evidence to get the authorities involved.

It's time to put Rehka to work on this.

It was near midnight in Peru, but his IT consultant, Rehka Gyan, would be at her desk in the home office he'd arranged for her halfway around the world in Mumbai, India. In one of the first missions he'd taken on after his 'death' in the ambush, Rex had freed Rehka from a life of slavery in a Saudi harem. He'd learned how capable she was, and when they got back to India, he'd hired her to handle this type of investigation when he needed it, as well as tracking down and recovering assets he'd liberated from a few of the criminals he'd eliminated.

Quietly, so he wouldn't wake the Markses, he slipped out the door, Digger following, and walked a few hundred yards up the mountainside with his encrypted satellite phone. She was not only his friend but also his technology expert, virtual assistant, and researcher. With a master's degree in computer sciences she had exceptional skills in programming and online research. If anyone anywhere left a digital footprint, be it on social media, email, or online searches, she could track that person down. She had enough black hat and gray hat skills to operate anonymously on the Darknet and get unfettered access to some of the most secure private, government, and law enforcement databases across the globe without leaving so much as a hint that she had been there.

They hadn't known each other for long when he hired her. The circumstances under which they met had been tense. He'd taken an almost paternal, or at least brotherly, interest in her. She and six other women were his first 'rescues' in his new life after he and Digger survived the ambush in Afghanistan and escaped to India.

Before making the call, Rex took a moment to compose his thoughts and prepare himself mentally to be Ruan Daniels—the only name she knew him by.

"Rehka, good morning. It's Ruan."

"Good morning, boss. You know, you always say that. Who else would be calling me on this number?" It was a ritual they went through every time he called. Each time, he had a different answer.

"The Crown Prince of Shambhala might."

She laughed. One of the most pleasant things about her was her enjoyment of his humor, which even he admitted was lame at times.

"How's your dad? Found any more victims to beat at Chaturanga? He's a shark, you know. The only redeeming value he has is he doesn't bet on the games."

"Don't even suggest that to him! He'd start. He and my mother are doing well, thanks to your generosity, Ruan."

"Have you seen Aarav lately? How is he?" Rex referred to Aarav Patel, a police detective and valuable contact he'd made in Mumbai. He had introduced Rehka to Aarav, whose family had virtually adopted her.

"He's undercover again. His wife and I have a standing dinner engagement, and then we watch Disney movies with the children. Where are you now, Ruan? And how are you and my friend Digger doing?"

It was part of their telephone ritual. She always asked him where he was, and he never told her.

"We're both fine. We're here and there, everywhere and anywhere."

Rehka started laughing. "And let me guess, you're doing this and that, not much of anything?"

"Exactly. You know me too well," Rex replied with a big grin. It also pleased him to hear that she was so cheerful lately. He took this as an indication that on the psychological front she was getting over her terrible experience in Saudi Arabia.

The niceties behind them, Rex asked for a report on her progress in tracking down the dozens of secret accounts belonging to a few of the bad guys he'd eliminated. Their money he considered the spoils of war, and Rehka's top duty was to find it, secure it, and invest some of it and distribute some of it to the victims of those bad guys, under his direction. She efficiently gave him the numbers and the new accounts she had tracked down and cleared out and what she'd done with the funds since their last conversation.

Although she had set up spreadsheets in a shared encrypted Cloud-based folder, and Rex looked at them on a regular basis, he still liked to talk to her about it because it gave him the opportunity to praise her for the excellent work she was doing. Part of her psychological battle was her lack of self-esteem.

Finally, they got to the purpose of Rex's call when he asked Rehka to investigate the name Walter Henry Roper—aka Junior, along with modern versions of the salted mine scam.

Early the next morning, the Markses were still asleep when Rex and Digger had crept silently out of the house. Rex paid one of the local women three dollars for a breakfast of quinoa and alpaca meat for himself. He shared a few shreds of the roasted meat with Digger to apologize for the bowl of kibble he'd eaten unseasoned with tastier food before they left.

He went to Alexandro's house to wake him and ask to be taken back to the site, even though he was sure he could find it again on his own. He didn't want Alexandro up in arms, not yet. But he also wanted the man with him to keep an eye on him, in case he was involved in what was beginning to look like an elaborate scam.

Sometime during his sleepless night, while he was thinking about genuine versus fake artifacts, the word 'salted' popped into his head. He'd read many stories about those kinds of scams playing out during the gold rush days of California, when con artists placed lumps of rich ore in worthless mines to convince naïve buyers to pay exorbitant amounts for the land.

He still had to confirm it, but if his subconscious had tossed that up from the mismatched pieces of the past few days' events, he had a suspicion he'd find the artifacts were fake, and the Markses had been scammed. And, admittedly, he'd been played for a fool as well. His pride was at stake, right along with the Markses money, which would no doubt be winging its way into untraceable accounts very soon, unless he could stop it. He had maybe twenty-four hours, maybe even less, from the time Junior had left the village yesterday. Junior had a twelve-hour head start. He'd be arriving in Santa Teresa sometime today if he wasn't there already.

Alexandro didn't answer Rex's hail from outside his house, and the sun was climbing rapidly. Rex considered whether to leave before the Markses awoke, even without Alexandro, or whether he'd be in trouble with all of them if he went on his own. The fact that he could travel faster on his own was the deciding factor. He snapped his fingers for Digger to follow and strode away from the village at a miles-eating clip. Maybe he'd even be back before Alexandro and the Markses became alarmed at his absence.

He made good time, but he was still feeling the lack of oxygen when he saw the partially-fallen wall of the site. Digger waited patiently when Rex sat on the wall to catch his breath before beginning his search. Even though he'd been here only yesterday, the ruins were in such a jumble that he wasn't certain of the place where he'd seen the arti-facts. It took him an hour or more – he wasn't looking at his watch – to locate it again. When he did, he eyed the struc-ture to determine how much damage he'd have to do to reach the artifacts.

While he was studying the walls of the structure, Digger went exploring. Rex didn't pay much attention. Try as he might, he couldn't see how to get to the artifacts without dismantling a wall or two. He was looking in from a different window slot to get a better angle on it when Digger appeared on the other side of the wall from him and let out two short barks.

"Digger! How did you get in there?"

Digger barked again, and then disappeared from view. A few moments later, he reappeared at Rex's side.

"Show me, boy. Show me how you got in there."

Digger tilted his head in that questioning gesture, and Rex tried to think of a command that would get the response he wanted. Before he could think of one, Digger started trotting away. Rex followed.

Disappointed that they were moving away from the structure with the artifacts, Rex started to turn back, but Digger stopped, sat down and stared at him.

"What is it, buddy?"

Digger got up and resumed his path. Rex decided there was something the dog wanted him to see and resigned himself to follow. Digger led him into another crumbling structure, this one using a small cliff for its back wall. Inside, Rex caught a glimpse of Digger's hindquarters and tail as they melted into a shadow that turned out to be a hole in the cliff face.

Rex couldn't call it a cave, because it was clearly man-made. Wondering how stable it was after centuries, he followed cautiously. He'd crawled only a few yards on hands and knees in the dark when the tunnel terminated at an intersection with one that ran perpendicularly to it. The second tunnel was wider, and the roof had fallen in here and there, letting in sunlight and obstructing the passage to some degree. Digger was nowhere in sight.

"Digger! Where did you go?"

In a flash, Digger was back. He'd wriggled through a passage at one of the cave-ins to Rex's left. Rex said, "Where are you taking me?"

In response, Digger turned and went back through the narrow hole in the rubble. Rex followed, pushing aside stones and dirt to make a wider passage.

When there was no longer any light from the cave-ins, Rex wished he had a flashlight, but all he had was his smartphone. Using the flashlight function on it would eat up the battery fast, so he belly-crawled a few more yards in the dark.

Suddenly, dog-breath assaulted his nose. "Digger," Rex said. "How much farther?"

Digger's answering 'woof' was deafening in the confined space. Rex felt himself wince. Then the air cleared of Digger's last meal and was only dusty again. Rex crawled forward.

In only three or four more yards, it began to get lighter again, and then suddenly Rex was out of the tunnel. He found himself in the ceremonial room, the artifacts within arms reach if he stood up.

Reverently, he picked up one of the statues. He was just about to carry it toward the windows from where he'd been looking in before, when he heard Flo's voice.

"Ray! Ray, are you here?"

He moved cautiously to the window slots and looked out. Flo, Barry, and Alexandro were outside, standing in a small circle and facing each other. He couldn't see any weapons, and the Markses seemed puzzled, not angry. Alexandro had a neutral expression on his face. He had to make a decision quickly, remain quiet and stay in hiding or tell them he was there. *Honesty is the best policy*, he decided.

"In here!" Rex called.

Flo's head turned quickly, and he caught her eye. "What are you doing in there, and how'd you get in?" she asked.

"Digger found a way in, and I followed him." He hoped his response was enough for them to not insist on knowing why he was there.

"Oh my goodness! Was that safe?"

"Probably not." He grinned. "I'm glad you're here. If it caves in on me while I'm trying to get out, at least there'll be someone to rescue me."

Flo assumed a scolding expression. "Don't even joke about that. What's that in your hand?"

"Oh. It's one of the artifacts we were looking at yesterday. I was just about to see if it's solid gold, or what."

"Well, is it?"

"I'm not sure. I'd just picked it up when you called. It's pretty heavy though."

By then, both men had wandered over to see what Rex and Flo were talking about. Alexandro didn't look pleased that Rex had the artifact in his hands. Barry looked excited.

Flo asked the others, "Is there any way to determine if that's gold?"

"It's gold," Alexandro stated flatly.

Rex frowned and stared at him, but Barry was already saying something.

"Gold is soft. You could probably dent it with a coin if you have one on you. Or scratch it with a pocketknife."

Rex reached into his pocket and took out his Swiss Army pocketknife. He turned the statue upside down and scratched the bottom of it, even as Alexandro shouted angrily.

"Stop! Do not deface the artwork of our ancestors! Our gods live in them."

But Rex ignored him and saw a dark gray streak where

the knife had scraped. He scraped a bit more from beside the first streak. More of the dark gray appeared. He held it to the light.

"What is that?" Flo said.

Barry stepped up for a closer look. "It looks like iron," he said. He turned to ask Alexandro what he thought, but all he saw was the man's backside as he was running away from the ruin.

"What the hell?"

Rex couldn't see what was happening. The slot was narrow, and the walls thick, so he could only see directly in front of him. "What's happening?"

"Alexandro's running off," Barry shouted.

"Shit. I was afraid of that… And now we know."

"Know what?" Flo asked.

"I'm afraid what we have here are some fake artifacts, a site salted with them to con you into parting with your money. I'm sorry."

Flo sat down abruptly, her legs refusing to support her. She landed heavily on the ground with a grunt. Rex pushed forward, pressing his face as far into the slot as he could to try to see if she was all right. She'd dropped from his view as if she'd been felled by an axe.

"Barry? Is she okay?"

Barry stood stunned. He didn't react to Flo's collapse or Rex's question.

"Barry! Heads up, man. We've got to go after Alexandro, because I think he's in on it. And we've got to get the authorities up here. Make sure Flo's okay, while I get out of here."

Barry nodded absently, still staring after Alexandro's vanishing form.

Rex left the other fake artifacts where they were but kept

hold of the one he'd scraped as he retraced his steps through the tunnel. At times, he had to push it in front of him and use both hands to pull himself back through the fallen rubble from the cave-ins. He couldn't help but wonder where Alexandro had gone.

He was out within a few minutes, carrying the fake artifact. Flo looked at it with disdain. "That's just gold-colored paint," she said.

"I'm afraid you're right. Just realistic enough for you to see it from a distance and believe it was real."

"But this whole set-up must have cost a fortune!" she said. "What did they gain?"

"Well, fifty-thousand from you that we know of. They've probably done it more than once," Rex said.

"I gave that little bastard fifty-thousand dollars!" Barry hissed. His face, which was red from anger, suddenly lost all color and he bent over, clutching his chest.

"Barry!" Flo screamed, she struggled to stand. Rex dropped the artifact and extended a hand to help her up while at the same time trying to support Barry with his other arm. As soon as Flo was on her feet, Rex eased Barry down and patted his pockets.

"Where are those nitro pills?" Before Barry answered, he felt the prescription bottle in a pocket and pulled them out. He twisted off the cap and poured a pill into his palm, then pushed it into Barry's waiting mouth, under his tongue.

Moments later, the pain lost its grip on Barry's chest and he wheezed, "We have to go after Alexandro."

"You're not going anywhere for right now," Rex answered. "And I'm not leaving Flo alone, with you out of commission. Don't worry, we'll catch him later."

Digger let out a short bark on cue.

Rex had left that morning before the Ministry offices were open, but now he felt he couldn't wait to get back to the satphone to call them, if he had a signal. He pulled out his smartphone and looked. Three bars. It would have to be enough.

───────

Hours later, he ushered Flo and Barry into their guest house and saw Barry settled to rest before he went to Alexandro's house. He suspected there'd be no one home, and he was right.

Rex could imagine several very bad scenarios coming down the pike, but it was useless to try to defend against them all. He'd been told the Ministry would send someone to investigate, but it would be several days before the agent got there. Their resources were stretched thin. However, Rex thought both the Markses should rest after three days of the strenuous climb to the ruins and then the shock they'd received.

And he wanted to investigate the extent of the scam. Was the whole village involved? Was the illness of the children real, or was it part of the scam? He wanted to talk to Pidro whose grandchild he'd met. He could at least do that while they waited for the authorities to arrive. Meanwhile, if Alexandro showed his face again, Rex would capture him and hold him until the Ministry's agent arrived.

It was too bad about the Markses money. But if Junior wasn't a master criminal who knew how to cover his digital tracks, Rex could track him down, with Rehka's help.

Before he went to find Pidro, he contacted her again and told her he'd try to get a photo to her if the Markses had one. He wanted her to apply facial recognition software to the problem.

"I want this guy, and I want him badly. Do everything you can to find out everything about him and track him down for me, okay?"

"I will get on it right away. Take care of yourself, Ruan."

Chapter Fourteen

Having set the investigation into Roper in motion, Rex returned to his sleeping bag for a few hours of deeper sleep. After breakfast, he set about getting answers to some of the questions he'd asked himself throughout the night.

The people of the village didn't give off deceptive vibes. He thought most of them could be taken at face value. However, the old man, Pidro, who'd approached him with a warning about Alexandro was different. Not that he appeared to be deceptive, but obviously he had a secret and didn't trust Rex with the truth, yet. What that truth was, Rex intended to find out immediately.

Because he'd promised Pidro, he hadn't said anything about the sick child to the Markses. Making an excuse that he wanted to continue his research, he left the Markses and went to speak to Pidro again.

He found the same group of old men who told him the tales a few days before, sitting on their benches in the sun. He caught Pidro's eye. With a subtle head gesture, he indicated the man should follow him for a private conversation again. Then he went to the same place up the mountainside and waited. As he'd hoped, Pidro joined him half an hour later, explaining that he didn't want to make the others suspicious by following immediately. That gave Rex the opening he needed.

"Is everyone in the village deceiving us about sick children and the pact you mentioned?" he asked. He wished he didn't have to be so blunt, but he felt there was little time to get to the bottom of it. If the whole village was criminally involved, it might be better to retreat and wait for the Ministry agent elsewhere, especially considering Alexandro's disappearance. No villager had remarked on it yet, but when they realized he was missing, what would they do?

Pidro's shoulders slumped. "We chose the wrong leader. I will tell you."

Rex patiently listened to the history of Alexandro's rise to power in the village. It seemed the position of *Inka Mallku* was not hereditary, as he had assumed, but came about when a person from their village proved himself worthy to be the leader in response to a threat.

In Alexandro's case, the threat was the children's illness. Alexandro had been on a sojourn away from the village for a long time, and shortly after he returned, the first child became more ill than usual from the bite of a sand fly. Normally, the bites caused no real harm, no more than the itching of a mosquito bite. But this one festered, from the description of the wound. After listening carefully and asking a few questions, Rex recognized it from his field medicine training as Leishmaniasis.

The condition was caused by protozoa deposited in the wound from an infected sand fly. Instead of healing as a bite from an uninfected fly normally did, the wound harbored the protozoa until it became a parasite, which formed a boil. Left untreated, it could cause disfiguring ulcers or morph into a more serious condition that could attack internal organs and eventually lead to death. Rex knew there was a treatment for it – intravenous injections of an anti-parasitic medication. In fact, the condition was well-known to medical personnel throughout South America. But this village didn't have a doctor – only a relatively ignorant leader who'd set himself up as priest and shaman and now deserted his people.

From what Rex could gather, Alexandro's solution had been to have the families of the children give them water from a sacred spring to drink, and bathe them in the same water. The spring was far away, but those of the village men who worked in the mines were tasked with bringing the water back with them, since the spring was near the mines.

When Pidro fell silent, Rex prompted him.

"And that didn't make them better?"

"No," said Pidro. "That's the problem. It has made them worse. But what are we to do? Our children die with or without the sacred water. The only comfort the children get is from the cool water in which they bathe while their skin is eaten away by the demons."

"What demons?" Rex asked.

"The demons who are angry with the village."

"And who told you demons were angry with the village?" Rex asked, already knowing what the answer was going to be.

"Alexandro told us."

Pidro went on to give his opinion that the demons were angry because they had accepted Alexandro as their *Inka Mallku.* "He no longer follows the old ways. Now he says his medicine isn't strong enough, and we must bring in a doctor from the modern world. But it is because he no longer makes sacrifices to the gods, and he talks to the demons through a modern idol he brought back with him. He should not have left the village. And we should not have chosen him after he returned."

Rex thanked Pidro. There were still missing pieces to the puzzle, but he was beginning to see part of the picture. Somehow, the local sand flies had become infected with the Leishmaniasis protozoa. The adults were probably immune to the bites from prolonged exposure, leaving the flies to feast on the tender skin and blood of the children, whose immature immune systems were more vulnerable.

What was still perplexing though was the role of the spring water. From what he'd gathered from Pidro, it was only after the sacred water treatment began that the children's condition deteriorated.

Thinking about the 'modern idol' Pidro spoke about, Rex remembered the ancient CB radio in Alexandro's hut. That was probably the 'idol' the old man mentioned, through which Alexandro communicated with demons. And Rex had a good idea just who those demons were.

One goes by the name of Junior Roper. But I'm sure there are more demons with CB radios out there.

Well, he could do something about Alexandro's demon-talking device. Before he called Rehka to ask her to investigate what might cause spring water to make Leishmaniasis more lethal, he surreptitiously entered Alexandro's hut. His first thought was to just destroy the CB and leave the pieces there, then he thought about taking it, but on second thought he carefully pried apart the casing and detached a few wires inside. The device was crude by modern standards, but he'd bet dollars to donuts Alexandro wouldn't know how to repair it, anyway.

After that, he contacted Rehka and requested more

research. Until he heard back from her, he wouldn't mention the children to the Markses. Barry was already on the verge of apoplexy because of his suspicions that Alexandro was in cahoots with Junior. Confirming it would do no good, and revealing the extent of Alexandro's harmful activities could excite him even more. Rex didn't know through how many crises Barry's supply of nitroglycerine tablets would last.

Rex spent the afternoon trying to determine how many children were sick, without betraying Pidro's confidence. It saddened him to think that this village, which had probably existed for centuries with no more strife than occasional familial squabbles, was now filled with suspicion and distrust. All because of the greed of one unscrupulous man. How many children had died already because of his incompetence?

If the original illness had been left untreated, no sacred water, would there have been a better outcome? Rex couldn't help but connect the dots between the water and the deterioration of the children's conditions and deaths. Was it possible that there was something in the water which Alexandro was not aware of? Could he be a victim of his own hubris? That didn't absolve him of responsibility for the problems, but it explained his motives, if Rex's musings were correct.

He also had some follow-up questions for his original informant. He'd been thinking about the fact that he knew this illness and what could be done about it. He wanted to know why Alexandro would want it kept secret. Was it possible that he knew the treatment he'd prescribed was less than innocent? If so, why keep it a secret? Maybe he was worried it would mar his reputation and standing in the community.

But Pidro was nowhere to be found.

Instead of spending more time looking for him, Rex assumed he'd gone on some errand or perhaps didn't want to be found. So, Rex turned his mind to figuring out how to finagle information out of the other villagers without revealing what he already knew.

He decided Digger would be part of the solution. The villagers had universally exhibited affection for the big black dog. In the past few days, from time to time, Rex had been forced to bellow a command through the village to lure Digger out of the dwellings where children and sometimes adults had lured him in with morsels of food. It didn't take Digger long to learn this bad habit. It was a dangerous one that Rex had to make him unlearn before some evil-minded person fed him poison.

However, for now, Rex was glad of it, because he could command Digger to go and scout, and then he could pretend to look for his dog, get himself invited in, and perhaps see the sick children for himself. He reasoned that those who didn't invite him into their homes as everyone else did were hiding something inside—more than likely a sick child.

The ruse wouldn't work if he made a systematic search, one house after another. He'd have to spread it over the next few days, pretending he was interested in other things between visits, and always acting casual about it.

Before beginning, he took Digger outside the village, ostensibly for a long run. However, the purpose was to sit him down and have a heart-to-heart talk with him.

"Digger, I want you to be as entertaining as you can, so

I can get into the houses. When you scout, don't be a military dog – be a friendly dog looking for a handout and children to play with."

Digger's ears went forward when Rex said 'scout', but he seemed to understand they were having a conversation rather than Rex giving him a command.

It was not as if Rex didn't know Digger wouldn't understand what he was saying, but over the time they had been buddies he'd been surprised at how many times it seemed as if Digger did in fact follow every word he said during these mission briefing sessions. Of course, there was also the factor that when Rex audibly verbalized his ideas it helped him to hear himself and adjust what sounded unworkable when he heard it for the first time.

Over the next three days, with Digger's help, he managed to get into most of the houses in the village, marking the ones where he hadn't been invited in or Digger had been turned out unceremoniously. No one commented on Digger's behavior, but the villagers gave Rex an idea of how they viewed the activity in their laughter, their welcome of the dog and him, and the apologetic looks he got when they shooed Digger out. He discovered only three more houses he thought harbored illness. He'd been able to confirm none of them, because those were the places where he wasn't invited in. There could be other reasons besides sick kids, but he couldn't guess what. However, Pidro would probably be able to tell him if he could get hold of him.

During this time, he also heard back from Rehka, who requested more information about the springs. She hadn't found anything that would indicate a correlation between the kids consuming or being bathed in spring water and their skin and general condition deteriorating. She wanted to know whether any of the other villagers consumed the water or bathed in it, and if so, whether they were sick.

On the fourth day after Rex's discovery of the fake artifacts, the Markses and Rex were eating lunch when a flurry of activity at the edge of the village reached their ears.

Rex stood up. "I wonder if that's the agent from the Ministry of Culture."

Flo suggested he and Barry go to investigate, while she cleared away the remnants of their meal. They could hear the crowd chatter getting closer as they approached the small square where all public events took place. Entering it, they were only a step ahead of the flock of women and children who were sweeping a single figure along with them.

The sun in his eyes prevented Rex from seeing well enough to make the person out, but his impression was of a short, slight figure in bush clothing like his own cargo pants and cotton shirt. It was only when they drew within a few feet of each other that he realized the figure was female. Another step, and he caught his breath sharply at her extraordinary beauty.

His usual confidence stumbled like a missed step. Fortunately, Barry moved forward, his hand outthrust, and introduced them.

"Barry Marks," he said, pumping the hand she offered in return. "And this is Ray Davis."

"Pleased to meet you, Mr. Marks, Mr. Davis," she said with a lilting Spanish accent. "I'm Luciana Mamani, sent here by the Ministry of Culture to investigate a claim of criminal activity involving antiquities. Would one of you be the reporting party?"

Whoever appointed this woman at the Ministry deserves a medal for good taste.

Rex found his voice and said he was the person who reported it. "I am the one who reported it, but it appears the message got garbled. I'm certain the objects I reported are not antiquities, but forgeries."

He barely heard her answer, lost as he was in the exotic dark eyes, liquid almond-shaped pools of the deepest brown he'd ever seen, almost black and slightly tilted as if her heritage included some Asian genes. In them shone a keen intelligence, always more attractive to him than the regularity of features that most people defined as beauty. Her black lashes were devoid of mascara, but still thickly framed those eyes.

Her face, though, exhibited all the traditional markers of beauty – glowing skin, a straight and well-shaped nose in perfect proportion to her face, and cupid's bow lips framing straight white teeth in an easy smile. Topped with lustrous mahogany brown hair to match her eyes, her oval face was perfection itself. She had pulled off a brimmed hat to better see the taller men, and the hair tumbled from it to her shoulders, slightly mussed. Rex had never seen such beautiful hat-hair before.

"Wait—you don't have arrest authority?"

Now her eyes betrayed amusement. He'd been caught out, staring like an adolescent.

"That's correct. My role is usually to recover stolen artifacts, backed up by local police once my investigations discover their whereabouts. I'm an independent contractor, paid a percentage of the value of the artifacts I recover."

Rex's face must have betrayed his frustration with the news, because she added she was sorry he was disappointed.

He wanted to say that just getting a glimpse of her beauty was reward enough for him, but the echo of the thought made him sound like a creep, and he'd already made a bad impression. Instead, he asked if there was anything in it for her if she caught the scammers and con artists who preyed on tourists interested in antiquities.

"Oh, yes. But not through the Ministry of Culture, which is who you called. I also freelance for the tourism department, again with the help of the police. They sometimes offer a reward, depending on the extent of the crime. Is this a police matter?"

"I think so, yes," Rex answered, feeling himself getting on more solid ground with his emotions.

Luckily, he couldn't see the smile on Digger's face who was sitting a yard or so away observing Rex's stupefaction.

Okay, Dalton, you were sixteen almost twenty years ago, get your shit together. Sure, she's beautiful. It's not like you've never seen a beautiful woman before.

With Barry's help to fill in the details about how Junior Roper took the Markses for fifty-thousand, and how Rex got involved, the trio wandered toward the guest house. Rex revealed that he had been working on an idea of how to reverse the con and would like to discuss it with Luciana, as his plan required not only her knowledge of it but also her help to stay out of trouble with the police.

When they reached their quarters, they introduced Luciana and Flo, and turned to a more immediate practical need. Where would Luciana find shelter?

Alexandro's disappearance from the village had left the village leaderless. Rex went to the old men of the village and asked where the 'new woman' might stay. After much discussion, she was shown to a small house only steps away from theirs. Flo insisted that Luciana have her meals with them for the duration of their mission, and to Rex's elation, she gladly accepted.

That evening, Pidro appeared at the door of the hut and asked to speak to Rex in private again. He knew the Markses couldn't understand the request, but Luciana's curiosity was manifest. He'd have to let her in on the other mysteries in the village soon if he wanted her to trust him.

"You have more questions," Pidro stated.

It was eerie in a way, but Rex understood the villagers were naïve, not stupid. His investigations had attracted notice from the villagers, and they were talking about it. Maybe the families of the sick kids had even appointed the elder to find out what he was looking for.

"I do," he said. "Why would Alexandro tell you to keep this a secret?"

"Because of people like you," Pidro answered. "Alexandro told us he had a plan to get money for a doctor. If outsiders know of our affliction, they flee, and money does not come, and we won't have the doctor."

"How many people like us have come?

Pidro shrugged. "Three. Four. Perhaps more. I do not pay attention. We do as Alexandro say, and go about our lives."

There was the confirmation Rex had been looking for, that Alexandro at least, and probably Roper, had perpetrated this scam more than once. He'd thought so. Most likely, they'd schemed to do it over and over. However, he couldn't think how they'd managed to get away with it more than once.

He asked once again why Pidro would only now reveal the secret and received the same answer. Alexandro was no longer trusted. Rex counted it as good fortune. Now he had hope to enlist the villagers to help reverse the con, and maybe there was also a way he could help them get the medical attention they needed.

Chapter Fifteen

Before they set up their sting, it would be Luciana's role to get buy-in from the Ministry of Culture, the tourism department, and the state and regional police. Rex's idea was complex and required the blessing of the authorities. In addition, it required cooperation from the Ministry in the form of an audacious request that meant the Ministry must trust them. Rex wanted to borrow a couple of genuine priceless antiquities.

But before that could happen, he had to gain Luciana's unmitigated trust, the plan had to be rock-solid, and the villagers had to buy into it and cooperate. Rex had already decided he would stay in the village for as long as it took to plan and execute what he had in mind. The Markses, however, were long overdue for their return to the States. Rex wasted no time in outlining his plan and asking the Markses if they were in or out for the duration.

"I don't really need you two to be here to execute my plan," he explained. "But I'd welcome your participation."

Flo answered for herself and her husband when she

said, "We've never been involved in anything so exciting! We're not going to miss it for the world." Her rosy cheeks and shining eyes confirmed her seriousness and excitement.

Rex looked at Barry. "Are you sure? It could get dangerous."

Barry scoffed. "Like Flo told you. We're not going anywhere. We'll see this through to the end."

Rex smiled. "That's the spirit."

He then explained his plan in detail. "We're not only going to get your money back, we're going to bankrupt them, put them out of business permanently. They won't ever do this again. And then, just for good measure, we're going to have the Peruvians arrest them for doing it in the first place."

By the time he'd laid it out and secured Luciana's assurances that she thought it would work and that she might be able to get the authorities to go along with it, Digger was insisting it was time to eat. Flo excused herself to go and trade for fresh food from the village women, and Rex bribed Digger to work first by showing him the Kong.

Luciana followed and watched the exercises with interest.

"He is so smart!" she exclaimed, when Rex had finally let Digger have the toy. "He is a police dog, no?"

"No, not at all. He's just a very clever service dog," Rex said.

Fortunately, she didn't ask why Rex needed a service dog. He would have hated to lie to her.

Digger always knew when people were talking about him. He dropped the Kong at Rex's feet and began to flirt with Luciana instead, first play-bowing, and then putting his head on her knee and looking at her soulfully.

She laughed and petted his big head, scratching

between his ears until Digger almost swooned with pleasure. "I like dogs," she said.

Rex answered, "Well, this one likes you. I'll have to be careful or he'll leave me for you."

She smiled. Digger was looking at him with a big smile, too.

At dinner, Rex and the Markses asked Luciana how she'd gotten into her line of work.

"I'm an archaeologist by profession," she began. "My mother's grandfather made his fortune in mining. Gold, silver, industrial metals. He was fortunate, but I'm afraid he didn't leave behind a good legacy as his mining operations created some environmental problems, here in Peru, in Argentina, and in other South American locations.

"We have tried to make amends. My mother was an environmental activist, and she fell in love with these mountains, the rich heritage of the Quechuas, and with a Quechua man who she met while protesting a mining permit that would have destroyed his village.

"Eventually they married, and I'm their only child. I guess I inherited my mother's genes, which means I soon became bored with simply cataloguing and studying antiquities that others excavated. I wanted a little more excitement, and, well, here I am."

Rex was fascinated. He and Luciana seemed to have the same restlessness and yearning for adventure and learning. To travel to places where his fancy took him and study the history he loved wherever he went. It was as if something had been either bred or trained into him that craved excitement. Maybe that's what attracted trouble to him like bees to nectar.

The four talked long after the village had gone to sleep, a fire their only light, sharing stories of their travels. Rex, of course, had to censor his stories. When Barry finally declared himself exhausted and needing sleep, the party broke up with promises that tomorrow Luciana would start negotiating with the authorities to support their plan.

As promised, the next day Luciana used her satphone to speak with her contacts in the Ministry of Culture, the tourism department, and the highest police authorities she could reach. When she'd spent several hours going back and forth between government departments, she reported to the rest.

"We have tentative support from Culture and Tourism," she said. "The police want to know more about the man who took your money, Mr. and Mrs. Marks. A representative will be here to interview you as soon as he can get here from Santa Teresa.

"They think these people, this Junior Roper and his uncle, have been operating in this region for quite some time and have scammed many people out of their money. Many of them have been tourists who were too embarrassed to admit how stupid they were, or they feared the trouble they could be in for trying to buy antiquities and just wanted to go home and not get involved in pressing charges."

Barry pressed his lips together, obviously angry. Flo was not as willing to censor her thoughts.

"Those *bastards*," she said. "Well, I'm embarrassed, but I'm not going to let them off the hook and go home. It's not the money—it's the principle. If we get the money back, we'll happily donate it to these people to get them their doctor."

"Agreed," said Rex.

Luciana had more to report, though.

"The Ministry isn't willing to risk real antiquities, Ray. I'm sorry. They don't know you, and they pointed out that neither do I, really. What they *will* do, is lend us some very high-end fakes. Will that be good enough?"

Rex took the time to think it through before answering. "We don't know how sophisticated Junior's knowledge of artifacts is. The crude fakes we found at the site indicate to me that they aren't experts at all. I think that would work."

"Maybe I should see this site for myself," Luciana suggested.

"Good idea. I was going to suggest we do it today. But your negotiations have eaten up half the day. We can't get there and back. We'll have to go tomorrow."

Barry spoke up. "Could the two of you do it without me to slow you down?"

Rex hadn't wanted to suggest it and offend Barry. Flo, however, endorsed the idea.

"You could, couldn't you, Ray? I don't know about you, Miss Mamami."

"Luciana please, Mrs. Marks. And yes, I'm acclimated to altitude, if that's the issue."

"First names it is, then," Flo said. "I'm Flo, he's Barry, and altitude is our nemesis."

Luciana smiled. "I'm game if Ray is."

Rex was outnumbered, and truthfully, he did think they could make the round trip if Luciana didn't want to explore too much of the ruins for now. Before they left, he showed her the fake they'd brought back the last time they'd been to the ruins.

"Definitely crudely done," she pronounced. "How could they think that would even fool anyone?"

"You'd have to see where it was. At a distance it's impossible to tell. I plan to put it back where I found it."

Flo quickly put a snack together from their stores of food and promised to get Barry to help her feed the llamas.

A little smile played on Flo's face when she said, "We'll leave a light on for you, and I'll have something for you to eat when you get here."

Rex and Luciana walked abreast on the trail, with Digger ranging ahead of them. On the way, Luciana questioned him about Alexandro's absence.

"We haven't seen him since he ran away when we discovered the fake. The villagers don't know what to make of it. Fortunately, they haven't turned against us. In a way, it's like they've decided to wait and see what happens, and then they'll make up their minds who to follow."

"You're probably right," she answered. "These people are wise in the ways to survive up here, and they aren't unintelligent. But they are gullible. They've had no experience of the modern world."

"Lucky them," Rex said. "Do you think it's wrong to enlist them to help us pull off this sting?"

"I think they'll take it as a great joke. But I'm worried about Alexandro's whereabouts. How will the sting work out if he's gone to Roper?"

"I guess we'll have to factor that in," Rex said. "I don't know how we'll learn whether he has or not."

When they got to the ruins, Luciana agreed with Rex that the artifacts looked authentic enough to fool a nonexpert, when viewed from the window slot. She was impressed that Digger found the way in. Rex took the time to wriggle back in through the tunnel and replace the artifact, and then they raced nightfall for the village, arriving as the last glow of twilight left the sky.

Two days later, a senior officer from the *Policía Nacional del Perú* arrived, bringing with him the promised high-end fake artifacts they'd need to pull off the sting. Before turning the fakes over, he insisted on interviewing all four of them, even Luciana, separately and then together. Only when he was satisfied that their stories were genuine and their plan solid, did he agree to work with them and 'deputized' Rex. Rex assumed it wasn't a legal deputizing, at least not one that would've been legal in the US since he was in Peru under a false name and forged passport. But, so long as his documentation held up, he supposed it would be fine. Besides, the planned actions were aimed at Roper and cohorts— there was no reason to scrutinize his background.

The officer had also offered to deputize Luciana, but when he explained that accepting could mean she'd lose her entitlement to the bounty she'd otherwise earn on the capture of a major league criminal, she declined. Rex and the Markses had told her they weren't interested in the reward; only retrieving the fifty-thousand dollars and putting Junior *et al* out of business. Anything more they got would be given to the villagers, who had heard over and over from Alexandro that their silence and cooperation would eventually improve their lives, and who had been disappointed time and again. It would be a major undertaking to gain their trust now, when their own leader had betrayed them.

Then the officer had left the fakes with them and gone back to Santa Teresa to make up a posse to hunt down Alexandro.

Now it was time to let the villagers in on the plan, because their support would be needed.

On the following day, Rex, Digger, and Luciana left with one of the llamas bearing what they'd need to camp near the ruins and prepare the site. They'd survey the ruins and select areas where they could begin a genuine dig, set the villagers to the work, and do a little 'salting' of their own. When they'd drawn the plans out with precise measurements, they'd return to enlist the villagers.

Chapter Sixteen

The set-up took three weeks. Luciana's training in archaeology and Rex's tireless work in the back-breaking task of measuring, cataloguing the true nature of the ruins, and helping set up the grids paid off when it was time to involve the villagers. A group of ten men who had lost faith in Alexandro's promises were being trained in the painstaking art of an archaeological dig, which sometimes more resembled fine sculpting than digging.

Luciana had placed the fake artifacts in such a way that they could be 'found' whenever Junior took the bait.

The rest of the village went about its usual business, though they were in on the secret. Alexandro had not been apprehended, but if he returned, he'd see nothing to cause him suspicion of the elaborate scheme afoot.

Rehka had contacted him a few days before to let him know she'd located Junior Roper in Cuzco.

At Luciana's request, instead of picking him up, National Police were watching him and trying to get a lead for where his accomplice, the man he'd claimed was his uncle, might be. There'd been no sign of Alexandro around him. That was good news. If Alexandro didn't get in touch with Roper, the sting had a chance of working.

Now there was nothing to distract him from the task at hand. The site was ready, enough time had passed to make the next step look plausible, and the Ministry of Culture was prepared to do its part. That day, the Ministry would release a press report saying a pair of amateur archaeologists had made an accidental but important discovery.

The report would mention the Markses, state they'd been given a limited permit to dig and had broken through to an older temple beneath the pre-Colombian ruins they were excavating. Within, they'd found countless artifacts of gold and precious gems, an unprecedented and invaluable treasure of the Incas.

It would go on to say that professional archaeologists were on their way to help catalog the hundreds of artifacts, and the Markses were seeking partners to fund a more extensive dig.

Rex had done his part by posting a few hints on his fledgling blog. It was taking shape, and he had received a sudden insight while asking Rehka to do some clever search engine optimization to get the blog noticed by Google and other search engines. While building the site with Rheka's help, it struck him that it would make a great one-time cypher device for future missions, if he needed one. Meanwhile, it would serve as the tripwire for the bait they were dangling in front of Roper. Rehka had reported the blog had one visitor prior to her publicity efforts. The IP address was from Cuzco—Junior.

He was the only one besides the Markses who knew of it yet. He must be keeping track of them by lurking on the blog. Rex hoped if the reports of a discovery didn't bring him running, Junior would at least contact him through the blog. The stage was set. All they needed now was for Junior to play his part.

———

Rex had done one other thing when he spoke to Rehka again. As usual, they'd talked of personal matters for a few minutes before getting down to business. But this time, when Rehka asked where he was, he told her—because of his need to find and hire a doctor for the sick children of the village. He didn't know how long they had before their illnesses couldn't be reversed, and in any case, he couldn't justify allowing them to suffer longer to guarantee his safety.

This situation with the children somehow also led him to the point where he had to take stock of his life since he'd escaped from Afghanistan and dropped off the radar. It seemed every time he tried to find peace and quiet, and just be a tourist interested in history, someone in need of his unique skills crossed his path. Rehka had been one of them. She'd begun as a rescue, but now he relied on her for her IT and hacking skills as well as to administer his money as he required.

If he could trust her with his money and with secrecy as to the odd information requests he'd made over the past year and a half, why not trust her to know where he was, at least this time? He'd have to also trust her enough to tell her why it was important his whereabouts were their secret.

So, he'd told her, "I'm in Peru. You probably guessed that."

Rehka admitted she had. "But I don't know where in Peru. Are you in Cuzco?"

"No, I'm in a village high in the Andes, and I have my

150

hands full here. But I need a doctor up here. Do you think you could find and hire one to come out here soonest?"

The line went quiet and Rex realized his choice of words could've upset Rehka. He imagined her staring at the phone with her mouth agape.

But before he could set her straight, she answered, "I'm sure I can, but I need more information. What do you need the doctor for, so I'll know what kind of doctor to seek? How will he or she know how to find you? What equipment or medications will be needed?"

As she peppered him with questions, Rex realized he didn't know the answers to most of them. He stopped her in midsentence and said, "Rehka, just take a few deep breaths first and relax, the doctor is not for me, it's for the children up here. Just find someone who knows about diseases in Peru. I think it started with Leishmaniasis, so antibiotics or antivirals or whatever they use for that. But something else is going on, and I don't have a clue, but it's killing the children. So I need someone who can think outside the box.

"As for the rest, set up an encrypted email for me and give the doctor the address. It would probably be best for us to speak directly."

"Okay, Ruan, I'll get right on it. One question, though. You've never told me where you were before, or what you do. Has something changed?"

"Yes, and I wanted to talk to you about that. But that'll have to wait until I can get back, so we can talk in person. In the meantime, all I ask is that you trust me a little longer."

"Of course, Ruan. I would trust you with my life. I *have* trusted you with my life."

"Then let me just say that I'm now trusting you with mine. There are people who would like to know where I am, and they may not have my best interests at heart. Do you understand?"

"I think so. If questioned, I don't know where you are or what you're doing."

"Perfect."

"But I'd like to." She laughed. "I think your life must be very exciting."

"Punctuated by moments of sheer terror," he quoted to her without context. "Rehka, we need that doctor ASAP."

"I'm on it."

They settled in for the wait for Junior but were surprised when at about midday on the day after the Ministry's press release, he turned up in person. Rex knew he must have been flown in by plane and helicopter to get close enough to make the trip from Cuzco, in a day.

He, the Markses, and Luciana had talked about how to respond to any overture Junior made, brainstorming the possible approaches he'd take and speculating on whether they'd be in person or long-distance. Now they knew it was a direct frontal assault, but of course Junior was a self-assured master con artist and manipulator.

He greeted them all with enthusiasm, even taking Luciana's presence in stride without comment or apparent curiosity. Of all the scenarios they'd considered, this one had eluded them. But they were not unprepared.

Junior didn't say a word about artifacts, obviously trying to create the impression he was totally oblivious about the 'discovery'.

Instead, he joyfully shared the news that his uncle had made a full recovery without the expensive surgery. He thanked the Markses profusely for their help and produced a big brown envelope and handed it to Barry. It contained fifty-thousand dollars, in cash.

Here it comes.

Four pairs of eyes, five if one counted Digger's, stared at him as they listened to Junior's suggestion that since he and his uncle hadn't needed the money after all, they just unwind the deal. He'd returned the money, and they'd tear up the deed he'd hand-written. No harm, no foul.

Rex reckoned he wasn't the only one struggling to suppress the urge to start smiling as Junior played straight into their hand. Rex kept his eyes on Junior, he didn't dare look at the Markses or Luciana, and he hoped they were also keeping their thoughts to themselves.

It was time for Barry to take over as they'd planned. Barry hadn't become a successful businessman because he was born with a golden spoon in his mouth. He became a self-made multimillionaire through astuteness and hard work. He was a skilled negotiator and dealmaker.

Walter Henry Roper—aka Junior, you're about to be handed your ass. Rex wiped his hand over his face to hide the grin he couldn't stop.

"Junior, hmm… well I'm afraid we might have a bit of a problem with that. You see, the thing is, after you left, we went to the site, found an entry, and examined the artifacts. Alexandro tried his level best to stop us from doing that, and at the time we couldn't understand why. But we soon found the reason. Those artifacts were fake, all of them, made from lead covered in gold-colored paint. That's when Alexandro ran away, and we haven't seen him since.

"So, I'm afraid Alexandro took you for a ride when he sold the rights to the site to you. We, Flo and I, have been thinking about it since we made the unpleasant discovery, but then remembered that you told us that you didn't have much interest in the site per se, but that you really just wanted to help his people to get a doctor for the village."

Junior feigned shock and surprise, even anger at what Barry told him.

He was good, but not good enough to fool Rex, who could see the young charlatan was in a tight spot. Rex, who was trained and had much experience in the art of interrogation, knew how to look for the micro-expressions which people unconsciously displayed when they were distressed or lying.

Barry continued, unfazed. "We're really grateful and happy that your uncle is okay and that it turned out to be not as serious as you feared it would be. So, now that Alexandro has left his people in the lurch, they are still without a doctor and there seems to be an urgent need to get one here without delay.

"So, Junior what do you say, we hand this money over to the villagers and let them use it for what you intended it for all along."

Junior didn't blink or hesitate, "Of course, no problem, but in that case, I would still like to nullify our contract. I take it that would be okay with you?"

Barry looked at Flo as if seeking her permission before he continued.

"I don't really understand why you want that to happen. I mean, you wanted to donate the money to these people to help them, and the rights to the ruins was just a means to an end. We, on the other hand, would like to keep the site and excavate it."

"But you just told me it's worthless. It was 'salted'. Why on earth would you want to keep it?" Junior replied. It was obvious he was having difficulty mustering enough control over his emotions not to snap at Barry.

"Well, you're right. What Alexandro showed us *is* worthless. No doubt about that. But I take it the fact that you've been on the road over the last few days traveling to get here prevented you from seeing the news about the momentous discovery we've made?"

Junior's performance was expert. He asked for details. His pretence of surprise looked genuine, and he congratulated them with evident sincerity.

Barry then deferred to Luciana. "Luciana is our consultant from the Ministry of Culture. Why don't you tell him a little about our find?"

She picked up the cue with aplomb. "Of course." She proceeded to describe the site they'd prepared in superlative terms, throwing in 'solid gold', 'precious gems', and 'priceless artifacts' generously. She finished by saying it was fortunate for the Ministry that the entrance to the cavern was so well-hidden in the ruins, or it would surely have been looted by now.

When she fell silent, Barry said they were grateful for the introduction to the site but unfortunately, they had no intention of canceling the agreement.

"So, as you can see, circumstances have changed, Junior. We've made an important discovery, and we can't let it go."

Junior couldn't subdue his frustration any longer and turned to Rex. "*You* know I wouldn't have sold it if I wasn't desperate. How is this fair? Can't you talk reason into them?"

Rex took up his role with relish. "I'm afraid not, buddy. Flo and Barry were kind enough to let me in on the opportunity. We're partners now, and we've got a sweet deal going here. Miss

Guzman here," he said, indicating Luciana, "has made us aware of a way to profit from the find in a way… how shall I put it… geez… well, let's just say the Ministry won't know about it.

"All we need are the permits, and we're in business."

"So, you were digging without the permits?" Junior asked.

Rex could see the scheming going on in his eyes. He twitched the line, teasing the hook far enough away for the fish – Junior – to create the fear of losing it and luring him to snatch it.

"No, we got the permits for the site Alexandro showed us. But the site we discovered is *below* that level. We need special permits to allow us to send the locals down in an underground excavation, instead of an open one. We've brought up one of the artifacts to examine and establish the authenticity. We've determined without a shadow of doubt those artifacts are indisputably genuine. And the great thing is, there are so many down there, no one will know if a few go missing, if you know what I mean."

Junior had become feverish with his pleading but after a while appeared to give up and asked to see the item they'd brought up from the purported underground cavern. Barry and Rex looked at each other, hummed and hah'ed and pretended to be very reluctant. Junior said it was the least they could do, since they'd snatched up the opportunity for a song and weren't being fair about letting him back in on the deal. In the end, they 'let' Junior 'persuade' them and told him to come by a bit later to look at it.

As they all walked back to the hut, Rex dropped back and spoke to Luciana in a whisper. "Thanks for going along with that."

"Why did you give him a false name for me?"

"Because, if he decides to double-cross us and report this, he won't have your real name."

"Ah. Good idea." She smiled. "But that means he also won't have my real name if he decides to investigate my bona fides, though."

"No chance of that. He's a crook, through and through. You can bet he won't want to have anything to do with the Ministry."

"Let's hope you're right. Even though the Ministry knows what we're trying to do, this thing is so twisted and convoluted they may not understand it, even if they try."

Rex chuckled under his breath. "I'm counting on that. If *they* don't, neither will Junior."

Chapter Seventeen

Junior hadn't counted on Barry Marks' response—his resilience was surprising and even more so his willingness to buy or steal antiquities. There was nothing in his past dealings with the Markses which gave an indication that they would be prepared to get involved in anything illegal.

Junior's plans were in turmoil. What he thought was going to be a straightforward transaction; give back the money, unwind the deal, and then do exactly what Barry had hinted at – pick off a few choice pieces before everything had been catalogued, had now turned into a headache. Nonetheless, Uncle Rich had the black-market connections that could help them make a fortune, if he could only get in on the Markses venture.

I need a new plan. Quickly.

Junior mumbled an apology, broke off from the group and headed for Alexandro's house.

Rex just smiled when he saw where Junior was headed. Sorry to disappoint you, but the CB ain't working no more.

On arrival at Alexandro's hut, he went straight for the

CB to report the new development to Uncle Rich. They'd be able to brainstorm a solution together. When he picked up the handset, he noticed the channel indicator wasn't lit. He checked the batteries, but they gave him that signature jolt when he touched his tongue to them. The power button was turned to on.

What the hell?

He clicked the transmit button and said, "Breaker, Rich Uncle, come back."

No response.

"Rich Uncle, Breaker, come back."

He kept on calling Uncle Rich, but didn't get any response and eventually gave up.

Nothing. Dead, deceased, kaput, done for. Crap.

The loss of communication was an issue. Without Uncle Rich's input, he'd have to wing it and trust that Uncle Rich would buy into it. He stood thinking for a few minutes, and then decided he needed to find Alexandro as a matter of highest priority.

He thought it was also important to go and ask the Markses and Davis if it was an appropriate time to see the antiquities before doing anything else.

They agreed, and Barry went into the second room and came out with an item wrapped in canvas, apparently heavy from the way he handled it. He handed it to Junior.

The weight for its size was staggering. Junior made as if he was going to drop it and noted how all four of the others jumped forward, hands outstretched as if to catch it.

Hmm, that's a good sign. This must be genuine, or at least that's what they seem to believe.

He unwrapped the canvas and gasped.

The item in his hands was a fine piece of Inca art. The statue appeared to depict *Viracocha*, the creator in Incan mythology. The meso-American features on his flat face were exquisitely sculpted, his sun-like crown wrought in delicate gold filigree, with insets of emerald crystals, which also dangled from gold wire extending from the crown. In his ears, opal insets represented large earrings, and his eyes were made of turquoise. His hands clasped ceremonial blades as tall as the central figure at the ends of outstretched arms, and each blade's hilt was created in obsidian.

No wonder they almost fell over their feet to stop me from dropping it.

Any of the gems could have come out, but most worrisome were the wires, dangling gems, and outstretched arms. So delicate, they could easily have bent, damaging the piece badly. Repairs would have lessened the value.

The piece was exquisite – and priceless.

Junior's hands froze into claws, so reluctant was he to hand the piece back. He willed himself to let go. This piece alone was worth more than a million dollars, by his best guess. Whatever it took, whomever he had to kill or injure, from whomever he had to beg, steal, or borrow, this artifact he had to have. But he must play it cool and come up with a plan that would push the Markses, Ray Davis, and this new woman, Lucy or Lucia or Lucinda, or whatever, out of the picture.

He needed Alexandro.

"I'd like to get my hands on that scoundrel, Alexandro. He sure had me fooled," he said, after forcing himself to let go of the statue when he handed it back to Barry. "Does anyone have an idea where he could be found?"

"Like Barry said, we, and that includes the villagers, haven't seen him since he ran away from the ruins when we found the fake," Rex answered. "We thought maybe he went to tell you the scam had been discovered."

"*Me?* You thought *I* was in on it?" Junior pressed his right hand to his chest to emphasize his shock and outrage.

"What else were we to think?" Flo injected.

"I can assure you…"

Barry interrupted. "No need to respond Junior. It was just a passing thought at the time when we were still in shock. We now know you were not in on it. Alexandro is the perpetrator here. Please accept my apology on behalf of all of us." He swept a hand around to indicate he included Flo and Ray.

Junior nodded his head graciously. "I can't blame you. In your shoes, I would've thought the same. I accept your apology.

"So, Alexandro is beyond our reach, unscathed. Pity," he added. "But now I'd like to propose we join forces. An excavation at this location will be expensive. Are you able to handle it yourselves? My uncle has connections in high places. If you'll let me buy in, he'll help us get grants and investors to fund the dig."

Junior examined each face in turn. Barry and Flo looked as if they could be interested, with more information maybe. Ray looked doubtful. The woman looked neutral.

"Face it, since you said the word of the discovery was out, you're going to have to post guards as well as hire labor for the excavation."

"Yeah, we're aware of all that. But what has changed in your circumstances? Not long ago you told Barry and Flo you *and* your uncle were broke – destitute – because of that scam someone pulled on you," Ray objected.

"That's true, but no doubt you also know sometimes it's all about *who* you know. My uncle has very influential contacts in all the right places, I also have some, but no one nearly as good as his.

"Come on, there's enough here to go around for all of us. I don't want to really say this, but if it wasn't for me you wouldn't be in this position. I'm sure you'll agree that's true. And frankly, it would help my uncle and me get back on our feet."

Rex began, "I don't know…"

But Flo interjected. "Barry, Ray, I'm on Junior's side on this one. He's right. We actually do owe him a debt of gratitude. None of this would have happened if he hadn't brought us here and sold the site to us. And I agree there's more than enough to go around. What's one more artifact out of the dozens we've seen? And who knows how much more is buried under those? Give the boy a chance."

Junior smiled gratefully at Flo as she put her hand on her husband's arm, pleading with him. Over Ray's frowning objections, Barry finally relented.

"Okay. Truth be told, we could use some help. Luciana is taking care of the permits, so that won't be a problem. She assured us it has actually been approved, they're just issuing the paperwork, we should have that within the next week or so. The help we need is for a quick cash injection to kick the project off. As you can imagine, we need to move at speed here before we get inundated with government officials, police and such. We urgently need the money to hire workers, buy supplies, hire guards, and buy weapons, too. Once word gets out about what we have here, every criminal on the planet will want to relieve us of our fortune, hence the need for guards and weapons.

"By my calculations we need about two million US to get going. Flo and I have already put half of that down, and as we free up some of our investments in the US we'll be able to fund the rest.

"So, I guess the question is can you put up a million in

the next week? I know it's a lot of money, but the payback is probably going to be tenfold, at the minimum. I'll understand if you can't get the money. I have a few potential business partners lined up back home. But as Flo said, we owe you a favor, so if you can put the money in, we'll be good to go."

"For what percentage?" Junior asked.

"Twenty-five," Barry replied without blinking an eye.

"What! No way. I put up half the money and I get a quarter share? That's daylight robbery. I thought I could count on your good will, but it seems to me I've been mistaken."

"Hang on, Junior. You obviously didn't pay attention. We need two million just to start this thing up. Ray and I have put half of that down already. Our estimates are that we'll need in the order of four million or more, in total. So make your calculations."

"Hmm... yeah well... okay. I see what you're saying. Okay, it's a deal." He stuck out his hand to shake Barry's to seal the deal.

Barry didn't reciprocate. "Not so quick, Junior. Let's just dot all the i's and cross all the t's before we shake on the deal. We're in agreement that time is of the essence here. Right?"

Junior nodded.

"Okay, we need the million in cash in the next week. You deliver the money on time, and we have a deal on which I'll shake hands. Otherwise, the deal's off and we go with our other options."

Junior smiled from ear to ear. "Thanks for the opportunity. It shouldn't take long to get the money."

Early the next morning, Junior left a note for the Markses and Rex that he'd started early to get back sooner and headed down the trail the four of them had originally taken to get to the village. He didn't want company, because he would need to leave the trail at a hidden branch not two miles from the village.

The concealed trail led another five miles to a small valley where his helicopter and its pilot waited. When he'd convinced Uncle Rich that the investment would be worth it, he never dreamed that in the months they'd been running this scam, they'd been unknowingly sitting on top of a major fortune.

It was too bad they hadn't discovered it themselves. If they had, the Ministry would never have heard of it, and he and his uncle could have sold off every artifact one by one. They would never have had to expose themselves to risk for chump change like fifty-thousand dollars again in their lives. But he'd come up with a plan to get fifty-*million*. It just required patience and what he and Uncle Rich were best at – the double-cross.

All he had to do was convince Uncle Rich to go along with it. The artifacts had to be worth many millions, if what he'd seen was any indication. He'd trade one-million for fifty-million or more any day.

Digger alerted Rex to someone moving around outside, and he was awake instantly. He gave Digger the hand signal to be quiet and rose soundlessly. The rustling had stopped, but Digger was still on high alert.

Checking outside, Rex almost stumbled over the rock holding down the paper with a note from Junior.

"Made an early start so I can be back sooner. See you in a few."

Rex snapped his eyes from the paper to the spaces between the houses, but he couldn't see Junior. He quickly pulled his pants and a t-shirt on and slid his feet into his boots. There was no time to waste if he was to catch up to Junior.

"Scout," he said quietly to Digger. "Stay close."

As Digger moved out, Rex tied his boots and jumped out the door to follow.

With his second command, Digger would know not to lose him as he followed as quickly as he could. Within a few minutes, they'd caught up to within thirty yards of Junior, and Rex signaled Digger to follow at a distance. When Junior disappeared into the jungle after reaching the tree line, Rex knew he was on the verge of discovering the secret to Junior's speedy travel.

He called Digger even closer to him to avoid any nasty surprises in case Junior had made them and set up an ambush. Consequently, when the noise of the helicopter starting up reached their ears, he and Digger were still well within the dense jungle. He began to run, and Digger soon outpaced him. The helicopter was well above when they got close enough to see the end of the trail break through the trees, and by the time he'd managed to stop Digger going into the clearing and peer out from cover, it was too high for him to see the call numbers.

At least now he knew he'd been right. The bastard had been able to travel close to the village all along.

Rex returned to the village with the news. "I suspect we'll see him returning much sooner than he indicated. He must think we're idiots not to catch on."

"He's used to dealing with gullible people," Luciana

said. "But that's in our favor. He'll be careless, thinking he's got you where he wants you. He won't even suspect the shoe is actually on the other foot."

"Let's hope you're right. And that the money he's going to bring with him is really theirs, not from some grant they can get. We don't want government money, we want Roper and his uncle's money."

Luciana smiled. "I have no doubt it's theirs. I just heard from the Ministry. They finally got word from the National Police, and they've confirmed these two have been on their radar. No organization would give them a grant, definitely not the government. They're on a watch list, but without victim and witness cooperation, they've avoided prosecution and jail."

The day proved even more eventful when Rex checked his email. The new one Rehka had set up for him had its first message, from a Doctor Elena Martinez. The email introduced her and indicated in direct language with no frills that she was aware of his request for a doctor, familiar with Leishmaniasis and other diseases endemic to Peru, and would be free to come to the village within a week. She named her price and asked for directions to the village.

Rex admired the no-nonsense approach and emailed back immediately that the terms were acceptable. He asked if she would require a guide or if she had any more questions about the illness.

The answer came immediately. No guide needed, just give her coordinates for the trail head out of Santa Teresa. And please forward close-up pictures of the skin deterioration he'd described.

Rex acknowledged the email and said he'd forward pictures as soon as he could. Then he found Pidro and asked to see his grandchild again.

"A doctor is coming," he said. "She must see pictures of your grandchild to know what medicines to bring."

It was probably more complex than that, he thought, but rather than try to explain modern medicine to Pidro, the simplest explanation that would satisfy the man would be best.

Rex noted that the child seemed sicker than before. Pidro's daughter reported that her son couldn't swallow and was having diarrhea. The two symptoms together were life-threatening. Rex observed that the child was now almost completely bald and was wheezing. These weren't symptoms related to Leishmaniasis, to the best of his knowledge.

"Try to get more water down him," he advised. "Just a few drops at a time, but frequently." It was all he could do. He just hoped the little one could last the week until the doctor arrived.

Chapter Eighteen

Now that they had the fish on the hook, so to speak, Rex asked Pidro if he could gather the villagers. The ten men who had been training to appear to be archaeological diggers had agreed to help him explain to the rest of the village what had been going on in relative secrecy right under their noses.

It was clear to Rex that village affairs had been deteriorating in Alexandro's absence. He thought it was time for a new leader to step forward when it became clear that Alexandro would not return. Until someone told the village what was afoot, they wouldn't know they needed a leader.

The adults of the village gathered in the square, and Rex sent Digger to help the older children keep the younger ones entertained, so none of the adults would miss the meeting. He didn't see any sick children, so he made a mental note to check on them after the meeting.

The chatter among the villagers, who were sitting cross-legged in the dirt of the square, died down as Pidro took his place next to Rex and asked them to attend the words they would hear. He said he had come to trust the foreigner as a friend to them. Then he took his place among the rest, and it was Rex's turn to speak.

"My friends, we thank you for your hospitality in the weeks we have stayed among you. We are honored and privileged to be allowed to live among you. Now it is time to tell you why we have stayed so long, and what we think has happened to the *Inka Mallku.*"

In the next few minutes, he explained how he and the Markses had discovered an evil plot involving the sacred ruins, and that Alexandro had been frightened by the discovery. It was too soon to try to convince the entire village at once that their *Inka Mallku* had been one of the plotters. He'd let the ten men who already believed it explain that. However, he told them that Junior was the bad man and part of the wickedness going on.

"In the next few days, we expect the visitor who comes often, Junior, to return. He is the person responsible for setting up the whole scheme, and we have made plans to capture him and prevent him from continuing with his immoral actions."

After that, he had the ten men stand and explain what Junior had done and what they were doing to help capture him. The rest of the villagers seemed spellbound, until one of the ten mentioned Alexandro's part in the plot. Then chaos broke out, with arguments, raised voices, and finger pointing springing up among them like wild fire.

To Rex's surprise, more than half the village was willing to agree that Alexandro had been a bad leader. About half of the rest were unsure and therefore remained quiet. The remainder were Alexandro supporters, the ones starting arguments, and it was getting out of hand.

Rex called Digger back to him and commanded, "Sound off."

Digger responded with a howl that raised even Rex's hackles. The villagers quieted immediately and looked toward Digger fearfully. Digger sat down and smiled, apparently pleased with the result.

Rex had never used that command before, didn't know how he'd remembered it in the moment. It must have lodged in his subconscious from when he'd watched Trevor practicing with Digger so long ago. For a moment, he stared at Digger, astonished at the incredible volume of the sound he'd unleashed. But it had the effect he'd hoped.

"We may have made a mistake in believing Alexandro ran away because he was guilty. Maybe he was frightened. If he comes back, we will give him a chance to explain himself. Will that satisfy everyone?"

Murmurs of assent rose, and then everyone fell silent. Rex judged that most of them agreed, so he asked, "Can we count on your silence and cooperation when Junior comes back?"

A few shouts of *yes* and none of *no* assured him that his gamble had paid off. Now he asked Pidro to come and stand next to him, and then suggested they choose a new leader.

If this is not subtle influence, then I don't know what is. He subdued a smile.

Not surprisingly, they chose Pidro, but not as *Inka Mallku*. He refused that title, because he said he was not a healer. His title would simply be leader, and he would step down when Alexandro returned and proved to be innocent or a new *Inka Mallku* took Alexandro's place.

A few hours later, Rex, Luciana, and the Markses were relaxing after dinner and discussing the meeting when a commotion outside set Digger to barking in alarming tones. Rex immediately recognized the agitation in Digger's bark, sprang up, and rushed out to see what was going on.

The others were only a step behind him, and they found themselves staring at the business end of the automatic weapons in the hands of four mean-looking strangers. The men shouted in Spanish, but Rex had already raised his hands. Now the others followed his lead.

Rex immediately saw this was an explosive situation, and the only way to not escalate it was to be nice and submissive. Unarmed people seldom win aggressive arguments with people who had guns pointed at them. The most important thing to do now was to not piss these guys off— try everything he could to defuse the situation, keep everyone calm, and protect Digger who was all tensed up, growling and restless. One wrong move from the dog, and these bastards would shoot him. And if they did that, Rex knew he would not be able to control himself. He snapped his fingers to get Digger's attention and said softly, "Quiet boy. Stand down. Relax. I'll handle this."

Then he turned to the four men and said, "Good evening gentlemen. To what do we owe the honor?"

"Shut up and listen," said one of them. "We know you have discovered treasure. It belongs to our people. We're here to collect payment. You pay us money, you can keep the artifacts."

Rex could hardly believe it. A protection racket. Peruvian mafia? All the way up here in the Andes. I would not have believed it if anyone told me before tonight.

"We don't have a problem to pay you. The problem we

have is we don't have money with us. You'll have to give us time to get it for you."

He felt Luciana stir beside him, grabbed her hand, and gave it a slight squeeze, hoping she would get the urgent mental message to go along with whatever he said. Apparently, she did, because she kept quiet.

"Listen gringo, we will be back in three days. You'd better have ten-thousand dollars ready when we come, or you will die without illness."

"All right. We will try."

"Well, if you know what's good for you, you won't try, you'll make sure."

The men melted into the darkness, and the last thing Rex saw was the shine of the quarter-moon's light on the barrel of one of the men's rifles. He sighed in relief and turned to the others.

"That went fairly well, I reckon."

"What are we going to do?" Flo asked.

Rex could hear her effort to say it calmly, not quite succeeding. He gave her props for not wailing the question.

When he answered, his voice had taken on a self-assured tone none of them had heard before. "We're going to prepare for their return…"

"What! Are you out of your mind? We must get out of here. That's what we should be doing right now!" Barry snapped.

Rex held his hand up and stopped Barry from launching into a tirade. "As I said, we're going to prepare for their return, and what I was about to say was, and then we are going to kick their asses for them. Those that are fortunate enough to survive what I have in mind will never want to get within a hundred miles of this place ever again."

Into the stunned silence that followed, Luciana said, "I should have seen that coming."

"What?" Barry asked.

"They were probably Shining Path," she answered. "An insurgent group you three would have no reason to know about. When I approved Ray's plan, I should have known the publicity would bring them out. I blame myself. Maybe we should just pay them off."

"I don't pay extortionists, never have and never will." Rex spoke measuredly.

Luciana stared at Rex, puzzled. The Markses stared at him, bewildered.

"If any of you want to pay them, you're welcome. I suggest you pack your stuff, go to Santa Teresa, and get the money. I'm not doing anything of the kind. I'm going to teach these hooligans a very painful lesson. And when I'm done with them, if you still feel like paying them, then you can do so to those who you can find and who still want money."

The three of them were silent for a while. Then Barry spoke. "I guess you're right, they have to be stopped from doing this, not encouraged to continue by paying them. Pay them once, and they'll be back for more."

"Yes, dear, that's all nice and dandy, but how are you—we—going to do it? We only saw four of them. How many more are there? If they're terrorists, as Lucania said, they'll be armed. How exactly are the four of us going to take on an army of revolutionaries?" Her gaze moved between Barry and Rex while she talked.

Barry looked at Rex and said, "How?"

"I'll tell you in the morning. Let's turn in. We have a lot of work to do tomorrow. Those of you who want to go and get money will need an early start. It's a long way there and back. Those of you who'll stay and help me sort this out will also need an early start."

Rex was in a foul mood. There was nothing in this world that could put him in a bad mood as quickly as terrorists, drug dealers, human traffickers, arms dealers—in short, all scum had that effect on him. He didn't have time or mental energy to comfort his three friends—he had a war to plan.

He was wakeful all night, cataloguing what resources he had and how he could deploy them under several different scenarios.

To the best of his knowledge, there were just two firearms in the village – his Sig Sauer P226, and the hunting rifle he'd brought with him. It wasn't much against automatic weapons. But in his line of work, he'd learned that necessity is the mother of invention. He'd seen no weapons of any kind in the village, but there'd been no reason he would. Maybe they had something. He'd ask in the morning.

How many of the insurgents would come? Did his apparent cooperation buy them enough trust that the same four would come, or would they come with a larger force?

As far as troops were concerned, Rex had the villagers and his companions. He doubted Flo and Barry would be any help. Although Barry's mettle had surprised him over the last few weeks. Luciana was an unknown, but he had watched her closely and suspected she had some useful skills. Maybe even a firearm. Of the hundred or so villagers, excluding the children, more than half were women. He'd need some of them to herd the children to safety before the shooting broke out. That there was going to be a shootout he didn't doubt.

In the absence of weapons, there were a few tricks up

his sleeves, but some required material he wasn't sure was available. The rest, he could teach the villagers to prepare.

He'd been right. They'd have a busy day tomorrow. Before the first light of approaching dawn pinked the sky, Rex closed his eyes and went to sleep with a final comforting thought when his secret weapon, Digger, sighed and snuggled up to him seemingly sensing that Rex had worked through the plan and he could also get some rest now.

Rex and Digger rose only two hours later as the noise in the room indicated Flo was at work fixing breakfast. But when he opened his eyes, he discovered it wasn't Flo but Barry bustling around to get the fire in the stove going.

"Hey, Barry. How did you sleep?" he asked, wriggling into his pants inside the sleeping bag.

"Not a wink. I'm thinking we should pack up and hightail it back to civilization. We're in over our heads."

Rex nodded thoughtfully. "You know, that might be a good idea for you and Flo. Luciana, too. I'm sure she could guide you back."

"We wouldn't go without you," Barry answered. "We got you into this."

"Not really. I asked to join you, remember? And I already told you, I have a different idea about how to handle this." Rex kept his tone neutral, but Barry took issue with his statement anyway.

"You reckon just because you're forty years younger you can handle this kind of danger, and we can't?" He bristled like a wet hen.

"Yes, there's that, and the fact that I've had military training, as Flo probably would've told you."

"Yeah, she told me. But that doesn't mean you can take on an insurgent group by yourself."

Rex was out of the sleeping bag by then, pulling on a

shirt. He padded over to the stove in his stocking feet and set a kettle of water over the fire to start some coffee.

"I wouldn't be by myself. And I can't leave the villagers to face the threat alone. It's our fault – *my* fault – they're in the middle of the situation."

"How is it your fault?" Barry asked.

"My cockamamie plan to reverse the sting – my fault."

"Okay, I can see I won't change your mind. What's your plan now?"

Rex was still explaining his plans for fortifying and arming the village, with Barry loudly scoffing at some parts of it, when Flo came in, her hair awry from not having been brushed yet. "Why are you two making all this racket?"

As soon as she'd heard Barry's case for leaving the village and Rex's for not leaving, she made her pronouncement. "I'm staying right here. Rex is right, honey. We can't leave the villagers."

Rex and Barry answered hotly at the same time.

"I never said *we*," Rex said.

At the same time, Barry said, "I don't want you in danger, woman. Can't you understand that?"

Flo looked at them, each in turn, put her fists on her hipbones, arms akimbo, and said, "Which one of you thinks you can make me do or not do anything? I'm not leaving. Deal with it."

Luciana poked her head through the door hangings just in time to hear Flo's announcement. She started laughing.

"What did I miss? Sounds entertaining."

Later, after they'd eaten and cleared away the dishes, with Digger helping take care of the leftovers, Rex had to repeat his litany of makeshift weaponry and booby traps. Luciana confirmed she had a sidearm, with a spare clip, thirty bullets in total. They finally came to the consensus that Rex should enlist the villagers to set up what they could, and that it wasn't any safer for Flo or anyone else to leave the village before the insurgents came back.

Luciana summed it up. "They'll just kill you on the trail. They probably have the place surrounded."

With that decided, Rex and Luciana, who also spoke Quechuan, divided the town between them and went to speak to the villagers. They met again for a noon meal and to report their findings.

Rex had turned up two ancient rifles in his half of the village, but there wasn't much ammunition for either, and they weren't the same caliber. Luciana's half yielded three more with the same issues. The villagers used them for hunting when the alpaca herd wasn't adequate for their needs.

Despite their haste to get ready, both had been subjected to lengthy explanations about the reason there were guns in the village. To Rex's annoyance, Luciana decided to explain it to the Markses. Baby alpaca, or *cria*, were carried for eleven to eleven and a half months, so the *hembras*, or females, were off-limits. Every year, most of the males born that year were *wethered*, leaving only a handful of the strongest for breeding purposes. If more females than males were born, the harvestable males of the herd became too few to support the village for a few months in late summer. In that case, the owners of the rifles went out to hunt the wild camelids, such as guanacos and vicunas, along with the rarer taruca, a species of deer, to supply them all with meat. And as if the villagers' and Luciana's insistence to repeat the explanation was not enough irritation for Rex, who understood the urgency here, Flo started her own thread. She was appalled to learn that their presence had put more pressure on the alpaca herd, since it was only late spring, and spring-born alpacas were less hardy than those born in the fall. The hopes of the village were pinned on the almost-year-lings from the previous fall and the *cria* that would be born in a few months.

At another time, Rex would've been very interested to learn all about it, but now was not the time. He was only interested in how much firepower they had, and after pooling their information, he and Luciana concluded it wasn't enough. Nowhere near enough.

They'd have to get creative.

Because the village was above the tree line, there was no cover to speak of, other than the stone houses and occasional boulders deposited in the valley by ancient glaciers now played out. Rex's usual traps – tripwires, underground pit blinds, and shooting holes – would be spotted instantly unless the attack came at night. He had none of the ambush-type munitions that he and a team would usually rely on. To defend this village, he'd have to resort to his knowledge of methods that were used in the Middle Ages and whatever the oldsters could remember of Inca warfare. Getting it all ready would be a mammoth undertaking.

After their meal, Rex went to talk to the old men about Inca weapons and methods of war, while Luciana inquired of the women where they could find ingredients for some of the thermal devices Rex had described, and to solicit volunteers to construct methods of deployment.

When Shining Path returned, it was as Rex had feared, though he didn't know it yet. They came in numbers. However, one of his scenarios, and the one he and Luciana thought most likely, and the one Rex preferred, if he had a choice, was that they would attack at night.

The bandits didn't disappoint - they arrived at night.

Their first indication they were there came from Digger,

who gave one sharp bark that was answered by gunfire. Rex, who'd been sleeping in his clothes since the morning after the first Shining Path visit, rolled out of the sleeping bag, instantly alert.

"Get Luciana," he whispered to Digger. The black dog would be impossible to see, since the moon hadn't risen yet. Digger left his side, and Rex did a quick mental review of his plan.

The villagers had helped to dig a few trenches just outside the village, where the trail ended, and the well-worn paths of the village began. If the insurgents had approached from that side, he'd see and hear the evidence any minute, as the oncoming insurgents fell into the trenches filled with brush and pine resin they'd collected from the forest below them. One match, lit by an insurgent to see what he was up against, or thrown into the trench by a villager who would be creeping toward the trench for that purpose, would ignite the brush as if it was soaked in gasoline.

If they'd come from another direction, the trenches would be a liability, because once the designated villager lit it, it would backlight the entire village and anyone moving within it.

Rex barely had time to think through all of it before the flames erupted on the other side of the village from his location, and inhuman screams confirmed a few of the insurgents had fallen in and been trapped by the fire.

Digger was back, with Luciana in tow, her sidearm in hand. "How many?" she said.

"Not sure, but there are definitely already a few less than they came with," he said grimly.

"Where are Flo and Barry?"

If they'd done as planned, they would've belly-crawled

to the nearest houses and begun alerting people. The whole village should be alert by now. "They're telling the villagers to light the torches. We'll soon be able to see what we're up against."

The torches they'd prepared with scraps of wool, fat from the Peruvian chinchilla known locally as *vizcacha*, and aged deadfall from the forest, were a double-edged sword. They'd reveal the insurgents, but they'd also reveal the villagers. Rex had taught the villagers to stay low as they made their way to their assigned torches, already set up in holes in the ground to support them upright, and then drop low again after lighting them with the matches he provided.

Those who had guns were to use the oil lamps inside their homes to adjust to the light, then rush outside and surprise the insurgents caught unawares when the torches lit them up and blinded them at the same time. There'd be a few seconds at most when it would give the riflemen an advantage. Right on cue, Rex watched as torches all over the village flamed into life, followed by gunfire.

Okay, so far so good.

Now it was time for the surprise Rex had arranged, something that ought to strike terror into any insurgents that hadn't already been wounded or killed. Before he resorted to his rifle or his Sig, which would be useless against a charging enemy once he ran out of ammo, he'd use a cross-bow one of the villagers had produced during the weapons inventory.

It had six bolts, and Rex intended to make each one count.

He'd prepared the bolts like fire-arrows, but instead of merely tipping them with ordinary flammable material, he'd collected the limestone and guano he needed to fabricate quicklime and calcium phosphide. He'd added pine resin to hold the mixture together and ignite it. And voila! Greek fire. Any insurgent hit by the bolt would die horribly as the unquenchable fire burned right through him. Rex would aim for center mass, the torso and belly.

Meanwhile, Flo and Barry would separate and make for the berms of mixed animal fat and sand that surrounded the rest of the village. They'd been quicker to construct than the trenches at the head of the trail, so he'd had the villagers place them around the rest of the area. Flo and Barry would light them and then retreat to the nearest stone house to take shelter for the duration of the fight.

As Rex went over the defenses in his mind while waiting behind cover for the approach of an insurgent leader, he noticed a dark figure holding what could only have been a rifle darting from house to house, backlit by the numerous fires now burning. He whispered to Digger, "Heads up, here we go."

He quickly lit the Greek fire at the tip of the bolt already seated in the cross-bow and took aim at the next place he'd be able to see the approaching man silhouetted by the fire.

There!

He pulled the trigger.

The bolt flew true, and Rex watched dispassionately as the insurgent's belly bloomed with flames. The man fell, screaming, and two others ran toward their fallen comrade. Rex put the next bolt in one of them.

Luciana's handgun barked just a split second before the other reached the first man. Her target fell next to the screaming human torches. He had a merciful exit from this world compared to the two he wanted to help.

In the next few minutes, the first fallen man became the foundation of a funeral pyre with several more falling on top of him. Rex hit four more with his remaining bolts, six out of six—a perfect score. Others tripped over sprawled limbs of Luciana's kills and fell into the flames, which caught and consumed them indiscriminately. By the time Rex was out of bolts, he'd counted nine insurgents down between them. For the couple of minutes that took, Digger sat quivering beside Rex, who would have recognized the dog's eagerness to get into the action if he'd had time to notice. But he hadn't commanded Digger to do anything, so the dog waited for instructions.

Gradually, the noise of combat died down and it became apparent the insurgents had enough. They were obviously not prepared for such a welcoming party. It was impossible to tell how many of them arrived, how many were killed and wounded, and how many escaped.

Rex considered it prudent to wait for morning before they attempted a pursuit, even if that meant losing the trail. He didn't want to risk them walking into an ambush. He told everyone to go to bed and try to get some sleep, knowing that no one would sleep.

The attack had been too swift to execute the escape plan he'd devised for the children and a few women to shepherd them to safety, so he and Luciana once more divided the town and went door to door to be sure everyone was okay.

Sadly, two of the oldest village men had succumbed to gunfire. Miraculously, those were the only casualties on their side. The casualties on the enemy's side would be revealed when the sun came up. For the moment, Rex was deeply in need of sleep.

"Digger, guard." The dog would know that meant 'stand guard' instead of 'guard someone'. Rex didn't know how he knew it, but he did. Rex had used the command before when he should have stayed alert but needed sleep.

Rex woke with a start to find Luciana leaning over him, a soft smile playing on her lips.

"Wake up, sleepyhead," she said.

He flailed wildly, disoriented for a moment that someone could have sneaked up on him.

Where's Digger? Oh – I left him on guard outside.

Luciana must have read his mind, because she said, "I fed Digger and let him in. The sun's up, and half the village is in the square waiting for you to tell them if we're safe now and what they should do. We are safe, I think. I doubt Shining Path will want to walk into that buzz-saw again."

He scooted up to a sitting position before he remembered he wasn't dressed. Then he remembered he'd crawled into the sleeping bag with his pants on after the battle.

Luciana had walked away, and now she was back with a cup of coffee and an admiring look at his bare chest.

Oops. I did take off my shirt.

Rex slurped the coffee gratefully. His brain fog was dissipating. His eyes scouted the floor for a flat place to set the cup, so he could grab his shirt and pull it on. He thought he caught a fleeting look of disappointment on Luciana's face, but when his head popped out of the neck of the shirt, she had her neutral expression in place.

What the hell is wrong with me? This woman is messing with my brains. Damn, but she's beautiful. She may do that any time she wants.

Digger sat a yard or so away staring at rex and Luciana in turn—and he smiled.

Rex made an effort to collect his scattered thoughts and asked if Luciana had been out to count the bodies that morning.

"No. Waiting for you. I don't care to see them, if that's okay with you."

Her squeamishness surprised him. She hadn't hesitated to pull the trigger last night. As soon as he finished his coffee, he'd need to take care of business. Dead bodies in the middle of the village would quickly become a health hazard, not to mention a psychological shock for the villagers, and it was definitely not a sight children should see.

He took a huge swallow to finish the coffee and stood up.

"No worries. I'll go arrange to get rid of the bodies. I wish we could know how many of them were in their group. Depending on that, we'll get an idea if they might regroup and come back."

"Impossible to tell," she replied, "maybe if you question everyone who was involved in the fight to find out how many they saw from their positions you could come up with an estimate?"

"Hmm, that's an idea, and maybe we can also check out their tracks as well."

Luciana nodded.

"I'm going, then," Rex said, "Want to head over to the square and tell them I'll be along in a few minutes?"

"Okay."

He started with the pile of fused, burned bodies only a few yards from their door. It was a mess, but he counted six heads, or rather six skulls. Some of the faces and skin were burned off right down to the bone. He didn't think Greek fire would consume bone to ash, so he took that number as accurate. Three more lay in sprawled heaps nearby. Luciana's kills, from the bullet wounds in their faces and chests.

From there, he walked around the village, counted three more in the underground pit traps, and another five gunshot and lying here and there in the spaces between the village houses. Seventeen. A strange number. He hadn't seen the one who'd done the talking on the first night. Was he missing, or was he one of the faceless victims of the Greek fire?

After Rex reported the death count to the village and consulted with Luciana and the Markses, he oversaw the men Pidro had detailed to help dig a burial pit a mile from the village. Other men from the village dragged the bodies to it with the help of Rex's llamas, and they tried to burn the remains again before they buried what was left after the fires went out.

During the project, Rex couldn't help but notice his helpers were looking at him with a mixture of awe and superstitious dread. He supposed they were wondering if he was a demon or magical being who could command fire that wouldn't go out. Or if they wanted him to be their new *Inka Mallku* because he was the first one in their lifetimes to stand up to these evil men who raided their village with impunity.

He thought two of the bodies were those of two of the four men who'd come to demand protection money in the first place. One had been sandwiched face down in the pile of six burned men, so he hadn't recognized him before. The other, he hadn't recognized at all, but Barry had.

The spokesperson was still not accounted for.

Rex had asked Flo to accompany Luciana, and set the two of them to find out what, if anything, they could do for the villagers to get them settled back to normal again. Though normal, he assumed, would elude them for a while. He didn't suppose this village had heard of a raid like that for hundreds of years; not since the Conquistadors had swept through and destroyed the village represented by the ruins they'd visited.

When they finally all came together again, Rex told them the bad news. It looked like the leader of the insurgent group that had attacked them had escaped.

He proposed to go after them, if Digger could get a scent to track. Flo dropped her head into her hands, knowing from experience that when Rex was determined to do something, she would never be able to talk him out of it. Barry made a half-hearted offer to go with him, which Rex declined. Luciana's offer, though, he accepted. She'd proved herself a worthy teammate, and he figured he and Digger could use her help.

There was no time to waste if they were going to have a prayer of tracking down the Shining Path survivors from the previous night's raid. Already, scents would have faded or been confused by activity in the village today. Rex and Luciana left with only their backpacks containing food, water, their weapons, and remaining ammunition. Digger also carried his backpack with three days' worth of kibble and some water.

If they didn't catch up with the insurgents or locate where they turned off the trail in that time, they'd be in Santa Teresa and there'd be no chance of finding them.

They went to the trail head, just beyond the pit trap. He studied the tracks on the ground and found a set he was reasonably certain belonged to one of the attackers and followed it for a few yards. Then he knelt to have a talk with

Digger, pointing to the tracks on the ground and saying, "We need to find those bad men. Can you do it?"

He got no answer except a swipe of Digger's tongue across his face.

The dog dropped his nose to the ground and snuffled for a second or two, looked up at Rex, and waited for instructions.

"Yep, that's right, boy, track."

Digger was on his feet, nose down, following the tracks.

Rex and Luciana followed.

Digger went about twenty yards, stopped, and looked over his shoulder. He lifted his head and barked, a fierce, protective bark.

"That's it, boy!" Rex exclaimed. "Find them!"

Luciana looked down as she and Rex caught up with Digger, and she saw what Digger had detected.

"Look, Ray! One of them is wounded." She pointed to a tiny drop of blackened blood in the dirt.

"Now I'm sure he'll be able to find them. Let's go!" Rex said. They quickened their steps even more, breaking into a jog as Digger kept going. The two of them were pelting downhill so fast Luciana soon became breathless, and Rex had to call to Digger to slow down, so they were able to keep up.

Their quarry had a twelve-hour head start.

After a couple of hours, Luciana needed a rest stop, so Rex called Digger back for a drink and some well-deserved praise. It wasn't long after they started up again that Digger followed the tracks along another hidden branch in the trail, which led off to the opposite side of the trail from the one on which Rex and Digger had followed Junior a few days before.

The main trail was proving to be more than a minor

route from Santa Teresa to the Quechua village. It was a regular 'superhighway'.

On the first day, after turning off the main trail, they traveled what Rex reckoned was about twelve miles before it got too dark under the forest canopy to continue. They stopped for the night and unrolled their sleeping bags next to each other in the shelter of a tree that had low-hanging branches to conceal them.

After a quick meal of jerky and a few bites of cold cooked quinoa, they climbed into their sleeping bags and told themselves to go to sleep. Their breathing told Rex that Luciana and Digger were asleep within minutes.

Rex, however, was too keyed up to sleep. It was not as if he was on a mission with a few highly-trained, trusted, and well-equipped Special Forces operators. He would have been happier if he'd had a few grenades, an accurate idea of the enemy's whereabouts, the ability to use his and Digger's coms without awkward questions from Luciana, and while he was wishing, a rocket launcher or two and a drone or two overhead.

Eventually, he was able to quiet his thoughts and get some sleep. It seemed like it had been only a few minutes, though, when Digger stirred. Shortly after that, Luciana woke up as well. It was still dark enough under the tree that Rex doubted it was morning, but the twitter of the birds set him straight.

"We might as well get up," he muttered. "The avian alarm-clock can't be set to snooze."

Luciana's delightful tinkle of laughter answered. "You're right. And nature is calling me anyway."

They settled for having breakfast to go, chewing jerky as they walked. While Luciana made her quick side trip, Digger gobbled his kibble and a piece of jerky.

They'd been traveling around the mountain peak on a relatively flat route since leaving the main trail. Today, however, the trail led distinctly downward. Rex asked Luciana how well she knew these mountains, whether they might be heading into a valley.

She started to explain, but before she could get two words out, Rex noticed Digger had stopped and was alerting to something. He touched her arm and put his finger to his mouth. "Something or someone is up ahead," he whispered. "Stay here and stay quiet. I'll check it out."

Luciana stopped in her tracks, nodded her understanding, and melted into a squatting position just off the trail. When Rex looked back a few steps later, he noted with approval that she'd disappeared from his view.

That woman is not just a beautiful face.

He crept silently to Digger's position—the birds had fallen silent as well. Digger's stance was unmistakeable. There was some threat up ahead.

When he reached Digger, he quickly saw the alarming truth. The trail turned sharply there and dropped steeply. The trees were thinner, and through them, Rex could see a mile or more down the zigzag of the trail. In the distance was what looked like a tent city. And between the tents and their position, he and Digger could see a group of men, six to eight, coming up the trail toward them. The distance, the trees, and rugged terrain made it hard to tell accurately how many they were. But he could make out the long guns they were carrying. The bottom line was, he, Digger, and Luciana were outnumbered at least two to one in the best-case scenario.

Only help for that is an ambush to level the odds a bit.

But there was precious little time to set it up. A faint

echo of sound from downhill assured him that the insurgents were not expecting any trouble.

He sprinted for Luciana's position.

"They're coming our way, and they're armed for bear—six to eight of them."

"We aren't. What do we do?" she asked.

"We'll have to ambush them, unless we just hide and follow. But that leaves the village and the Markses as sitting ducks. I think we should take them on here."

"How much ammo do you have left?"

"One clip. Fifteen rounds. You?"

"I have twenty-eight. That's enough as long as we can surprise them and make each shot count.

"Okay, you stay where you are. You're in a good spot right there; they won't be able to see you. Fortunately, they've not spread themselves out. They're bundled up in a small group. Obviously not expecting any trouble—all working in our favor.

"I'll go down about twenty yards from here toward them. They'll pass me first, and as soon as the last one is past me, I will attack them from the back. Some of them might run toward you, and some might turn around to face me. So, your job is to shoot anyone coming your way, and I'll take care of anyone coming my way. We need to hit them hard right from the beginning, get their numbers down as quickly as possible while chaos reigns in that first few seconds."

"I will. Good luck," she said.

Rex just nodded. He never really cared much for that expression. The concept made him think of the two sides of a coin, which meant he had fifty-fifty odds—chance or antichance. It implied that luck, not skill, would determine success or failure. Luck was not a strategy or a plan, and luck also had nothing to do with what he was about to do to the insurgents. However, he didn't give Luciana a piece of his mind. He just thanked her and left.

He'd left Digger on guard to warn him when they got close, commanding him to hide and guard while he spoke to Luciana. Rex ran back to Digger's position and found a place where he could hide.

He then walked a few yards back toward Luciana and set up the hunting rifle with a trip-wire made from a vine he hastily braided into a sturdier rope. One round from the rifle could take out at least one insurgent, and depending on how close these goons were to each other a single shot might get two or three of them.

After setting up the trap, he went back to his chosen position, next to Digger.

There was no time for anything else.

The wait seemed interminable but was only about fifteen minutes in truth. Digger's soft, low growl warned him a few seconds before the first of the group came into Rex's view. He let them pass his position. There were eight of them. They were talking and laughing, without a worry in the world.

Boys do I have a nasty surprise for you, Rex grinned.

The rifle trap was about ten yards away, halfway toward Luciana's position.

The first man in the line, who Rex recognized as the leader of the group who visited them the first time, walked up to the vine crossing his path and kicked it out of his way.

Bang!

The .308 bullet went through, shattered his right arm, penetrated his chest, and blew his heart to pieces, then exited just below the left armpit and lodged in a tree trunk two yards away. If one of his buddies had been next to him, there would have been two dead men instead of one.

Digger exploded out of hiding and tackled the last man in the file, his standard operating procedure for a situation like this. It ensured he'd take out at least one enemy before the others realized what happened.

Rex opened fire. The next man went down, and then a second.

Three down, five to go.

Before the remainder of the thugs could figure out what was happening, and in which direction they should return fire, Rex had moved to a new position. He saw one point his automatic rifle and start spraying the position Rex had left. Rex shot him in the face, and the man fell backward, his rifle continuing to spew rounds into the air.

Four down, four to go.

Rex caught sight of Digger, who had ripped out the throat of the first guy he'd attacked and was engaged in a rolling, snarling fight for his life with the second. Rex shot one of the two remaining insurgents, and the last one dropped his rifle and lifted his hands in the air. Both had been aiming at Digger, unable to fire because they'd risk hitting their own man.

Rex rose and kept his gun pointed at the last insurgent. "Down on the ground, face down and hands behind your head!" he shouted in Spanish.

The man dropped down and did as he was told.

Rex walked up to him, picked his rifle up, and put his right boot between the man's shoulder blades to keep him down before turning to see how Digger was doing.

Digger had his man down, and so far he'd been able to prevent the guy from getting his hand on his sidearm.

"Just hang onto that arm buddy, I'll be there in a

second." Rex hit his captive behind the right ear with the Sig and his body went limp. He sprinted over to Digger. Seeing an opening, he moved in and kicked the insurgent in the ribs hard enough to lift him off the ground. He'd meant to get him in the head, but either way, it worked. The guy folded like a pierced balloon and went quiet—out cold. Digger shook himself loose and took a step back, ready to attack again. Only the guy's desperate attempts to keep Digger away from his throat had saved him.

"Okay, you did great boy. Stand down."

Rex then called out to Luciana that everything was under control.

The wide-eyed, pallid Luciana joined him a few seconds later and looked at the carnage in shock. Rex felt sorry for her, a battlefield in the aftermath was a gut-wrenching experience, even for battle-hardened soldiers.

He walked up to her, put his arms around her, and gave her a hug, and then gently guided her to one of the trees and helped her to sit down. He spoke gently, "Sit here and take a few deep breaths. I'll take care of the prisoners."

She just nodded dumbly.

He went back to his position where he started the fight, picked up his back pack, and retrieved flexi-cuffs which he used to tie the two captives up.

After tying up the last man, Luciana ran to him, throwing her arms around his neck and hugging him tightly.

He submitted to the hug, and when she pulled her head back to look up at him, there were tears in her eyes. He lowered his face and kissed her gently on the lips, and then retrieved his handkerchief to wipe her tears away. He held her in a tight hug like that until he heard the first prisoner stirring, then said, "I think we have to get moving."

She nodded, sniffed loudly, and said, "Yes, the quicker the better. How many dead?"

"Six."

"What about the rest of the camp?"

"Their leader is dead. He was the guy who took the first shot you heard. The one who was the spokesman the first night they visited us to demand the money. Without their leader the rest of them will either disband or find another group to join, but in any case, they aren't our problem unless they show up in the village again."

Digger was growling menacingly at the survivor who'd surrendered.

"Call off your dog, man. He's creeping me out."

Rex reckoned the man had been trying to escape his bonds, and that's what had set Digger off. Rex made a hobble out of a string of interconnected zipties. No worries about the guy getting out of those – he'd be too busy carrying his wounded buddy.

When Rex had hefted the unconscious man in a dead-man's carry over the other's shoulders, he said, "Let's go."

They set off in single file, Digger first, then the prisoners, then Luciana, then Rex bringing up the rear. It was going to be a long and slow walk back to the village.

Late in the day on the second day after Rex and Luciana had ambushed the Shining Path insurgents, they arrived back at the village. The prisoners were in bad shape. Rex had seen no reason to relieve the able-bodied one of his burden, so he was tired and staggering under the dead weight of his companion by the time they got to the village. The wounded one was near death. Digger's mauling hadn't done him any good, but Rex's kick had ruptured something inside him. Rex suspected internal bleeding and thought the thug would probably die before they got there. But to his surprise, the guy was still breathing, barely, when they reached the fortifications on the outskirts.

Rex marched the prisoner to the square before he allowed him to roll the half-dead punk off his shoulders and sit down. On the way, they'd collected a gaggle of villagers, who were peppering Luciana with questions. But the biggest surprise was a new face, a handsome woman in her fifties, who came out of one of the houses closest to the square to see what was going on.

"What is the meaning of this?" she asked, addressing Rex in a brusque tone.

"This is what's left of the group that attacked this village a few days ago," he answered in a matching tone. "Who are you?"

"I might ask you the same thing, but I suspect you are Ray Davis, in which case, I'm the doctor you requested."

Rex immediately dropped his guarded attitude, wondering quietly if he told her he was not Ray Davis if that would change her into something other than a doctor. He smiled. "In that case, I am Ray Davis. I suspect you must be Doctor Martinez, and I've brought you a new patient."

He stepped aside so she could see the two prisoners, one sitting wearily on the ground, dejected. And one lying in a motionless heap.

"Good heavens, what happened to him?" the doctor asked. She made a cursory inspection of his mauled arm, which had stopped bleeding and crusted over. "Did that dog bite him?" She looked disapprovingly at Digger.

Rex decided it was past time to set the record straight.

"Look, Dr. Martinez. I don't know how long you've been here, or whether my friends the Markses have told you about the events of the past few days…"

"I just got here an hour ago," she interrupted. "And I haven't met anyone named Marks. These villagers don't speak much Spanish, so I don't know anything, except a very old man met me when I got here and brought me to this hut." She indicated the house she'd come out of. "And brought me a severely ill child."

"Then let me back up and try to fill you in," Rex answered. He succinctly recounted his discovery of the sick children and the Shining Path attack, his and Luciana's trek to follow the survivors of the attack and their success, culminating in bringing the prisoners back. Because it wasn't germane to the immediate necessities, he left out the scam and reverse scam. He didn't know why the Markses hadn't been notified the doctor had arrived, or why they hadn't come out to greet his and Luciana's arrival, but that wasn't important at the moment, either.

"So, as you can see," he finished, "the new patient is this man. His needs are urgent, I assume. The wounds you see came from my dog, yes. And just so you know for future reference, that's what happens to any person who points a gun at him or me or my friends. My dog attacked him while I was busy fighting off about five of his fellow gang members who were trying to kill me and my friend, Miss Mamami.

"But, don't let me keep you from doing your job. Treat the children first. That's what I hired you to do. I suspect the villagers are going to find these men guilty of murder and attempted murder and extortion. I don't know what the penalty is, but I doubt anyone will mourn if this man dies."

A wail from the second prisoner earned a glare from Rex.

"What caused internal injuries, if your dog is responsible for his condition?" Dr. Martinez asked, ignoring the rest of Rex's speech.

"Well, ma'am, he was trying to kill my dog. So I kicked him. Meant to connect with his head, but he moved, so I nailed him in the liver."

Dr. Martinez's jaw dropped.

Rex was starting to enjoy the torment he was putting the doctor through.

"Very well," she said. "Bring him inside. I've already started an IV drip to rehydrate the little boy. I'll check this man next."

Rex grudgingly helped the other prisoner and Pidro carry in the unconscious man and place him on a pallet on the floor.

The doctor said, "If you can have these people supply a table of any kind, it will help me work better. And I thought you said there were several sick children."

"Yes, there are. I'll get them here," Rex answered.

He went outside, motioning Pidro to follow. "The doctor needs a table, and some light. Can your people supply those things?"

Pidro nodded.

Rex continued. "Why haven't the other children been brought here?"

"My people fear the outsider. They wait to see if she cures my grandson."

"Do they trust me?" Rex asked.

"Yes. You helped us repel the invaders."

"Then tell them that they can thank me by bringing

their sick children to see the doctor. She can't help them if she can't see them and treat them."

Assured that Pidro would do as he'd asked, Rex turned his attention to the other two things on his mind.

"Where are the Markses?"

"They went to work at the site of the ancient ones," Pidro confided. Forestalling Rex's next question, he asked what he should do about the second prisoner. Rex had directed the guy to return to the square sit down, be quiet, and not make trouble if he knew what was good for him.

"Whatever you want," Rex said. "He is one of those who attacked the village. It is up to you to as leader to decide what to do with him."

In fact, it was probably up to Peruvian national authorities, but Rex was in a savage mood. Frontier justice, he'd decided, was the way to handle it, but he'd leave it up to the villagers.

His next move was to get some decent food and some well-deserved sleep.

Chapter Nineteen

The Markses returned at dusk and their return woke Rex and Digger. Rex was disoriented for a moment, because the last thing he remembered was Luciana telling him she needed some rest. For some reason, he was surprised to find her missing. Then it occurred to him that the last time he slept, she was in her sleeping bag right next to his, with Digger ensconced in the middle like a black, furry chaperone.

"Where's Luciana?" he asked.

"Sleeping in her own quarters, I assume," Flo answered. "Welcome back. We saw the fruits of your labor in the square."

"Oh, the prisoner? I don't know what the villagers intend for him. Did you meet the doctor?"

"Yes, we did. Why didn't you tell us there were sick children here?"

"I promised Pidro I wouldn't, when Alexandro was still here. Evidently, he had some hold over them and didn't want outsiders to know. After that, things got busy, and I had it under control anyway. I guess I didn't want you to worry."

Flo seemed disappointed, either in him or in his answer, but Rex had bigger fish to fry.

"Have you talked to Pidro? Do you know what they're planning for the prisoners?"

"You know we haven't learned enough Quechuan to speak extensively with him. The doctor says there's little chance the injured one will survive. She said you kicked him?"

Flo's expression expected Rex to elaborate, but all he said was he'd intervened to save Digger's life, and she seemed satisfied with that. Before they could discuss the second prisoner's fate any more, Luciana arrived. She looked fresh as a daisy, as if she'd had a bath and a full night's sleep. Rex could hardly believe his eyes, and when she smiled at him, his heart skipped a beat.

"Flo, can I help get dinner ready?" Luciana asked.

"I'm fine, dear."

"Do you mind if I borrow Ray? I have some questions for him," Luciana said.

Barry entered the hut at that moment and greeted Rex and Luciana. "Ray, I just came from the square. Do you know what Pidro's up to?"

"No, and I can't say I care, unless he's about to turn the bastard loose. What's going on?"

"I'm not sure, because it was all happening in Quechuan. But there are a bunch of villagers surrounding the prisoner and yelling at him, and Pidro is among them. I've only ever seen public executions in the movies, but I'd say what's happening out there will soon be one of those."

"Okay, no worries I'll go check it out."

Luciana said she'd go, too, and the two of them walked

back to the square with Digger padding patiently on one side of Rex and Luciana on the other. She reached out and caught Rex's hand.

"I want to talk to you in private," she said again. "Will you come to my place after dinner?"

"Sure."

"Bring your sleeping bag."

Rex's heart missed a beat, or it could've been two or more, but before he could respond, they'd arrived at the square. Barry's account had been accurate. The only part of the public execution missing was that the thug hadn't been tied to a stake with brush and firewood around him. The man was standing, shuffling in a circle to meet each shout by facing the shouter. He looked exhausted, and Rex wondered how long this had been going on and how much longer it would continue before the crowd was in such frenzy that they'd kill him.

He and Luciana found Pidro and, with Digger, hurried to his side.

"What's going on?" Rex asked.

"We are questioning this man," Pidro answered.

You could've fooled me. I usually question people in a different way. But I guess cultural differences can explain that.

"He is being called to account for the raid on our village and other misdeeds that have happened here and near here in the past."

"Like what?" Rex asked.

"We want to know if he and his group are responsible for our sick children."

Just then, Dr. Martinez materialized at Rex's elbow, nudging Digger aside with her foot. Digger growled but gave way.

"Doctor, just a gentle piece of advice. Do not antagonize my dog. He can be a bit short tempered if treated rudely," Rex said mildly.

"Or what? He'll maul me like he did that poor man inside? And if I defend myself, you'll kick me and lacerate my liver?"

Rex had had enough of the doctor's attitude. "Doctor, I get the impression you've made up your mind without having considered all the facts. So, I want you to listen carefully. That 'poor man', as you like to refer to him, was part of a group entering this village four nights ago with an automatic rifle, demanding a payoff not to kill everyone here. Then a few days later he returned with an army of his goons, attacked these defenseless and innocent people, and killed two old men trying to defend their homes.

"After fending off that attack, Miss Mamami and I followed the remaining assailants and caught up with them. They'd regrouped and were on their way back here to launch another attack on the villagers. They were all armed with automatic rifles. We engaged with them in a gunfight and stopped them. During that gunfight I ordered my dog —by the way, his name is Digger—to do what he did.

"Now take note, while Digger was doing as he was told, I killed five others. So, if you've got a beef, tell it to me and leave my dog out of it. He acted on my instructions, and also note, it was with his help that we prevented another attack on these people."

During Rex's account of the events, the expressions on Dr. Martinez's face shifted from surprise, then outrage, and finally it became apologetic. "I… I apologize. No one told me."

"As you mentioned, you don't speak Quechuan, so they couldn't have told you. If you want to know anything, just ask Miss Mamami or me instead of jumping to conclusions, Doctor. All is not as it may seem here.

"Now, did you have something to tell me or ask me? If not, you might have noticed I'm a little busy right now."

"I wanted to tell you that the boy has symptoms of radiation poisoning. I need you to ask his grandfather where he could have come in contact with the cause, and for how long he's been exposed."

It was Rex's turn to drop his jaw.

Radiation poisoning? What the hell? How the hell? And why is it only the children?

Now he wanted to know if Shining Path was responsible for it, too. He led the doctor back to her quarters, with Luciana and Digger trailing. Once out of the noise of the crowd, he asked the doctor if she had any idea what substance might have caused it, mentioning that according to Pidro, only a few children had fallen ill.

"I haven't seen the others yet, but you were right about this one having Leishmaniasis. I've begun the proper antibiotic treatment through the IV drip. But the cluster of symptoms that led me to conclude the child has long-term radiation poisoning have nothing to do with Leishmaniasis. Whether it's the same for the other sick children, I'll know only after I can examine them. And only then can we begin to track down the cause. It will be something the others have also had contact with, that is, if they also have radiation poisoning."

"Tell me this, doctor. Will this kid and the others die?"

"Again, I can't say until I've examined the others. This one is very sick, but I may be able to save him. Unfortunately, he'll be on thyroid medication for the rest of his life."

"Thyroid medication?" Luciana questioned.

"The symptoms indicate severe thyroid deficiency, if not

cancer. The only thing I can think of that can destroy such a young child's thyroid function is exposure to radiation. That's how I made my diagnosis. Do you have medical knowledge?"

Rex left Luciana with the doctor and ran out to find Pidro again. Seeing him at the front of the crowd again, Rex strode through, weaving between the ranks of angry Quechua, who were now shaking their fists and shouting threats.

This guy is going to be toast soon.

He grabbed Pidro's arm and swung him around to face him.

"We need the other kids at the doctor's hut immediately! Are their parents here?"

"The fathers are, or probably are. The mothers care for the children."

"Well, get their attention and get them to bring their children to the doctor, right now."

Pidro looked a bit bewildered, as if he had no idea how to get anyone's attention amid the chaos.

Rex looked down and said to Digger, "Sound off," hoping to quiet the crowd so Pidro could be heard. And just like the previous time, the ear-splitting howl had the desired effect.

In the immediate silence that followed, Pidro said in rapid Quechuan that any man whose child was ill must take the child to the doctor right away.

Six men peeled out of the crowd and ran in different directions. Before the crowd could work themselves up again, Rex walked up to the prisoner and got in his face.

"Did you or any of your group give the children of this village anything to harm them?" His expression was so menacing that the man shrank what seemed to be at least four inches in the face of it.

"No! I swear, we didn't do anything to the kids."

Rex wasn't convinced and called Digger over. Digger had an uncanny second sense about liars. He asked the man again, this time accompanied by Diggers bared teeth and low growl.

"NO! I swear, we didn't. What are you saying, man?"

Rex looked at Digger. Digger looked back. He didn't give any indication that he detected a lie.

"All right. I'll tell them," Rex said. He returned to Pidro's side. "It wasn't them. It was something else that made the children sick."

Using the silence, Pidro shouted to the crowd to disperse. The village council would decide the fate of the man, who was sagging in relief. Rex didn't know whether he should be relieved or not. Maybe this thug and his cohorts hadn't hurt the kids, but he'd been involved in the raid, and the village was owed retribution for its two elders who'd died.

There was no more to be done until the doctor had finished her examination of the rest of the kids. He returned to her hut and entered, finding the doctor and Luciana in animated conversation.

"Excuse me, ladies. Am I interrupting?"

Luciana gave him a heartwarming smile, but it was the doctor who answered. "I owe you an apology, Mr. Davis. Ms. Mamami has explained what you've done for the villagers, and I'm appalled by my bad manners toward a man who is nominally my employer. I apologize for my behavior. I am truly sorry about that."

Rex was relieved not to be at odds with the woman anymore. "Accepted. The villagers will be bringing the other children shortly. I think there are six more. Do you need more room? Anything I can help with?"

"Not at the moment, Mr. Davis."

"Ray," he answered automatically.

She raised her eyebrows askance.

"My name, you may call me Ray."

"Thanks, I will."

"Then can we bring you some dinner? I'd prefer you be here when they start bringing the children, if you don't mind."

"Thank you. I would appreciate that."

Just then, the first of the other children arrived, a girl carried by a worried father, with a frantic mother in tow. Rex explained in Quechuan that the doctor was skilled and that Pidro's grandson was already being helped. Sometime during all the chaotic events of the past hour or two, a table had been brought to the hut, and the doctor indicated the father should put his little girl down on it.

Rex signaled Luciana to come with him and went to get some food from Flo to keep his promise. They'd gotten just beyond the square when Luciana caught his hand again and tugged.

"Stop a minute."

He stopped, and suddenly found Luciana in his arms, pressing a kiss to his lips.

"You are a good man, Ray Davis."

He smiled down at her. "Miss Mamami, the kiss I like… very much. The good man thing… hmm… you better hold off on that until you know me better."

"Just an observation," she answered.

Late that night, dinner over, the Markses filled in on the details of the mission to find and eliminate the Shining Path chapter, and the doctor still attending to the children who had been brought one by one, Luciana urged Rex to go with her to her quarters and in a whispered reminder, not to forget his sleeping bag.

Rex couldn't help but notice when the Markses gave each other significant looks, and Flo held out her hand. Barry dug in his pockets and came out with some Peruvian coins, which he dropped in her palm. She refrained from saying the hateful "I told you so."

If she did, Rex didn't hear it.

Luciana wasted no time in coy misdirection. As soon as they walked through her door, she pointed for Rex to put his sleeping bag down next to hers, and then she knelt to arrange a bed with one spread out to its full width, and the other spread on top. They were different brands, and the zippers didn't quite match up, but it wouldn't matter.

Moments later, they were sitting cross-legged, facing each other on the joined sleeping bags.

But before she made another move, she had those questions she'd mentioned before.

"Who are you really, Ray?"

Nervous, he asked, "What do you mean?"

"You knew what to do for the village to defend themselves. As if you're a trained warrior—more than that... a skilled and experienced one. You took out five men single-handedly with five single shots. You're an obvious professional at jungle warfare. Who are you? CIA?"

Rex grinned. It was too close for comfort, he had to stop this line of questioning in its tracks. He leaned closer and pushed the strap of her tank top off her shoulder. "I'd tell you, but then I'd have to..."

She started laughing before he finished the sentence. Rising effortlessly on her knees, she lunged forward to tackle him and landed on top of him. Kissing him fiercely, she murmured, "We'll see who kills whom."

Rex laughed and pushed her back gently. "Just one second. He raised his head and said to Digger, "Boy, I need you to guard outside."

Digger started smiling and tilted his head.

"C'mon Digger be a good buddy and help me out here."

Digger woofed once and left.

Rex turned his gaze to Luciana and said, 'Okay, now what was that about who was going to kill who?"

Chapter Twenty

As if the time since Junior had left to raise one million dollars was not filled with enough trouble of its own, the latter turned up on the morning of the sixth day with much more than just the money. Rex met Junior, who was accompanied by twelve heavily armed men on the edge of town after the village men who were guarding the trailhead stopped them.

Rex needed only one look at Junior and his throng of louts to see straight through his plans. He was surprised, but he didn't show any signs of it, though he chastised himself in silence for ever thinking Junior would not have a few tricks up his sleeve.

Aha, so that's how its going to be. You're not going to share it—you're going to take it all. Well, young man, we'll have to see about that.

Nevertheless, he kept an easy smile on his face as he greeted Junior. "Whoa, Junior. Seems like you've saved us the trouble of having to make a trip to go and hire guards."

"Yeah, well I had a bit of spare time, and Uncle Rich

managed to pull a few strings with a friend of his who oper-ates a security company. I am glad you agree that it will save us time. That's what I intended."

Rex kept the smile on his face and nodded while he made a quick assessment of the twelve men. It didn't take him much more than forty seconds to surmise that these 'guards' were a bunch of amateurs, yobbos hired off the streets by Junior for a dime a dozen, so to speak. But Rex knew that a stupid guard with a gun was just as lethal as a clever one.

This bonehead has turned a non-violent situation into a potential war. As if we didn't have enough trouble already. You've now put us and the villagers in harm's way. But if trouble is what you want, trouble is what you'll get.

Rex looked down at Digger who was staring up at him and let out a soft yelp as if to say, "I'm ready, just tell me when."

"Okay, I guess we need to go and figure out where we're going to put the men up?" Rex said.

Junior answered, "I think we'll have half of them guard the site, and the others can keep an eye on the village while they wait to change shifts."

Rex had controlled the urge to sigh in relief as he imme-diately grasped what Junior hadn't – the idiot was dividing his forces.

Divide and conquer – and he's done the dividing for me.

Obviously, Junior's reason for the suggestion was so that he and the men could control the dig and hold the village under virtual siege at the same time. But Rex knew as soon as Junior discovered that there was actually no dig, all hell would break loose.

Without hesitation, he told Junior it was a clever idea

and changed the subject. He asked Junior if he'd seen the pit trap nearby.

"I did. We had to detour around it. I meant to ask you what that was all about."

"We had a *'friendly'* visit from the local chapter of Shining Path," Rex replied. "They wanted money to leave us alone. We decided we didn't want to give it to them."

"Wow! What happened?"

Rex couldn't help the feral grin that emerged as he answered, "We arranged a welcoming party for them. Seventeen of them are still guests of the village, you might say. You'll find them buried in a pit a mile or so outside the village."

Junior's face paled. "Seventeen?"

"Yes. Soon to be eighteen, unless the doctor has performed a miracle, and maybe nineteen. The last one's fate is to be decided by the village elders. Oh, and we left six more dead on the trail between their encampment and the main trail."

Rex was watching Junior's reactions closely, and he was certain Junior had known about the attack, but probably not all the details about the final results. But aside from the autonomic facial and body reactions, over which he had no control, Junior didn't give any indication the news was anything but a surprise.

Rex didn't care about that. His purpose was to put a bit of fear into Junior and keep him off balance for as long as was necessary to allow him to put the plan that had been forming in his mind the last few minutes, into action. The first part of it was to prevent Junior and his entourage to go up to the dig right away.

He led Junior and his men to the village square and asked him to wait while he found Pidro and got instructions for housing the half who would be posted in the village.

Junior said they had tents, and he'd just have them set up in the town square.

"That may not be possible. The prisoner will be kept here, and a public execution may be in the offing. Let me just talk to Pidro."

"Who is Pidro, by the way?" Junior asked.

"One of the elders. He was elected leader when Alexandro disappeared."

Junior's bewildered expression indicated Rex hadn't given him enough information to allow him to adjust to all the changes. But that was all the information Rex was willing to give him for now, though. "I'll be right back. Just have your men relax right here."

He hurried to find Luciana and brainstorm how to stall the rest of the plot until they could get reinforcements for the police, who had arrived before he and she were back with the Shining Path goons and were camped at the coordinates they'd chosen near the ancient site.

To keep Junior from immediately dispatching half his men to the site, they decided the best way to stop that was an 'impromptu feast' to celebrate Junior and his men's arrival. Luciana went to enlist Flo in the preparations and then to call for police reinforcements, while Rex searched for Pidro to get him to rally the villagers for the feast.

Before he found Pidro, the doctor intercepted him. "The man you brought here injured expired last night," she said.

"Not unexpected," Rex answered.

"I didn't have the staff or equipment to repair his liver. I'm sorry."

"Don't be sorry. I'm not sorry, and you'll find neither

will the villagers be," Rex said. "What about the children? Anything else to report on their situation?"

"They're all in a stable condition for now. All of them are suffering from both Leishmaniasis and varying degrees of radiation poisoning. I've begun treatment for both conditions. I suggest you and the parents get together and determine how and where they got exposed to radiation, to prevent other children from being exposed."

"What about the sand flies?" Rex asked. "Any help for that?"

"I doubt it. But it wouldn't hurt to find out where the children play and try to eradicate the source. It won't be a long-term solution, but there is effective medication for Leishmaniasis, and they will eventually build up antibodies. The main worry is the radiation poisoning."

"Thanks, Doc," Rex said. "If you'll excuse me, I'm on an urgent errand."

"You aren't plotting something against the ruffians who arrived this morning, are you?" she asked, an artificially sweet tone in her voice.

"I'm glad you and I are in agreement about their personality types," he said, grinning. He left her staring after him and continued to Pidro's house.

The more urgent errand was to detain the ruffians until Luciana could get police reinforcements up here. Once they'd handled that, Rex would turn his attention to tracking down the mystery of the radiation poisoning. It weighed on his mind, though. That it only had affected the children, and only some of them, was puzzling.

Within the hour, preparations for a feast were well underway. Rex returned to Junior and told him unfortunately there was going to be a delay, because the villagers insisted on a proper traditional feast like they did for all newcomers, and that it would offend them if they didn't attend. So, frustrating as it was for him, it was going to take time to roast the alpacas and get everything ready.

Junior was not happy. He kept on mumbling and grumbling.

"Relax, buddy, you're on Andes time. There'll be plenty of time to get your men to the site," Rex said cheerfully. "It isn't going anywhere."

Rex ignored Junior's increasing anxiety and pretended he didn't notice it. "Your men will have to share quarters, I'm afraid," he said. "There are only three more empty huts. Will they mind?"

Junior appeared annoyed, but he answered mildly enough. "I'm sure it will be fine. If it's too small we can use the tents. Where will I be staying? In the hut next to where you and the Markses were before?"

"I'm afraid that one's now occupied. You can take your pick of the three Pidro has indicated, and your men can share the other two."

Rex urged Junior to follow him as he led him to three widely-separated huts. At least one, he knew, had been hastily vacated by a young couple so the plan would work. With the separation and subtle surveillance, the thugs wouldn't be in a position to mount a surprise attack. Rex suspected Junior wouldn't deploy them that way, anyway. He assumed they were supposed to take over the antiquities site and carry off the spoils.

Junior selected one of the houses and ordered his men to split up and move into the other two. There was grumbling in the ranks, but he quelled it with a few sharp words, and the men complied. Rex saw them settled and went to tell Pidro it was done.

Pidro wanted his advice. They didn't have a problem

executing the Shining Path member, he said. But someone had mentioned it might be better to let official authorities deal with him. What did Rex think?

Rex assured him he thought that was the way to go. "I think we can make a case that we did the right thing when we killed the attackers," he said. "But executing one without a trial might be a different matter."

"We have given him a trial," Pidro remarked. "We found him guilty."

Rex suppressed an indulgent smile. No doubt there was a trial, what was in doubt was the fairness, and then by whose definition of 'fairness'. "And what was the penalty?"

"Death. That's what I am asking you. Should *we* execute him, or let the police do it?"

Rex solemnly assured him that letting the police do it was the best policy. With the evidence they'd provide, the police would have no choice but to take custody of him. What happened after that would take place far away, in Cuzco or even Lima. And even if the guy somehow got off on charges of murder or terrorism, he'd no doubt avoid this place.

Pidro seemed to be happy with Rex's advice and left to tell the rest of the elders.

Next, Rex rejoined Luciana in the Markses' hut, where she and Flo were preparing their contribution to the evening's feast. Flo had mastered the intricacies of the primitive stove and was coaxing it to produce, of all things, peanut butter cookies. For a moment, Rex wondered where she got the ingredients, but they must've been in the supplies that they brought up the mountain with them. He didn't spend too much time thinking about that or bother asking. He loved peanut butter cookies and thought the villagers would go wild for them as well. For a fleeting moment, he questioned the wisdom of introducing sugar-filled bakery goods to the village, but the assembly line was already in operation. So, he was working on a plan to get his hands on one of the cookies. Flo was too busy to see Rex wink at Luciana and put his finger on his lips, and when she turned to take a pot off the stove, he filched a cookie off the table.

Luciana had a hard time not laughing out loud.

While Flo was none the wiser about one of the cookies missing, Rex munched on it while he filled everyone in on the doctor's report and Pidro's plans for the prisoner.

"What about these thugs Junior has brought?" Barry asked. "What are we going to do about them? We had a simple plan. Get the cash from Junior, introduce him to the cops. Get him arrested, find his uncle to arrest him, and everyone live happily ever after. Except Junior and his uncle."

"Well, things have changed. But depending on whether Luciana was able to get the police reinforcements organized, we can still sort it out."

She nodded. "They'll be at that valley Junior uses for his infiltration in about four hours, they told me. I suggested they stay out of sight until morning. They'll have an easier time capturing six men than all twelve."

"That's as good a plan as any," Rex said. "Once we have the six here in the village secured, we can head for the site to help. We shouldn't be too far behind Junior and the six with him. And just to be sure, I will take care of Junior and the six up there. You all will stay here."

Luciana harrumphed but didn't say anything.

Rex was satisfied with the arrangements, and for the rest of the afternoon he would make the rounds of people who might need his help with the feast arrangements, offering it where he could. But first, they had to try to play out the reverse scam. Junior might have brought the million dollars with him to lower their guards until he had the treasure site secured. If so, Rex intended the Markses and the villagers to have it.

He suggested to Barry that they should confront Junior about the money. They'd play good cop, bad cop if necessary, with Barry doing the talking as good cop.

Rex had left Junior cooling his heels in his assigned hut. On reconnaissance, it seemed Junior felt safe in the village. In any case, he hadn't set a guard outside his door.

He and Barry approached and called out a greeting before entering the door opening through the alpaca-wool hangings. They found Junior just sitting up from where he was lounging on a sleeping bag.

"Barry! Good to see you, man! Ray. To what do I owe the pleasure?"

As planned, Barry, with a bland expression on his countenance, answered. "If you'll remember, we had a business arrangement. Did you bring the money?"

"Yessir, I surely did." Junior got up and crossed the few feet to his gear. From the pile of bags he'd dumped there, he pulled a battered-looking briefcase. Rex was astounded it wasn't inside a more easily carried duffle or backpack.

Junior hefted it and carried it to the rickety table in the room and said, "Sit! Sit! Make yourselves comfortable." He took a three-legged stool at one side of the table. On the other side was a wide bench, where Rex and Barry crowded to sit.

Junior hunched to read the silver dial of the combination lock and thumbed it back and forth while mouthing the combination to himself. When a subtle click sounded, he pushed the buttons to open the latches on either side of the briefcase. With a flourish, he twirled the case to face Barry and Rex and opened the lid in almost the same motion.

The case was tightly packed with banded one-hundred-dollar bills.

"There you are. One million US dollars," he announced.

Barry reached for the case and pulled it toward him. Rex was stunned. He hadn't actually expected Junior to have the cash, he was more prepared to listen to some cock and bull story about why he didn't have the money or why he wouldn't hand it over yet. It seemed Barry was also sceptical, as he reached in and selected a bundle and broke the band, flipping through the bills with his thumb.

"Barry, dude," Junior said with a nervous laugh. "Don't you trust me? It's all there."

Barry smiled. "Sure I do, Junior. But my motto is, 'trust but verify'. That's okay with you, isn't it?"

Junior replaced the stricken expression on his face with a sick smile. "Sure, Barry. No problem, it's a lot of money. I would've done the same."

Barry didn't break the bands of the other stacks of bills, but he did take each one out and flip through the ends to make sure what was inside was actually money. Everything appeared to be in order, so he re-stacked the bills.

"May I keep the case? Or would you like me to transfer the money to one of my bags and keep it."

"No worries, man. Keep it."

"Okay, you kept your end of the deal, so we're partners, now," Barry said. "I look forward to a profitable venture."

He reached out his hand to Junior for a handshake. Junior took it and offered a more confident smile.

For the first time since they'd arrived and asked about the money, Junior seemed to relax. Rex wondered if he thought his uncle might have double-crossed him somehow.

Barry was taking his leave of Junior when Rex stood and, without ever having spoken a word, held back the door coverings for Barry to exit. He followed and accompanied Barry back to his hut.

"Put that where neither Junior nor his goons will be able to find it easily. We aren't out of the woods yet," he advised.

Chapter Twenty-One

To Rex's delight, the villagers' mood had returned to their former, happy-go-lucky state. He asked Pidro how this could be, when they were still mourning the two elders who'd died.

"*Chica de jora*," Pidro replied. "My advisory council and I decided it is ready, and we will enjoy it at this feast. The people look forward to it, and to the sacred coca leaves as well."

A feeling of foreboding invaded Rex's overtaxed brain. It seemed he'd been stamping out fires for days.

What the hell is chica de jora, and what do sacred coca leaves have to do with a fake feast?

He'd learned about the coca ceremony, first from Alexandro, and then from the group of elders who'd given him much of his knowledge about the Quechua culture and history, as well as immersing him in the language until he was now near-fluent. In his minds-eye he could see the coca ceremony getting out of hand. He betrayed none of his misgivings, though, as he questioned Pidro about the *chica de jora*.

"It is an ancient drink," Pidro answered. "Fermented corn." He used the Spanish word *maíz*, one of the words that had infiltrated the Quechuan from outside since the fall of the Inca empire.

Corn mash... Distilled? The Andes version of white lightning? Moonshine?

A few questions about how the drink was prepared set Rex's mind partially at ease. It sounded like beer, which he assumed wouldn't be very high in alcohol content, since it wasn't distilled after the corn fermented. The coca ceremony though, might still be a problem, depending on how accustomed the thugs were to the drug. However, he knew that the coca ceremony was sacred, and he elected not to cast doubt on Pidro's plan, for fear of offending him. He'd just warn the others to be alert.

Pidro also let him know that the prisoner would be moved from the square and not allowed to participate in the feast. He delegated Rex to inform Junior and the twelve men he'd brought with him to gather there at dusk.

———

Just before dusk, villagers began gathering in the square. Rex was there to direct Junior and his men to the center, where they were to be guests of honor. As far as he could tell, Junior seemed to have relaxed, accepting the festivities had to happen, and there was no way out of it for him and his men. Rex saw the thugs had left their heavy arms behind and most of them were unarmed. Only four of them were carrying sidearms, old fashioned six-shooters. Rex was relieved. At least if a riot broke out, it wouldn't involve too much of a gunfight.

The feast began with Pidro making a speech about how happy the villagers were to have honored guests, and how pleased they were to celebrate with food, drink, and a sacred ceremony. Then he poured onto the dirt of the square a libation of the *chica de jora* as an offering to *Pachamama*, Mother Earth. Next, he raised the half-empty cup to the sky to salute the mountains. With each gesture, he thanked the gods for the fertility of the fields and the water they were receiving in bounty to nourish the crops. Last, he took a ceremonial sip from the cup, with his eyes closed in ecstasy. Then he opened his eyes, smacked his lips, and raised the cup toward the crowd, who roared their approval.

Rex observed the locals and their joy in the feast and wondered how many of them knew it was a ruse to keep the brutish visitors in town to avoid springing the reverse scam on them too soon. They gave every indication they were attending a real feast, joyfully drinking the *chica de jora* and serving all the delicacies of the region he'd come to enjoy, including perfectly roasted alpaca. Then he noticed that the locals drank sparingly, while filling the guests' cups every time they were half-empty.

You cunning little buggers.

Rex had tasted the drink as a courtesy and found it not to his liking. It was thick, almost like a thin corn chowder. It tasted as if someone had added licorice to it, along with mint, a combination that didn't strike him as fortunate. He took Pidro aside and asked about the flavors, only to be told that it was fennel and yes, mint. Pidro explained that each person who made it added their own flavorings, which might include chamomile or cinnamon or the two flavors Rex had detected.

"We mixed two batches together to have enough for the feast," he explained. "But you and I, and some of the men who volunteered, must drink sparingly. You especially. If you are not used to it, it will make you *very* drunk."

Rex didn't have a problem drinking sparingly. The first couple of sips were all he could stomach anyway. To his amusement, Barry offered to finish his cup, and having already finished his own, was well on the way to oblivion. Flo was giving him glances of alternate indulgence and exasperation as he cracked silly jokes in English and then couldn't understand why no one else was laughing.

"I take it he's a cheap drunk," Rex said to her, smirking.

"The cheapest," she answered, laughing hard enough to squeeze a tear out of her crinkled eyes. "And I'm not much better. Goodness, I'd better slow down!"

Rex could see Digger didn't quite know what to make of the carousing, either. But he seemed to have accepted that the humans were enjoying themselves and he should relax. He had on his biggest smile, and when anyone thought to give him a pat, he leaned against them affectionately. Except, Rex noted, for the guests of honor. Digger didn't like any of them, so instead of accepting their pats, he ducked and slunk away whenever any of them came close to him. They didn't seem to care. Soon Junior and all twelve of his men were shouting, singing, and staggering around the square.

"We could probably wait until they pass out and tie them all up," Rex mentioned to Luciana. She'd abstained from drinking any of the *chica de jora* at all, explaining that she didn't care for it. "Anything that smells that bad can't taste good," she concluded. No one seemed to be offended by her excuse.

However, because Junior seemed to be watching him closely, he did take a cup anytime someone offered him one, and he sipped a little each time to avoid offending the bringer of the gift. As he got used to the taste and the texture, it wasn't such an ordeal. Before long, he'd lost track of how much he'd consumed.

He caught one enterprising teenage boy sneaking a cupful from the clay vat and took it from him, frowning in disapproval. The kid just laughed at him and skipped away out of sight. Rex sighed. He could keep an eye on the beer, or he could keep an eye on as many of the thugs as he could keep track of, but he couldn't do both. Luciana advised him to leave the kids alone. The parents could take care of their own.

The two of them were circulating, trying to ride herd on Junior's thugs. He wasn't certain Pidro or anyone else was drinking sparingly, as Pidro had advised they should. No one seemed as sober as he and Luciana. The villagers had either forgotten this feast was a ruse, and they were supposed to be on their toes, or most of them didn't know it was a ruse, or they were great actors.

As the night deepened and the moon rose, more and more people, including most of the thugs and Junior, had collapsed all over the place and were now snoring heaps of human flesh.

When the moon had cleared the nearest peak and shone full and majestic in the night sky, Pidro caught Rex's attention.

"We have been blessed by the gods. The strangers are disarmed, if you will observe. It is time to give thanks."

He held a bundle of three perfect coca leaves aloft in

one hand. The other was also raised but empty. He began to intone an ancient chant, and Rex recognized it as a prayer. When it was done, Pidro reverently balled the coca leaves and tucked the bundle into his cheek.

He then went around to the men of the village who were still on their feet, to the two thugs who remained awake, and finally to Rex. To each, he gave a small bundle of coca leaves. He had to show Rex how to ball them up and tuck them into his cheek. Rex started to object, but the thugs were watching, so he submitted, thinking he'd spit out the leaves when no one was looking.

Luciana approached and asked him in a low voice if he knew what he was doing.

"Not in the least," he answered. "But I don't see a way out of it. Keep an eye on me, will you? I'll try to get out of the worst of it."

She nodded and took his arm. Pidro hadn't offered her any of the coca leaves, nor had he offered any of it to the other women.

Hmm, not a women thing then, Rex thought.

Flo and Barry had staggered to their house an hour or more ago. Whether they'd managed to reach their hut, Rex didn't know. Wherever they were, they were most likely busy sleeping off their indulgence.

Luciana saw that Rex still had the leaves in his mouth, looked at Digger, and said, "Looks like it's going to be just you and me, boy."

Digger *woofed* softly in response.

The bitter taste of the coca leaves made it hard for Rex to refrain from spitting them out, though the pinch of something Pidro called *lejía* helped the taste some. He knew from what he'd been told about the ritual that the qualities of the drug wouldn't begin to affect him unless and until he began chewing them with some kind of alkali, but they first required softening. Nevertheless, the place where he had them tucked into his cheek felt numb, as if he'd been given an injection by a dentist. He assumed the *lejía* was the alkali, though he didn't know what was in it. He couldn't decide whether to spit out the excess saliva caused by having the leaves in his mouth or swallow it.

Assuming that swallowing it would add to the effects, he almost spit, but saw Pidro was watching him with knowing black eyes. And he wasn't spitting. He nodded to Rex and started chewing slowly.

Shit. Now I've got no choice.

Under Pidro's watchful eyes, Rex had no choice but to imitate him.

Rex woke the next morning with a fuzzy head and the memory of an angel in his arms. He slowly opened his eyes and located Luciana lying next to him.

"How the hell did I get here, and what happened last night?"

He didn't realize he'd spoken his thought aloud until he saw Luciana smile and open her eyes.

"You're heavier than you look, Ray Davis," she said.

"You carried me here?" Rex was confused. *She couldn't possibly have...*

"No, silly. It took two of the villagers to drag you here, though. It was all I could do to keep Digger from shredding them. He was very worried about you."

"Speaking of which, where *is* Digger?"

"I sent him to keep an eye on Junior and his gang," she said.

226

"Wait, he obeyed you?"

"He did. All I had to do was give him those commands I've heard you give him. He followed me after I tucked you in and assured him you were okay, just tired. When we got to the square, I pointed to the thugs and said, "Guard." And he did. He stayed right there when I told him I was coming back to take care of you."

"I'll be damned. That's surprising."

"Not really. He's observed us, seen our interactions. I guess he's allowed me to be part of his pack, at least temporarily."

Rex's head was beginning to clear, but he badly wanted a cup of coffee. As if she'd read his mind, Luciana got up and went to the stove, where the familiar coffeepot from Flo's kitchen sat over a low flame.

"Flo was kind enough to lend me this, after she and Barry had their fill."

"They're up already? That's surprising. They were both three sheets to the wind when they left the party."

Luciana began to laugh. "It's past noon, Ray. They've sobered up and have gone to smooth things over with Junior. He's convinced the villagers poisoned him."

Rex looked at his wrist, realized his watch wasn't there, and pushed the sleeping bag back to get up and get it. That's when he realized he was bare as the day he'd been born.

What the hell?

"Luciana?" he asked tentatively.

"Yes, mi corazón."

My heart. Oh, lord, what have I done?

"Um. Did the villagers undress me, too?"

"No, *guapo*, that was my doing."

Rex wondered if he'd missed the night of his life. If so,

that was a regret he could probably live with, though it stung a bit right then. But what was he going to do about this woman who'd apparently fallen for him?

He decided his head was in no state to handle complex issues like that now.

A problem for another day.

"I guess I don't need to ask you to turn your back while I get my clothes on?"

"Correct." She started laughing. "Unless of course, you think there is something I have missed and am not allowed to see."

Damn! That's what I was afraid of.

Chapter Twenty-Two

Rex thought it was his involuntary participation in the coca ceremony that was causing his hangover. He managed to pull his clothes on, though his head felt like it was splitting in two, and he wished it would go ahead and finish him off.

"Shit. I'll never do that again," he muttered.

"Never do what?" Luciana asked.

"Chew coca leaves. My head is killing me."

"*Mi amor*, that is not why you have a headache. Coca is an anesthetic, it doesn't cause a hangover, though it might cure one. Your hangover comes from too much *chica de jora*."

Rex tilted his head in an unconscious imitation of the gesture Digger made when he was confused or curious. "But I had very little!"

"Not by my count. You had very little at a time. But there were too many times."

Rex managed to slowly and with a lot of pain turn his gaze to her, "But…"

She held her hand up to stop him, "I take it you learned

some math at school, yes? So, you would know drinking three pints slowly or quickly makes no difference—it's still three pints. Then on top of that, even though you have been at this altitude for a month or so, you still aren't acclimated enough to indulge in so much strong drink, irrespective of the speed at which you do it."

"Okay, okay you win. I get it, I can't take my *chica de jora*, please just promise me next time you see me even thinking about drinking it you'll prevent my suffering by shooting me in the head."

Luciana's laugh, which Rex liked so much before, now felt as if it was piercing his skull, and he gritted his teeth.

After a few more minutes, the coffee was beginning to help him concentrate a bit more, and he suddenly had a clear image of Junior and his thugs lying in heaps in the square. Had they recovered before him?

"Shit!" he exclaimed again. "Junior and his men! Are they still here?"

Damn it to hell, this was not in my plan. No more chica de jora for me, ever!

"Relax. Six are still here, nursing hangovers worse than yours. Junior and the rest staggered out of town about a half hour ago, moving slowly. I think their hangovers are just as bad."

With that news, Rex jumped up but almost lost consciousness from the pain in his head, and he doubled over holding his head in both hands.

Luciana started laughing.

"What?!" Rex snapped. He immediately regretted his tone. It wasn't Luciana's fault – it was his. He softened his tone. "What's so damn funny?"

"You. Listen, if you chew some more coca, you will feel much better very quickly, and we can easily catch them."

"No, thanks," he said emphatically, with a bitter twist to his lips. "I've had enough mind and body altering substances for now. I'll tough it out. Come on, let's go! We have to catch them before they get to the site and over-whelm the police there."

"Well, I don't think that's going to be as big a problem as you think."

From her expression, Rex could tell she had more to reveal. This time he guarded his tone when he asked, "What? What haven't you told me."

"Well," she said again, with evident reluctance. "Everyone was sleeping so peacefully, I thought... hmm... well, how can I put it? The thing is, what's a girl to do when her man is naked but passed out? I had to do something more useful than watching you sleep. So, I..."

Rex raised his eyebrows, "Luciana, what is it that you're trying not to tell me? Out with it already."

"I thought it might be good to... er... remove the firing pins from their automatic weapons."

"You what?!" Rex shouted. Then he clapped both hands to his head and moaned, "Shhh... I've got a hangover."

Luciana's silvery laugh pealed again. "I hope I did the right thing?"

"Damn straight, you did the right thing. But... well, brilliant as it was, I'm not happy that you've put yourself in such danger... I..."

She shrugged. "Danger. What danger? Those men might as well have been dead. They never posed a threat to me."

"How the hell... sorry... but how did you know how to do it?"

"Ah, that's going to remain my secret. You have your secrets – I have mine," she teased. "But if you want to catch up to Junior and his group and get in on the fun, we should leave now."

"What about the six here in the village?"

"Oh, they're already in custody. The police I called for yesterday moved in right after Junior and the others left. The thugs he left here are all in handcuffs, they just need to wake up and discover it."

"Let's go, then. Or wait. On second thought, you've done so well so far without my help, why don't I go back to sleep and you sort the rest of it out? Wake me when you come back."

Luciana laughed. "Sure, no problem, I can do that for you, but I have a feeling you're not going to let me."

"You see, that's the problem a man has when a woman knows him too well. Okay, I want you to stay here where it's safe."

"Mister Davis, I thought we were getting along very well, especially lately. Don't ruin a good thing. I will not stay here. This is my collar, and you won't take the final fun and glory from me. I'm going. And if you don't start behaving, I'll be having a quiet word with Digger about your manners."

"I see, not only have you hijacked my operation, you've also corrupted my dog."

Luciana didn't reply, she just held his gaze.

Rex hesitated. The joking was over, and this was serious. She *was* going whether he liked it or not. The only thing he could do was to try and protect her. "Okay, you can come with me."

"I didn't ask your permission."

Rex held his hands up in surrender. "Let's get going. Now, you didn't say anything about their sidearms. Did you disable them?"

"Well, yes and no. The guns and two of the pistols they left in the huts, yes, I have disabled them all. Obviously, there was nothing I could do about the revolvers. They don't have firing pins, as you know. I didn't want to touch the sidearms the men carried on their persons, in case they woke up."

"Brilliant! Oh, but where are the Markses?"

"There's no problem with the Markses. They're both under the weather. I've already suggested they stay here, and they were happy to oblige."

"Okay, then there's nothing else to do but lead you into battle. Please follow me and try to stay out of the way of flying bullets, will you?"

"I promise I intend to do exactly that. I'm out of ammo."

"You can have the rifle. With that you can stay out of the thick of it and be our sniper."

Rex went outside, gave a piercing whistle for Digger, and then went back in, grabbed his Sig and magazines, the Winchester and a box of cartridges, and slung his backpack over his shoulder. Luciana had thought of everything. The weight indicated the water bladder was full, so he didn't bother looking for food. She'd have taken care of that, too.

Digger appeared, panting and eager to work. Rex put Digger's own backpack on him, too. He'd already discovered Luciana had even packed the kibble and water Digger would need. When he straightened, Luciana was waiting for him, her backpack on already, her arms akimbo on her hips again.

"I'm not kidding about the coca, Ray. It will give you extra energy and take care of your hangover."

He held up a bottle of aspirin. "I took some of these, thanks."

Without another word, he turned and headed for the trail to the ancient site, moving fast in the hope of catching Junior.

Two hours later, Rex doubted they'd be able to catch up before Junior and his thugs surprised the two policemen who were waiting to arrest Junior. No one had been able to notify them that Junior would have six men with him. Although they were armed, they expected Luciana and Rex to be with Junior, not Junior and six armed men.

Even though the goons had only sidearms that could fire, the cops would still be outnumbered. He tried to go even faster, but he was at his limit for effort, probably because of the damned fool stunt he'd pulled drinking all that beer when he thought he'd been careful.

But kicking himself now would do no good, so he took his mind off it and pushed harder. Luciana was having a tough time keeping up. Digger was ahead of him. Thank goodness for Digger. Maybe *he'd* catch them and provide enough distraction for Rex to get there.

"Go get 'em, buddy," he muttered under his breath. Digger was too far ahead to hear him.

It wasn't long before a commotion up ahead and a look at the nearby landmarks let Rex know that the group had reached the site, and Digger had caught up with them.

Gunfire!

Rex began to run. Digger knew how to keep himself safe, if he wasn't sacrificing himself to save someone else. Rex didn't know if he'd instinctively protect the police or not. But he didn't know the police, and nevertheless, from the sounds of it, someone needed help.

He practically stumbled over the first casualty. One of the thugs was cursing and sweating, one leg badly mauled – Digger's doing. When Rex rounded a boulder and almost stepped on him, the man had his pistol pointed at Digger and was pulling the trigger repeatedly, but nothing happened.

Thanks Luciana! You're a star.

With the sounds of gunfire still going on beyond and Luciana coming up fast, he had no time to waste. He put a bullet through the thug's shooting arm and kept on going, leaving him screaming and cursing even louder.

One down, six to go.

He wanted Junior most of all. The bunch Junior had brought with him weren't professional soldiers or guards. If they were professional at anything, it was probably at being thugs, and thugs needed a leader. If Rex could take Junior down, the rest of them might just surrender and no one had to die. If they didn't surrender, they'd probably just abandon their mission and run, every man for himself, which would make it easier for a disciplined soldier to neutralize them.

With all this going through his head, he ran up the trail toward the gunfire, but more cautiously, staying low and darting from boulder to boulder for cover.

A whistling noise near his ear sent him back behind the last boulder whose cover he'd left. He was close enough for them to see him, now. And as if the uneven number wasn't enough, the police didn't know him from the thugs. They'd never seen him. He'd have to avoid friendly fire as well as what was coming from the thugs.

"Luciana, stay back!" he yelled. The last thing he needed in this situation was to have to worry about a noncombatant as well as himself, Digger, and two unknown cops.

Rex heard shots pinging off the boulder behind which he was pinned down. He turned his back to it and crouched, thinking. What he needed was a distraction. He whistled for Digger.

A few moments later, his furry black buddy was all over him, wiggling with joy and thankfully uninjured.

"Good boy!" he praised. He ran his hands over the dog, assuring himself that his first impression was correct. No blood, no other apparent injuries. Now he had to send his best friend back into harm's way. He quickly removed Digger's backpack so that he could move more easily.

"Quiet attack," he said, pointing in the direction he wanted Digger to go. Digger stopped trying to kiss him and went into alert stance. Then he tore back around the boulder the way he'd come, and a moment later, Rex heard screaming.

Attaboy.

Rex used the distraction and went around in the other direction, running at top speed to the next boulder, where he dived for cover, then peeked around trying to get a look at the lay of the land. No shots followed.

Digger must be occupying the shooter who had me pinned down before.

Before he decided which way to run next, Luciana startled him by nudging him from the back. He hadn't heard her coming over the screaming of Digger's target.

"What are you doing?" he whispered urgently. "I told you to stay back."

"And I told you this is my collar," she said. Then she launched herself out from behind the boulder and ran toward the screaming.

"Shit! Woman, you're going to be the death of both of us," he yelled as he followed her.

They were on the scene of Digger's fight in a few yards. Digger had the thug pinned, his pistol beyond his reach, and was worrying at his shooting hand. The guy wouldn't be shooting with that hand again, ever. His trigger finger was missing, and several others were hanging by mere threads of skin.

"Digger, out," Rex commanded.

The dog immediately stopped biting the guy and backed off. Rex picked up the pistol and shoved it into his waistband. This guy was out of commission, crying, nursing his hand. He'd pissed his pants.

"Two down, five to go," he said to Luciana.

They were at the ruined wall of the site Junior had salted, and now the maze of half-fallen buildings provided both cover and danger, because the rest of them and the police could be anywhere. In a hurried conference with Luciana, Rex decided that the best way to proceed was not to. They'd wait, concealed, until they could figure out where everyone was, or Digger found someone else.

"Quiet attack," he commanded again.

Digger seemed to understand the danger, too. Instead of exploding from behind the wall where they were crouched, he dropped to his belly and slunk around. He'd keep that stance for as long as necessary to flush someone out of hiding.

The next thing they heard was another shot. Rex's heart leaped to his throat.

Not Digger! Please, don't let Digger be shot!

Without a second thought, he jumped from his position and ran in the direction Digger had gone. Seconds later, someone rose from behind another wall and aimed a pistol at him. Rex didn't slow down. On the run, he fired first, nailing the guy between the eyes, and kept on looking for Digger.

A shout in Spanish rang out. "Halt! Police! We have you covered. Drop the gun and raise your hands!"

Cops? Only one way to find out.

He kept his pistol in firing position. "Show me a badge!" he yelled.

"Mr. Marks?" came the reply.

Luciana jogged to his side. "Luciana Mamami," she yelled. "This man is with me."

Moments later, Rex, Luciana, and the two policemen stood together.

"What happened, Luciana?" one of the cops asked. "You were supposed to lead this Junior Roper to us and let us arrest him. Instead, seven men show up, all armed."

"Slight hiccup," she said. "Let me introduce Ray Davis, and his wonder-dog, Digger. With Digger's help, we've neutralized three of them. Where are the rest?"

"As soon as we met them and they pulled their guns on us, we took cover," he replied. "They headed further into the ruins, and then your dog came running up and chased one of them back the way they'd come. One other followed. A third has had us pinned down."

"Probably the three we've dealt with," Rex answered. "How do you propose we flush out the rest?"

"Let them come to us. Sooner or later, they'll have to come back along the trail. We can ambush them then."

It sounded like a reasonable plan to Rex. He'd have said the same thing. They weren't likely to strike out through the countryside off the trail, and even if they did, they couldn't get far without being spotted if he, Luciana, the police, and Digger were concealed strategically. Since they were well above the tree line, the boulders were the only cover. If he and the others simply went back and spread out, chances were Junior and his men would think his three goons had killed them. He'd probably come marching down the trail with mayhem on his mind.

"Let's do it," Rex confirmed.

Chapter Twenty-Three

Luciana settled the question of who would lead the effort to deploy their forces in ambush.

"Ray has demonstrated some sophisticated jungle warfare techniques against the Shining Path guerillas," she said. "I assume you men are equally competent – in the city but not out here? Am I right?"

The senior of the two police officers nodded.

"Then I suggest we defer to Ray for his expertise. You men are the arresting authority, however. Is that agreeable with you?"

The officers didn't have a reason to disagree.

Rex considered his options. For him, it was merely an exercise in logic.

First, they had to make sure the two wounded goons who they neutralized before were properly secured and silenced. The four of them took care of that quickly, and then Rex assessed what he had available to work with. Luciana had demonstrated during the raid that she was a crack shot. He didn't know about the policemen, but he assumed they were at least competent. Luciana was the only one armed with a long gun, so he could put her in a safer position some distance away.

He also didn't know how many working firearms were held by the four men still unaccounted for. Although Luciana had disabled all she could find, it was prudent to work on the assumption that all of them could return fire.

Prepare for the worst, hope for the best. It was the motto drilled into him by the CRC instructors from day one. And the application thereof had kept him alive on many occasions.

With those factors in mind, he decided it was best to let most of Junior's party get all the way outside the ancient site's walls before springing the ambush. Otherwise, they'd just retreat into the site and hole up. On the other hand, he couldn't allow any of them to get too far beyond the last ambush position, where he would place Luciana, lest a target escaped while they were occupied with the others.

Accordingly, he placed Luciana at the farthest point of concealment he thought would allow the thugs to clear the site, even if they were going to walk through the ambush one by one, spaced out, rather than bunched up. That's the way he'd have led his men out, if he were in the same position. Junior had proved himself clever, and Rex knew to never ever underestimate the enemy.

In the middle, between himself, close to the site, and Luciana, farthest along the trail, he placed the two cops. If they were good shots, there was no harm. If bad, he and Luciana would be the mop-up crew, whichever way the enemy ran. Rex kept Digger by his side so he could give him the appropriate commands when necessary. He made sure that each of his troops chose a good place of concealment where he'd deployed them and settled in to wait.

They had a four-way bet going about how long the wait would be. The cops thought it wouldn't be long. One said an hour at most. The senior man gave an optimistic estimate of half an hour.

Luciana said she thought it would be longer. Maybe as long as four or five hours, but certainly in time to return to the village before full darkness.

Rex told them he hated to say it, but Junior was a clever adversary. He thought Junior wouldn't move his men out before nightfall. Again, that's how he'd do it if he were in Junior's shoes.

He relied on Digger to alert him well in advance of the louts reaching their position. If they couldn't capture, injure, or kill everyone on the spot, he at least wanted to know as quickly as possible that they'd escaped, so he would know to head at speed for the village to protect the Markses and the villagers.

The cops both lost their bets. Rex considered his and Luciana's a draw. When Junior made his move, it was when twilight had fallen, but not yet full dark.

Junior had also deployed his troops in the best way he could. He sent two goons out with a hundred yards between them. Close on the heels of the second one, he came, clutching an automatic rifle. Only a few yards behind him was his third man, with the last man a few yards behind him. As they passed, Rex estimated that the first one would reach Luciana any second. The third thug was just passing Rex's position when Luciana fired a round over the head of what Rex assumed was the first one, as they'd planned. He and the others didn't want a bloodbath, preferring rather to capture the criminals.

He heard her yelling, "Halt! You're surrounded. Drop your weapons."

242

A few seconds of silence followed. Rex was frustrated that he couldn't see what was going on down the trail, but he followed the plan. His target had taken two running steps when Rex shot him in the leg. The man fell, screaming, and Rex ordered Digger to secure the wounded man.

By the time Rex tried to draw a bead on Junior, he was out of range. He left his cover and jogged toward his first target, pulling a pair of flexicuffs from his pocket as he moved.

He picked the man's revolver up, shoved it into his belt, and cuffed him. Then he said to Digger, "Come" and ran toward the next place he knew one of the cops was concealed. Before he got there, he spotted the cop and one of the thugs locked in hand-to-hand combat.

"Digger, attack."

The dog went flying down the trail, leaped the last two or three yards through the air, and sunk his teeth into the thug's arm as he was trying to draw a fearsome-looking knife to fight off the cop. The thug screamed and dropped the knife as Digger's hurtling sixty pounds smashed him into the ground. Within seconds, the cop was able to overpower him with Digger's assistance. By the time Rex reached them, he was cuffed and lying on his stomach, and the cop was using his handkerchief to make a tourniquet for the man's arm.

Digger had backed off, of his own accord. He looked at Rex, eagerly waiting for his next instructions.

"Good boy." Rex gave Digger an affectionate rub of his ears and asked the cop if he had everything under control.

Before he was finished with his sentence, rapid gunfire alerted him to trouble ahead. He left the cop to deal with his own prisoner and ran down the trail. Digger soon outpaced him. As he neared the place where the second cop should have been, he saw the officer hit the trail up ahead and swerve, running and firing at the same time.

Junior. Shit, I wanted him alive.

Where's Junior?

Digger was out of sight, but not for long. Rex topped a low rise in the trail and almost stumbled over Digger, who was once again in the sights of a man whose gun didn't work. As he took in the scene, Digger lunged at the man, who threw the gun at him and turned to run. Digger took him down with a leap on his back and started to bite the back of his neck.

Rex had his Sig pointed at the man's head when he yelled, "Digger, out!" To the man, he said, "Don't move or the dog will kill you."

"Digger, out," he repeated.

Digger gave one last threatening growl and let the man go.

"Turn over, and keep your hands where I can see them," he instructed the guy.

When he complied, Rex asked him, "Where's Junior?"

In sullen tones, the man said he didn't know, that Junior had caught up with him and passed him. Maybe whoever was firing the rifle up ahead had killed him. Rex cuffed the man and continued down the trail to Luciana's position.

He found her in tears. At first, he thought she'd been hurt. He hurried to her and took her in his arms. "Where are you injured?"

"I'm not injured, you idiot. I'm mad! Junior got away."

She pointed across to the trail where the third of the thugs was sitting holding one mangled hand in his uninjured hand, trying to staunch the flow of blood from the bullet Luciana had put through it.

"I shot over his head, and he tried to pull his sidearm.

So I shot him, but Junior came racing past, firing in my direction. I returned fire, but I missed him. All I have to show for my effort is that miserable bastard. I couldn't shoot toward Junior, because one of the officers went after him and I was afraid I'd hit him."

"It's okay," he assured her. "So, we have three injured and captured. Junior's ahead and armed with a weapon that works and moving fast, and one police officer ahead of me, chasing Junior. Is that about it?"

"Yes."

"Are you still determined to capture him yourself?" he asked her.

"I'll never catch him, damn it. The officer is ahead of me."

"Then do you mind if I do?"

"Go ahead," she said, with a bitter twist to her lips.

"Why don't you see to rounding up everyone and follow?" he said.

"Would you just go already? You're not going to catch him, either."

Rex grinned, said, "Digger, come on, you're with me," and ran back to the trail.

He knew he had little chance of catching Junior himself. But Digger could. As they ran to the trail, Rex called to Digger, "Get Junior, boy!"

Digger knew who Junior was. They'd spent time on the trail together, and Rex knew it had been a trial for the dog. He hadn't liked Junior from day one. He simply lengthened his stride and took off. Rex marveled at how quickly Digger extended the distance between them. Soon, the dog was out of sight.

I still owe Digger a formal apology for not trusting his judgement of human character.

Rex didn't slow his pursuit. It would be full dark soon. Running full tilt down the mountain trail in the dark would be risky. He also didn't want to leave Digger alone with Junior for too long after the capture. He still wanted Junior alive, but he wasn't sure Digger did. However, Digger would not easily kill without Rex telling him to do so.

Rex reckoned he was within a couple of miles of the village when he passed the exhausted policeman sitting on the ground next to the trail. He didn't stop to ask what had happened – that could come later. Half a mile later, he caught up with Junior and Digger. Digger was sitting calmly a few feet from what was left of Junior. The man was alive, but not in good shape. He was bleeding from extensive bites on all extremities, and his face looked like he'd tried to run through a bramble thicket. Digger had taken his toll, and from the look of him, was well satisfied with his performance.

"Well, shit, Digger. You didn't leave me anything to do!"

Digger turned toward him and relaxed his muzzle into the smile that made him so endearing and belied his lethal capabilities. He expected praise, and he got it.

"Good boy! You did great! When we get home, you get a treat and the kong."

At the word treat, Digger pulled his smile in and cocked his ears. Then, without a backward glance, he trotted off down the trail toward the village.

Huh. I guess he figured the rest is my worry.

Junior wasn't a heavy man. Nevertheless, it was a little work to get him situated on Rex's shoulders for a fireman's carry. Once he was there, though, Rex made it to the village without undue strain. Now and then, he wanted to slug his burden, though, when Junior moaned and groaned as if he were the one doing the carrying.

Rex's progress through the village streets toward the square attracted a following crowd. When he reached the square, he dumped Junior unceremoniously, like a bag of sand. The villagers who were following him sent up a cheer when they saw who it was in the light of the fire that was going in the center of the square.

Pidro arose from the shadows surrounding the fire. "You have captured the evildoer, as you promised. We shall have a feast to celebrate."

"Hold that thought," Rex answered. "I still have to go back and help Luciana and the police with the rest of Junior's men. Where are the others? Did the policemen take them away already?"

"No. They are holding them in the quarters we provided. Do you want me to call for them to be brought here?"

"No, leave them where they are. This man needs the doctor to see to his wounds. Would you send for her?"

Pidro looked dispassionately on Junior, who was still lying in the heap in which he'd been dumped. He shook his head and said, "In due time. First, we will question his involvement in our children's illnesses."

"He's your prisoner now. Suit yourself. I'll be back soon with Luciana and the rest."

"We will be here, questioning this spawn of evil."

Chapter Twenty-Four

By the time Rex met Luciana and the two policemen with their three captives on their way down the trail, there wasn't much left to do. Luciana handed him Digger's abandoned backpack, and he turned to walk beside her as they returned to the village. The prisoners were in varying degrees of pain, but they would survive. Luciana told him they'd dragged the two dead men that had been killed outright, and the first one Rex had left injured before they reached the site, off the trail and left them to the tender mercies of the local wildlife, having no way to bury them.

"What happened to the first guy? I didn't kill him."

"Bled to death, I guess. He was dead when we went looking for him. I really should start carrying a shovel whenever I am with you and we're going after bad guys," she remarked.

We?

Luciana's statement forced Rex's mind to a topic he hadn't thought of for a long while—a steady relationship. Despite Luciana's stunning beauty and dazzling personality, he immediately realized he was not ready to discuss future joint expeditions to catch bad guys, not yet, and maybe not for a long time.

Unless there was a human villain responsible for the children's illnesses, his work in the village was finished. Junior would be brought to justice, along with anyone associated with him. The Markses would get their money back and arrange for a permanent doctor with the rest of the money they'd scored from Junior. Luciana would be compensated by the authorities, and the village would do fine without any of the gringos whose presence had disrupted them for the past several weeks. As soon as he was sure that the doctor had discovered the source of the children's radiation poisoning and knew they would be taken care of, he planned to hit the road again.

If Luciana wanted to join him for the rest of his jaunt in Peru, that would be nice, as long as there were no strings attached.

To cover his discomfort, which he was glad it was too dark to see, he answered mildly, "Maybe you should."

She moved closer to him, shoulder to shoulder, and said, "We deserve a celebration, don't you think?"

Pretending not to understand her meaning, he answered, "I think Pidro's already planning one."

She nodded and fell silent.

Rex immediately regretted his aloofness and rebuked himself in silence. Here you have one of the most beautiful women ever to be interested in you, and all you can think of is how to get away from her.

He looked down at Digger for help and saw his buddy was already studying his face as if he knew exactly what Rex was thinking. But Digger offered no advice, although Rex could swear if he had something to say it would've been something along the lines of, "Dalton, you're a total idiot."

But when all was said and done, the truth was, and Rex knew it, it was not wanderlust that kept him from a serious relationship, it was unfinished business. The unfinished business of revenge that he promised to visit on those who betrayed him and his friends. He had taken an oath, and until that promise was fulfilled, he wouldn't be able to settle down with anyone. Not even the dazzling Luciana.

The next morning, all six policemen left the village with ten prisoners in their custody. The Shining Path member, the six who'd been peacefully captured while they were stoned from chewing coca and drinking too much *chica de jora*, and the three they brought in the previous night.

The villagers flatly refused to let them take Junior until they had questioned, tried, and judged him.

Rex had an uneasy feeling, as if he hadn't done enough. His fists didn't ache from any close fights, which was a first for him on one of these impromptu missions. At first, he couldn't identify the feeling of something missing. When he did, he could only shake his head. This was supposed to be a relaxing vacation. What was he doing, pining for a fistfight?

He sat on a bench beside the village elders who'd told him the stories he craved and tried to keep his mind on his next destination. Digger lazed in the sun at his feet.

He should have been at peace, but he wasn't.

The village was preparing for the celebration Pidro had ordered, and as Rex watched women scurrying back and forth with baskets of items they were trading, he decided there was one thing he could do to relieve his itchy feeling.

He got up, called Digger to his side, and strode toward the doctor's place.

She came out the door before he reached it, so he greeted her. She said hello in a distracted manner and kept walking. Not to be foiled in his attempt to discover what was bothering him, he fell in beside her.

"You seem to be in a hurry."

"Not especially. This is my normal pace," she answered. "Did you want me for something?"

"I was wondering if you have any more ideas where the kids might have been exposed to radiation."

She stopped and turned to look at him. "I believe I suggested that you investigate that."

"Fair enough, but I've been a little busy since then."

"So I understand. Getting drunk on *chica de jora* and playing at cops and robbers."

"Now wait just a minute. I don't know what gave you the knot in your knickers, but I'm not the bad guy here. I found this situation when I arrived, and I've done nothing but try to help since then. Aside from the *chica de jora* incident, which only happened because I just didn't know how strong it was, or that I was overindulging while trying to be polite."

Dr. Martinez started walking again. "All right. I'll accept that. But I'm busy treating the children and the injured men you brought in. I haven't had time to investigate, and someone needs to do it before more children fall ill."

"Granted," he answered. "What I wanted was to learn the status of our knowledge about the source. Now I know we're nowhere, I can help. But I need some information first. What are the likely sources? I mean, I don't think there are any uranium dumps up here, are there?"

"Correct. I know of no such installations."

"Then what would be your best guess?"

She stopped again, this time to think. He watched her face as she apparently considered and rejected a few options.

"Natural radon emissions would be first. Do you know of any caves nearby? Or abandoned mines?"

"No, but I can ask around," he said. "What else?"

"Their homes aren't tightly built enough to allow radon to build up, and if it were radon, then I would expect the adults to suffer the same fate as the children. It would have to be a naturally-enclosed space like a cave or mine shaft."

Rex had a sudden thought. "There is a mine somewhere near here. But it isn't abandoned. Some of the men work there."

"What kind of mine? Uranium?" She looked doubtful.

"Gold and other valuable metals is what the elders told me. I think uranium does occur near gold, though, doesn't it?"

Rex noticed that Digger was watching them like people watching a tennis match, his head wagging back and forth to look at whoever was speaking. While he waited for her answer, he leaned down to give the dog a scratch behind his ears.

"I don't know," she said, finally. "If you could ask the men who work in the mines whether they bring home interesting crystals or pretty rocks for their children to play with, that might solve the mystery."

"I'll see what I can find out. Anything else you can think of?"

"Nothing likely."

Rex nodded and started to turn.

"Wait," she said. "Would the mine you mentioned have tailings?"

It was Rex's turn to think before answering. "Don't most mines? Why?"

"Because tailings dumps are highly dangerous if they contain traces of uranium. There have been cases of entire towns' water supplies being tainted, and...." She stopped talking because of the look on his face. "What?"

"The spring water!" he blurted. "Before you came, the local *Inka Mallku* told the parents to give their children water from a sacred spring to drink and bathe them in it to cure the Leishmaniasis rash."

She grasped the implication immediately. "Where is this spring?"

"They haven't told me, but Pidro said it was a sacred spring, and the miners brought the water from it when they returned from work each day. I'll go and find out. Maybe you can persuade the parents to stop those treatments until we can sort it out."

She nodded. "They've already been stopped, since I have the children in my hut, and I saw no reason to have anyone bring special water. But yes, I think you should find out about that spring."

"I'm on it. Thanks, doc. It's much nicer to be working together than at each other's throats, don't you agree?"

She smiled but didn't answer. Rex figured he was on probation.

Note to self. NO chica de jora tonight.

Rex needed to go back to the square, and if Pidro wasn't there supervising, he'd talk to the other old men. He bid her a good day and turned back.

The activity in the square was familiar by now. Rex

smiled to himself as Digger trotted ahead, straight for the old men lined up on the bench nearby. The dog was enjoying the extra attention he got up here.

Pidro was loitering near a trestle table some of the teenage boys had erected, snatching a treat now and then when the women weren't looking and preventing the boys from doing the same.

Rex strolled up behind him and said, "Are you authorized to taste the goodies?"

Pidro jumped half an inch off the ground and turned around to glare at Rex. "You startled me!"

"Guilty conscience?" Rex smirked and reached for a piece of fruit, only to snatch his hand back when Pidro glared at him.

"I am making sure the food is fit for consumption at the celebration," Pidro announced with injured dignity. "Did you want something? Besides to steal the feast food, I mean?"

Rex swallowed his laughter and straightened his face to a sober expression. "Yes, Pidro. I must ask you where the sacred spring is whose waters you have used to bathe your grandson?"

"That is not for outsiders to know, Ray. I am sorry."

"Pidro, it's possible those waters have been polluted, and that's what is causing the children's illness."

Pidro drew back in horror. "*We* have made our children sick?" The wail he sent up caught the attention of everyone around them, and soon they were surrounded by concerned villagers.

Trying to calm the situation, Rex put his hand on Pidro's shoulder. "No, not you. You did nothing wrong. It may not even be the water hurting them. We just have to check."

The nearest villagers heard what he said, and a cacophony of mutterings and louder voices began in the crowd.

"What water?" "How can water hurt?" "Who was hurt by water?" and so forth, all jumbled together. Panic was rising, and to make things worse, Digger had arrived, and it looked as if he had his hackles up prepared to protect Rex. He was growling at those who came too close and snapping at a few who tried to get Rex's attention by touching him.

"Everyone be quiet!" Rex snapped, raising his voice over the noise.

Since Pidro's distress had only grown with the pandemonium, Rex waited for the noise to abate, and then addressed the crowd.

"People, there is nothing to worry about yet," he said. "I just need to know where the sacred spring is. Its waters may be polluted, and that may be the reason the children are sick." He left out the Leishmaniasis connection.

An older teen stepped forward. "I will show you the spring."

Another round of protest went up, but the young man walked away from the crowd, and Rex followed. Some of them followed, shouting warnings at the young man, but he ignored them. When the followers fell away and went back to what they'd been doing before the disturbance, Rex drew even with his guide and asked why everyone had been angry.

"They are not ready for our way of life to end," he said. "It is foolish. You and others like you have made your way to our village. Already, we have changed. Those who do not wish to change will argue and want to keep outsiders away. My friends and I welcome change. We want modern life—what *you* have."

Rex walked along silently for a while. After a few minutes, he said, "Don't be so quick to throw away the old ways. Sometimes the modern world is not nice. People like me want to come to villages like yours to get away from it."

However, he couldn't disagree that if modern life was going to intrude on the village, it might bring diseases the old medicine couldn't cure, desires that the old ways couldn't fulfill, and envy of the outside. It might have been better to leave the village untouched. But it was too late for that already.

The boy didn't answer, and Rex didn't pursue it.

The spring proved to be about three miles from the village, in the opposite direction from the ancient city, but higher on an adjoining peak. They reached it an hour after leaving the village. Where they intersected it, it flowed in a narrow runnel among small boulders and a few hardy, but stunted, bushes. It didn't look special in any way. The young man knelt and brought a palmful up to drink. Rex stopped him and explained again that the water could be poisoned. Although, Rex couldn't yet see anything around that would indicate the stream was polluted. "Where does it come from?" he asked.

"The headwaters are the sacred pool," the young man answered. "The waters here are sacred, but less so. We will follow the stream from here." He got up and began walking upstream beside the water, occasionally having to detour around a large boulder or hop across the stream to continue without scaling a cliff.

Rex was getting thirsty, and so was Digger. Rex had to stop him from lapping water up from the stream. But he'd rushed away from the village with neither his backpack nor Digger's.

Another half hour brought them to a marked change in the terrain. To Rex, it looked like a landfill that had been recently covered with new dirt. Nothing grew there for several yards on either side of the stream, and it was a five-minute walk through it from end to end. It couldn't have been more alien to its surroundings if it had been a tar pit or an endless sand dune.

"What is this?" he asked.

"It is where the ore is dumped after all precious metals have been extracted," the young man answered. He seemed to think nothing of it, or of the fact that the sacred stream flowed through it.

"I need to take some of this dirt back with me," Rex said.

"Why? It has no more gold or silver in it."

"It may have what made the children sick in it," Rex explained.

The young man's expression was skeptical, but he waited while Rex scooped up some dirt and put it in a pocket, having nothing else to keep it in. They continued and soon were beyond the blighted area. Rex was convinced he'd found the reason, but his guide assured him they were near where the spring outflowed from the mountainside, the pool of sacred water. He reckoned he might as well see it.

In short order, they arrived. Again, it was not much to look at. Pretty, in an understated way, but it wasn't spectacular. The water didn't gush from a split in a stone, or anything dramatic. It bubbled up from under a small rock and made a pool no larger than an ordinary bathtub in area before tumbling over the lip that caused it to back up and becoming the narrow stream they'd been following. On one side of the rock, it wasn't there. On the other, it was.

Rex thought about it for a moment and concluded that the water here would not be polluted since the mine tailings were downstream. He told his companion so.

The young man knelt and scooped up a palmful. He trickled it over his head before repeating the action and taking a drink. Lastly, he scooped some up and dribbled it on the ground a few inches from the main stream. It appeared to be a minor ceremony. Rex likened it to the practice of dipping one's finger into a basin of holy water before making the sign of the cross in the Roman Catholic tradition.

He waited a few minutes and then respectfully asked if he might drink from the pool and, at the young man's nod, he took a knee to slake his thirst.

Out of respect, he led Digger back along the stream for a few feet before allowing him to do the same.

"I have seen enough," he announced. With no more discussion, they started back the way they came.

It wouldn't be confirmed until the dirt in his pocket could be analyzed, but the circumstantial evidence convinced him their theory was correct. Somehow, the water that the villagers were collecting downstream from the tailings dump was being polluted with a source of radon, most likely infused with it as it passed through the tailings.

All they'd need to do for now is avoid the water downstream and take their sacred water from above the tailings. Eventually, the mine owners should be encouraged to clean the polluted area, which would involve removing the tailings and some amount of dirt under them. Someone else would have to ramrod that. Rex felt he'd done his part by investigating it and finding the cause of the children's radiation poisoning.

When they got back to the village, Rex thanked the young man for guiding him and searched his pockets for something to give him. As soon as the young man realized what he was doing, he said no thanks were necessary and hurried away. Almost as if he didn't want to be seen with the *gringo* now that he'd violated the prohibition to show him the spring.

Rex called out another thanks, and then went to visit the doctor. She came outside the hut to talk with him, as the children were napping.

"Will they recover?" he asked after explaining what he found.

"They'll stop getting worse, at least for a time. With no further exposure, they're likely to survive. I can't say that they won't have health problems related to the exposure, sooner or later."

"What kind of problems?"

"They may develop thyroid problems, up to and including cancer. Bone density issues, maybe. Their immune systems will be compromised."

It saddened Rex and gave him renewed anger at Alexandro for his part in it. Rationally, he knew Alexandro probably hadn't meant his advice maliciously. It was more than likely ignorance. Emotionally, he couldn't separate it. He would have to process the circumstances before he'd be settled about Alexandro. Right now, he'd be grateful for a chance to at least punch him in the face.

Dr. Martinez was waiting patiently for Rex's response, he could see. She was staring at his face and ignoring Digger's attempts to engage her with a goofy grin.

"Did I miss something?" he asked. "Oh! Yeah. I have

some samples of the tailings. The spring, or rather the stream that comes from it, runs right through the tailings dump before it runs down to where the villagers usually take the sacred water."

"Where are they?"

"What?"

"The samples, Mr. Davis. Whatever has gotten into you?"

Rex wondered the same thing himself. His mind seemed scattered to the four winds.

"In my pocket," he said apologetically. "I didn't take sample bags or anything to carry it in."

She pressed her lips together. Clearly, she didn't approve of his unscientific methods. "I'll get a couple of vials," she said. She stepped back and disappeared inside her hut. She didn't invite him to accompany her. She was back in seconds, carrying two tubes that looked like blood collection vials.

"This is all I have," she said.

He took each tube from her and dipped them into his pocket, scooping as much of the dirt into them as he could, then handing them back to her to cap.

"I'll send them to a lab tomorrow."

"It *is* getting late, isn't it?"

She looked over his shoulder and said, "You're late to your own party."

He turned and looked around. Sure enough, the square was filling with people. He didn't see Luciana, and for a moment he had an idea he was going to regret leaving her alone all day while he pursued his investigations. But then he shrugged. They were soon going to have to part anyway. He'd rather she break it off with him than have to do so himself.

Confrontations with bad guys were one thing. Breaking up with a girl, he'd only done once in his life, and the scar on his heart was still tender, years later, though he didn't dwell on it anymore. He'd spent years not being able to dwell on it as a very real matter of survival.

Chapter Twenty-Five

Rex didn't rush to the guest accommodations. He was trying to decide if there was anything to keep him here after tonight. Now that he'd helped solve the mystery of the children's exposure to radiation to his satisfaction, he no longer had the nagging feeling that something was left undone.

Junior's fate would be decided by the villagers. They'd either carry out an execution or give him into Luciana's capable hands to be taken to Santa Teresa. Rex would prefer to accompany them if that were the case, but it should be decided before morning, one way or the other.

The Markses would be leaving soon, too, he assumed. It seemed like days since he'd talked to them, though in fact it was only a few hours since he'd seen them that morning. They had a bit more business to discuss – whether to ask Dr. Martinez if she could stay, or seek someone who'd be a permanent doctor for the village. Other than that, his work here was done.

Alexandro, of course, was a loose end. But Rex didn't have the resources to track him down. It was enough that he was long gone from here. If he came back, the villagers would no doubt deal with him. Rex didn't need to worry about it.

"What do you say, Digger? Have we been here long enough? Shall we head out tomorrow?"

Digger tilted his head at Rex's questioning tone. Because Rex was relaxed, the dog smiled at him and trotted happily beside him. There was something to be said about having just a dumb animal for a companion. Non-vocal, he corrected himself. Digger wasn't dumb by a long shot. He also wasn't demanding of anything but food and an occasional treat, didn't nag him if he didn't act as expected, and didn't talk his ear off.

He got amused at his internal argument, but he was at the door to Luciana's quarters. He hailed her from outside, unsure what their relationship was now. She'd separated their sleeping bags last night and rolled up in her own, with her back to him, though she hadn't suggested he go back to the Markses' quarters. When he got up this morning, she was gone. He assumed she was having her say in the discussions about what to do with Junior. He'd gone outside looking for her and run into Barry, who invited him for breakfast. He hadn't been back since.

Receiving no answer at Luciana's door, he went next door to see if the Markses were home. Flo greeted him warmly.

"Are you ready for tonight's feast?" She seemed as excited as if they hadn't attended two feasts in the village already.

"Ready as I'll ever be. No more of that *chica de jora*, though. That stuff's lethal."

The Markses both laughed at his rueful expression. Flo

dropped a morsel of leftover meat into Digger's eager mouth and rubbed his ears.

"I'm going to miss, you, pooch."

Rex looked curiously at her. "Did I miss something?"

"Barry and I are leaving in the morning. Luciana wants us to stop in Lima before we head back home and report everything that happened up here."

"Oh?" His questioning tone invited Flo to share more.

"She didn't tell you?"

"I haven't seen her since last night. No, she hasn't told me anything. What should I know?"

"Oh! Well, under questioning, Junior admitted that he knew about the Shining Path attack. In fact, it was Alexandro who told them to do it. When you drove the guerillas off, Junior had no choice but to bring the money to keep us in the deal. Otherwise, they'd have moved in, wiped out all of us and the villagers, and taken over the site on their own."

"Shit! I never would have suggested that scheme if I'd known it would put the villagers and us in such danger."

Flo put her hand on his arm. "I know you wouldn't, son. But you saved them. We can't always see the consequences of our actions. We just have to live and learn."

Rex felt sick to his stomach. He seldom had to second-guess his operations. He always did what he thought was right, and most often it was. The worst regret he'd had previously was leading his friends into an ambush that killed everyone but him and Digger. But that wasn't so much his mistake as someone else's betrayal.

Now, however, he couldn't help but dwell on what would have happened if his defenses hadn't held when Shining Path attacked. Even so, two village elders had lost their lives. He'd probably regret ever suggesting the reverse scam.

Truthfully, he'd known it was his scheme that drew them in the first place, but the fact that Alexandro was involved somehow made it worse. And he still didn't know what it meant that Junior had confessed it.

"So, what does that mean for Luciana, or me, or whatever you meant. Alexandro's involvement, I mean."

"Well, dear, it's not for us to say."

Rex noticed Barry rolling his eyes.

"But I think she wants you to help her catch him."

That news threw Rex into a minor panic before he controlled himself. It was already happening. She wanted to hunt down bad guys together. Should he do it? Was he ready to let her go if he didn't do it? Was he crazy for even thinking about staying with her any longer, when it could mean the end of his freedom?

Digger leaned against his leg, apparently sensing his distress. Absently, he reached down and patted his best friend.

"Well, buddy, I guess we'd better go and face the music."

To Flo, who appeared confused when he looked back at her, and Barry, who was studiously keeping his expression neutral, Rex said, "Ready? Let's go have ourselves a feast."

He didn't realize he'd spoken aloud to Digger.

Chapter Twenty-Six

Dusk had come on so gradually that Rex hardly noticed until they reached the square and the central fire lit it up brightly in contrast. The feast was in full swing, and in the center of the square, a sorry-looking Junior was tied to a post. Rex couldn't see any firewood stacked at his feet, but otherwise the situation put him in mind of an old Western movie, with Indians – the Native American kind – dancing around a hapless white man about to be burned at the stake. Digger went over and stood right in front of him, staring up at him with menace in his stance.

"Ray!"

Rex heard Luciana's voice calling, but he couldn't see her through the crowd at first. Then he did, and she was smiling. The way his spirits lifted when he saw her was a shock. When had he fallen for her? It confused him more than ever. When he noticed Flo's knowing look, he knew it showed on his face, too.

He consciously smoothed his features into a pleasant but otherwise neutral smile.

"I guess I'd better go see what she wants, if you'll excuse me," he said to the Markses.

"Of course, dear. I hope you work it out," Flo answered.

The happy noise of the crowd, the flickering firelight, and the sight of Luciana's exquisite face and figure combined to make Rex's progress toward her almost dream-like. Then she floated into his arms and they shared a kiss that could have lit the fire in the wood stacked around Junior, if there'd been any.

When she pulled away, Rex was reluctant to let her go, but he did.

"I hear you have plans for me," he said, forgetting Flo had intimated she shouldn't tell him.

Luciana gave him a puzzled frown. "I do?"

Now Rex was confused. "You don't?"

She laughed her magical laugh. "This could go on all night. What are you talking about?"

"Uh… Flo. Well, she kind of… Damn, I'm embarrassed."

"Don't be. I think I know what's going on. You know Flo has this romantic notion that you and I should be together and live happily ever after, don't you?"

He hadn't, but now that she said it, it made sense.

"Well, sort of…"

"So, she told you I'm going after Alexandro, and I want you to go with me."

"Something like that. And if you're going after that weasel, maybe I should."

"Ray, I don't think so. I've been in contact with the National Police. They have an idea where he is, and it's in the city. Lima. I don't have jurisdiction there, and it's not as informal there as it is here. It's best you move on."

Ray felt his jaw drop.

She's dumping me? Can't say I don't deserve it though.

It seemed he'd lost control of his face, because something in hers changed. They were standing so close that her eyes had to track his one at a time, moving back and forth. She took his face in both hands.

"I didn't mean to say that until the feast was over. Not until tomorrow morning, to be honest. I want another night with you."

Ray collected himself. "I can live with that. For now, let's not talk about it and enjoy the feast."

"Let's do."

Rex called Digger, who left his watch over Junior with a growl in his direction. The three of them ate and danced late into the night, before Luciana led Rex by the hand back to the hut.

Sometime since this morning, she'd put the sleeping bags back together.

Early the next morning, Rex woke from a peaceful sleep, the best he'd had in a week it seemed. He'd made love to Luciana as if it were the last time, and from her hints, he thought it might be.

His own thoughts on the matter were mixed, but it wasn't up to him.

The smell of coffee was what had awakened him. He sat up in the sleeping bag to see her fully dressed at the stove, pouring a cup. She turned and brought it to him, taking a seat on the top of the bedroll, her legs crossed.

Rex took his time with the coffee while Luciana petted and cooed at Digger. The silly dog rolled over on his back and let her rub his belly. It was a position of submission and trust, which told Rex, Digger was okay with Luciana being part of their pack.

When he'd finished his coffee, he slipped out of the sleeping bag. He pulled his clothes on, and then turned to find she'd stood up, too.

"So, we're moving out this morning?"

She turned to him. "I'm moving out. I take it you're going with the Markses? I think they could use your help with the llamas."

He bent to roll up his kit without answering. Soon she was doing the same with hers. When they stood, Rex could feel her pulling away.

"You're sure about this?"

She took his face in both hands. "Ray. If that's your real name. It's been wonderful knowing you. I could love you. I could.

"But I know you've got a restless soul, which prevents you from settling down. I'm not sure what it is, but I've sensed you've got something important you still must do—unfinished business. I won't be ready, and you won't be ready for commitments until you've closed that chapter."

It hit him, then, that her decision was final. And she'd hit the nail on the head, although it was a bit disquieting that it was so obvious he had unfinished business.

He turned her chin up and claimed her lips, one kiss to last a lifetime. When he drew back, a single tear tracked down her silky cheek.

He wiped the tear with his thumb and whispered, "I'll never forget you, Luciana."

"And I'll never forget you."

A FREE Novella from JC Ryan

vinci-books.com/no-doubt-free

Even paradise has shadows...

When a beautiful woman is found stabbed to death on the tranquil
island of Olib, police quickly blame her boyfriend. But, Digger, a
big black Dutch Shepherd, a trained military dog, and his alpha,
Rex Dalton, a former black ops specialist, know the police were
mistaken.

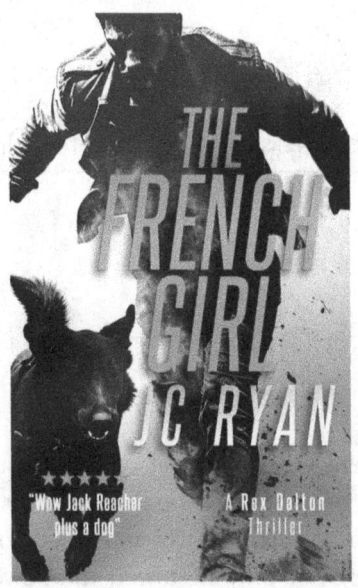

www.vinci-books.com/french-girl

A mysterious disappearance. A loyal dog.

A fight for justice.

When a captivating French woman vanishes and suspicion falls on Dalton, he and Digger are plunged into a dangerous investigation with far-reaching consequences. The duo must risk everything to save her.

Turn the page for a free preview…

The French Girl: Chapter One

Paris, France

French president Giles Raphael Aguillard raised his arms, one hand linked to that of his patrician wife's and the other to Lucien Laurent's, his newly-appointed Prime Minister. The Presidency not only bestowed the power as head of state of the French Republic on him, *ex-officio* he was now also the Co-Prince of Andorra, honorary proto-canon of the Basilica of St. John Lateran in Rome, and Grand Master of the *Légion d'honneur* and the National Order of Merit.

His triumphant smile marked the occasion—a rally and celebration following his election ten days before and today's accession to office. His teenaged and young adult children stood to their mother's side, and the Prime Minister's wife, along with several high-ranking ministers, stood to his. It was an illustrious occasion marred only by gray skies and drizzle, as the notorious wet and cold Paris January was barely begun.

Among the ministers and high-ranking officials stood a figure that had become a well-known accompaniment of the President before his election, and a frequent spokesperson since. It was the young, dark-haired, uber-intelligent head of Aguillard's communications team, Margot Lemaire, who'd engineered his resounding victory. The person who, in preparation for this occasion, rehearsed with the President until his speech was not only letter-perfect, but also pitch-perfect. Not that the new President would sing the speech—it was honed to precision to reflect the same public sentiment that had swept the President to victory in the special election.

His predecessor had served only two and a half years of his second and final five-year term when a diagnosis of aggressive brain cancer forced his imminent resignation and triggered the need for an early and abrupt election. There'd been hardly any time to campaign, but Aguillard's status as the hand-picked successor had overwhelmed the opposition party. His solemn promise to continue in the footsteps of his ill-fated predecessor, one of the most popular presidents in recent memory, and continue the most popular of his policies hadn't hurt any, either.

Margot Lemaire was content, actually, she welcomed this rare occasion to let others occupy the limelight today. She was confident of her importance to the President and of her bright future. Neither arrogant about her assets nor unaware of them, Margot was beautiful, though not spectacularly so, not at first sight. She was one of those women whose beauty proliferated the more time you spent with her. Single, friendly, and outgoing, and from a wealthy family, she moved with equal grace in the circles of the elite, the middle class, and the poor, which was what made her an excellent choice as Aguillard's campaign manager. Margot held a double PhD in political science and international affairs.

During the campaign, it had been she who graced the President's right side, where the Prime Minister stood today, while the wife and children occupied the left, closest to the President's heart as the campaign had subtly emphasized. The main planks in his brief campaign were family values and the promise that the electorate's wishes when they'd elected his predecessor for a second term would be honored; the most important of which were ambitious plans to address France's economic and immigration woes.

From the beginning, the people liked her. Before the campaign wound down, journalists and bloggers alike were writing about her elegance and unflappable demeanor under pressure, her quick understanding of any situation that might impact the campaign, and her firm grasp of the conservative principles of the prevailing party. A few bold pundits predicted that she'd be given a ministerial role in the new administration, but she herself knew she wasn't ready for that.

As the crowd roared, Margot bent down to attend to the distinguished guest seated in a wheelchair in front of her, who'd left his hospice bed to attend the inauguration of his successor.

"He makes a handsome figure, does he not?" she remarked.

"I chose well," the older gentleman said, nodding. "And you helped the people to accept that choice. Well done, my dear. Now, if you don't mind..."

"Of course." Margot's face showed sympathy and concern as she backed the wheelchair toward the stage's exit. It was too cold, and certainly too wet, for the former

President. It was her responsibility to get him out of the weather and back into the hands of his caregivers, who met her in the wings.

Rather than disrupt the speech, which was going well if the roars of the crowd were any indication, she stayed in the wings.

She shivered slightly when a light gust of ice-cold air hit her face. *It's cold. I wonder if he would allow me to take a holiday? I need it... and I think I deserve it. Somewhere nice and warm.*

As if Aguillard had eyes in the back of his head, he was aware, even as he continued his well-rehearsed speech, that Margot was leaving the stage, along with the former President.

He didn't miss a beat. Between the memorized sentences, he interrupted himself and announced, "Ladies and gentlemen, a round of applause for the able leadership of the great man who is leaving the stage. Can we all please stand and show him our support for his recovery?"

But there would be no recovery. The former President was worn out, and the doctors thought he had only weeks to live, if that. He had given everything he had to keeping a firm hand on the reins of government until the special election could be held, and Aguillard was grateful for that. He had an orderly administration to help him transition into office, though he'd shortly announce his own appointments.

Trust Margot to do the right thing. She is a gem!

After the roar of applause subsided, Aguillard went on with his speech, pausing in the right places for more applause and cheering, smiling when he imparted wit, looking fondly at his wife and children when he talked about how important they were to him, and how the nation must return to a time when family was everything. He had the crowd in the palm of his hand.

But while he spoke, Aguillard couldn't stop his mind from taking a subliminal detour to Margot. She had steered his campaign with the brilliance of a life-long politico. But unlike many campaign managers, who were at heart marketers and spin doctors, instead of attacking the opposition and making promises that could never be fulfilled, Margot promoted the principles of the party with conviction. It was a fresh new breeze in French politics, and the voters loved it.

When the election went exactly as planned, he'd offered her a junior minister position, and when she declined that on the admirable grounds that she was not yet experienced enough, he'd offered her an assistant role to a new position he was creating, like that of the Chief of Staff that American presidents relied upon. In a remarkable display of intelligence, she'd declined that, too, on the same grounds. In fact, it was she who suggested Communications was the more appropriate place for her, for now. There would be plenty of time for a ministerial assignment later.

Slightly taller than the President himself, she carried herself with the style and confidence befitting a member of the aristocracy. She dressed impeccably, as well. Unlike his wife, who'd been lovely in her youth but was now putting on weight around her middle and dressed like a dowager, Margot's attire was always at the height of fashion but appropriate for every occasion.

The sight of her long legs striding down a corridor with enough speed to lift her mid-neck length, dark, silky hair in the breeze set his heart racing. He couldn't help himself gazing at length upon her regular features—the strong, straight, well-shaped nose above full lips with just the right amount of pout, the high cheekbones leading one's attention to the wide-spaced, brown eyes and high forehead. The square chin, with just enough softness to it to make it feminine. The ear just peeking from the casual hairstyle...

He forced himself to concentrate on the speech, before he lost track of where he was. His eyes strayed back to the teleprompter.

Some of the media described Margot as part of the hope for the future of the party and France. The public and the other party leaders alike expected her to soon become one of the youngest ever junior ministers in the history of the French Republic, definitely a senior minister (*Ministre*) in the not too distant future, and some even predicted her to one day be the first woman President of France.

The only woman who'd ever come close to the position of President was Édith Cresson, who was the first and only French female Prime Minister, appointed by Francois Mitterrand in May 1991. She'd made a very bad job of her tenure and ended her career in April 1992 in a scandal of corruption within 11 months of taking office.

But this young woman was different. She was not going to disappoint the electorate. They loved her. Therefore, a cheer went up from the crowd when the President announced her appointment as his advisor in charge of press relations. Even the press loved her, as she was always good for a pithy quip, and of course, she was photogenic.

Therefore, at the first press conference after the inauguration, it was with surprise and disappointment that members of the press looked up at the podium to see, not their favorite, Margo Lemaire, but her first assistant, a decidedly less-photogenic young man.

Before he could even get the written remarks started, journalists were calling, "Where's Margot?"

"Is Margot ill? What's going on?"

The assistant was forced to answer before he could make the important announcement of several new appointments to various ministries. "Mademoiselle Lemaire is not ill. However, President Aguillard has granted her a holiday to recover from the strain of the campaign and election. Please allow her the well-deserved rest, and respect her privacy."

Some of the audience settled down. Others, employed by gossip rags, rushed out of the room to write their scoops: *Lemaire Exhausted by Campaign, Mystery Holiday for Lemaire*, and other headlines.

Meanwhile, Margot, dressed casually, wearing makeup different from her usual, large sunglasses, and a wide-brimmed hat that dipped below her eye level, boarded a Eurail train for Lyon for a brief visit to her brother before going to Italy, thence to her destination for the month-long holiday she'd negotiated with the President.

A faint smile made her expression pleasant as she handed her Eurail Pass to the conductor. He returned the smile, even though it had not been for him. Margot was thinking about her meeting with the President to request the holiday. At first, it had been contentious. He rightly pointed out that she'd only just begun her duties as his Press Secretary. However, she had made a persuasive argument, and in the end, he'd said only, "We will miss you. Come back well-rested."

She had given him her broadest smile.

"The press will not tolerate your assistant for long."

"He is completely capable. They will have nothing to complain about."

"Capable, yes. But not so pleasing on the eyes."

"Mon Président! You forget yourself!"

The French Girl: Chapter Two

Mumbai, India

Rex Dalton stepped into the baggage claim area in Mumbai's Chhatrapati Shivaji Maharaj International Airport to collect his best pal, his military-trained dog, Digger. Digger was a good traveler. It seemed as if he knew whenever he was put into a cage like that it was the beginning of a new adventure. So, Rex found him in good shape, not at all anxious. In fact, he was busy flirting with a member of the airport staff, who was showing him bits of something Rex was sure wouldn't be good for him. Digger didn't care about a healthy diet—as long as it smelled good, he gulped it up.

"Digger!"

Digger's head dipped guiltily, and he turned eyes full of innocence on Rex, who didn't buy it for a minute.

"You know better than to accept food from strangers," Rex scolded. Digger's happy smile seemed to say, "But surely this pretty lady is an exception." Rex frowned at him and then turned away before the smile could give away his amusement.

To the pretty lady in question, Rex explained in flawless Hindi that the dog was trained not to accept food from strangers, but that he only observed the rule when his master was in sight, and she was not to blame for the dog's disobedience. Nevertheless, she apologized and sent a look of regret toward the charming animal as she moved to another duty after inspecting the claim ticket.

Rex let Digger out of the cage immediately and put him on leash right away. Digger would have been perfectly well-behaved traveling through the busy airport off-leash, but the leash was required, and Digger didn't care.

"We are seriously going to have to get back to your training regimen, you hooligan," Rex said to Digger. The only word the dog understood was training, and Rex was sure he was intelligent enough to know it had been uttered in reference to his attempt at scrounging an illicit snack from that caring lady. His ears drooped momentarily. But he was soon his happy self again, as the familiar scents of Mumbai let him know where they were and maybe also realizing that he was soon to see one of his favorite human friends, Rehka, again.

Rex kept a small pied-à-terre in Mumbai as he had frequent business there. If he could be said to have a home, this was it, though he didn't think of it as such. It was merely the city where his financial administrator and IT specialist, Rehka Gyan, was based. How that had come about was a long story.

Rex could be referred to as a secret agent or special operations operative or an assassin or a spy. It was less than eighteen months ago when he still worked for a black ops outfit that went by the name of CRC – Crisis Response Consultancy. Nominally commanded by the CIA, it was actually a private company under the command of the Old Man – John Brandt – who called himself a private military contractor. Rex was their most coveted of assets – a stone-cold killer with a grudge against bad guys, especially Middle Eastern terrorists, who had killed his family when they blew up a train in Barcelona in 2004. But no one, least of all John Brandt, doubted Rex was his own man. Rex had his own definition of the 'liberty' aspect of 'life, liberty, and the pursuit of happiness'. And it didn't always coincide with his stated orders.

While Rex was on a mission in Afghanistan, Usama (the Lion), an Afghani drug lord, arranged an ambush that killed Rex's entire team, except Digger, the military dog trained and owned by the former Australian SAS operative, Trevor Madigan, Rex's good friend. Digger was now Rex's trusted companion because of a promise Trevor extracted as he lay dying.

Rex and Digger teamed up in the aftermath of the ambush and went in pursuit of those responsible. They soon caught up with them, and from the interrogation of Usama and his cohorts, Rex gathered enough information to conclude that the strings were pulled from America to get Usama to arrange the ambush. Rex also extracted from them the confession that the ambush was set up with the sole purpose to kill him and that he was presumed dead in the attack. Therefore, he'd elected to stay 'dead', take an extended vacation, and eventually determine who did it and why. He'd take care of that grudge later, when he knew more, and that was where Rehka's computer skills and Usama's money came in.

Soon after walking off the reservation and starting a new life in India, another bad guy, Prince Mutaib bin Faisal

bin Saud, had offended Rex's sensibilities by buying pleasure wives on the human trafficking market. Rehka, in fact,
was one of the victims. Rex had learned of her possible fate
from her father, whom Rex had met by chance. Rex had
investigated, found her, and taken her out of Saudi Arabia
after dispatching Mutaib, who was not only into human
trafficking but also an unscrupulous international weapons
dealer.

During her rescue, Rex learned that Rehka was an IT
specialist, and after he'd returned her to her family, he
proposed to hire her to break into the hard drives, locate
and secure the cash hidden in secure accounts all over the
world, and help him administer it for the benefit of the
victims of both bad guys.

Some of the hard drives he acquired from Usama and
Mutaib contained the information about their business dealings including the names and details of their contacts.
Those hard drives he'd placed in safe deposit boxes in a few
banks in Mumbai.

Rehka had contacted him just as his previous adventure
in Thailand was winding down and reported that she'd
found and secured all the ill-gotten money from both
Usama's and Mutaib's records. Now, what did he want her
to do with it?

From Usama, Rex had liberated cash, gold, gemstones,
and computer hard drives containing the whereabouts and
keys to retrieving secure bank accounts. He had no idea
how much money was in Usama's or Mutaib's accounts.

Tonight, after depositing his luggage and Digger's gear
at the studio apartment where he stayed, he intended to lay
in some food and other supplies, take Rehka out to a nice
dinner, and then get down to business the next day.

A few hours later, Rex and Rehka were enjoying the planned dinner, while Digger had been left at the apartment with his favorite toy, a Kong. The Kong was a hard-rubber item shaped a little like a snowman, with a hole running from the top of the snowman's head to the bottom. The hole could be stuffed with treats, and when Digger had finished teasing those out, he would pick the Kong up with his mouth and toss it. Because of its unusual shape, it bounced unpredictably, which delighted Digger as he chased and pounced on it. It would be good enough to keep him occupied until Rex had returned Rehka to her apartment after their dinner and gone back to his own in time for Digger's last walk of the night.

At dinner, Rex and Rehka caught up with the minutia of their lives. Rehka asked how he'd enjoyed Thailand, and Rex asked after their mutual friend, Aarav Patel, a Mumbai policeman who'd helped him while he was searching for Rehka's whereabouts. Rex watched her closely as she gave an animated anecdote about Aarav's children. She and Aarav's wife had become fast friends on her return to Mumbai, and the couple frequently had her over for dinner. He was happy to see how well she was doing emotionally after her ordeal in Saudi Arabia.

Rehka explained that she hadn't felt competent to advise Rex on the investment and distribution of his newly-gained wealth. She knew a little of what he wanted to do with it, because they'd discussed it before. But, acting independently as he expected her to, she'd researched until she found a discreet attorney who was also a financial planner.

"I haven't contacted him yet. I've been waiting for your

arrival so that I can show you what I've found, and after that, if you want to talk to him, I'll set up a meeting."

Rex appreciated her initiative and told her so. She was shaping up to be one of the best support assets he'd ever had, and that included the members of the CRC team that had backed him up on missions. When he'd 'gone rogue', his intention was to leave his profession behind, and he hadn't anticipated the need for his own team ever again.

Later, when he got back to his apartment and went walking with Digger along the dark streets to a nearby park where he could let his buddy off leash to run and do his thing, Rex reflected on the events of the past year. Nothing could have prepared him for the life he had now. He'd been afraid of dogs—a closely-held secret rooted in his child-hood. He'd been a highly-efficient black ops operator for CRC. Then he'd become a vagrant, but as much as he was not looking for it, it seems as if trouble had a habit of finding him.

He was enjoying his newfound freedom and his friend-ship with Digger. But in the back of his mind he knew at some stage he would have to leave his new life behind. He was not in a hurry to do it, but finally he would have to contact the Old Man and admit he was alive. If he did that, did it mean he'd go back to doing what he was best at on behalf of a country that might have betrayed him?

Digger interrupted his thoughts by returning from his own mission and leading Rex to the evidence, which Rex picked up in a plastic bag and deposited in the nearest waste receptacle on the way back to his apartment.

Well, I guess I'll think about that tomorrow.

The French Girl: Chapter Three

Mumbai, India

The next morning, he prepared a simple breakfast for himself, fed Digger his kibble mixed with some boiled eggs and a small tin of tuna in olive oil, and showed up at Rehka's apartment with Digger shortly after nine a.m.

He kissed her lightly on the cheek then unleashed Digger who immediately went over to Rehka to greet her with a wagging tail and a soft yelp as she scratched his ears. With a beaming smile, she said, "Welcome Digger. You can sit and lie anywhere you want."

She made a cup of tea for Rex and herself before they sat down, and she showed him how she used Usama and Mutaib's little notebooks in which they kept their encryption keys and pass phrases to access the hard drives and the various secret numbered offshore accounts.

She explained how, once she'd gotten access to the hard drives, it was not too difficult to get to the various secret bank accounts. Obviously, Usama and Mutaib had not been entirely paranoid about security. Maybe it was because they thought they were untouchable.

Rehka began by summarizing. There were three types of accounts.

First, money in bank accounts in their names in their own countries, i.e. Afghanistan and Saudi Arabia. That money was untouchable. There'd be tracers on the accounts against someone trying to access them, and in any case, the accounts would've been frozen while their owners' estates were being wound up.

Second, as Rex had presumed, there was money in nameless but numbered accounts in tax havens. Rehka had discovered secret accounts in financial institutions from Germany, Switzerland, and Luxembourg, none of which surprised Rex. However, there were others in such widely scattered areas as Hong Kong, Dubai, and Singapore. It seemed the demand for places where one could hide money from one's government, thanks to the globalization of economy and finance, had proliferated to include nations that weren't even dreamed of in the 1930s, when the Swiss had pioneered the strictest banking secrecy act in the world at that time.

As it turned out, from Mutaib Rex had liberated about fifty million US, which was deposited in numbered accounts to which no one without the number and security pass-phrases could get access. This was apart from the million and half US worth of gold coins and cash he took when he'd killed Mutaib.

Among Mutaib's assets were a handful of warehouses, spread across the world, packed with the stock of his trade —bullets and guns, rocket-propelled grenades, and such. These Rex would leave in place until he could go around and blow them all up. For now, leaving them to corrode away in leak-prone buildings was probably the safest option for the people living in those areas where their devious leaders, Mutaib's clients, had cornered the market on war, strife, senseless violence, drug smuggling, ethnic cleansing, and other 'peace-loving' activities.

Mutaib also had a luxury, mega-yacht cruising around the Mediterranean. This yacht, they discovered, was registered in the name of a shell company, and it took a bit of hacking and online detective work to discover that Mutaib actually owned the shell company. The company was registered in Luxembourg.

Rex was quite interested in this asset—in the back of his mind he had the idea that it would be nice to have it to cruise around Europe, off the grid. But for now, he didn't have a clue how to go about getting the ownership transferred. However, there was no urgency to get it done as it seemed Mutaib had arrangements in place with a timeshare company who had been managing and maintaining it while using it to cart people around European port cities on luxury holidays. The proceeds after costs were deposited into a secret numbered account in the Caymans.

There were also other tangible assets, some of which were inaccessible because they were publicly known, like homes and furnishings, vehicles, jewelry, and art works—all the trappings of a wealthy lifestyle.

"There might be others," Rehka said, "with possibilities for liquidation, since they'd been carefully hidden in similar fashion as the ownership of the yacht."

Rex asked her to investigate those, and unravel the complicated trail of ownership when she had some spare time. She'd discovered the assets through notes on the hard-drive records, references to this building or that warehouse full of goods. Knowing what to look for would make it easier.

As for Usama's wealth, it was mindboggling to learn that the man held in excess of forty-five million US in numbered offshore accounts. His net worth was somewhere north of seventy million, depending on how the non-cash assets were to be liquidated.

All these financial matters were a novel experience for Rex, and to be honest, utterly bewildering.

Rex had never had any other job than being a soldier, a Special Forces operator and assassin. He'd never had to worry about money. What he inherited from his parents he'd liquidated into cash and left in the bank. Most of the time, he didn't even have an idea how much money he had. He never had a need for a lot of money. The military had paid him, housed, and fed him. Later, CRC paid him, and they, too, provided food, shelter, and everything else he needed.

Save for the few thousand dollars per year he spent when he was on R and R, all of what he earned from CRC, which were not insignificant amounts, went into his savings accounts. A large part of the money he earned from CRC was placed in untraceable offshore accounts with the purpose to secure for an abundant retirement fund—if he survived the hazards of his profession for long enough to retire and enjoy it.

In short, Rex's financial experience was limited to checking his bank accounts online and withdrawing small amounts every now and then. But for security reasons, even that he hadn't done since he went rogue. By now, he had no idea exactly how much money of his own he had—by his rough calculations it could've been somewhere in the order of four million.

Nevertheless, he couldn't touch that money. Doing so would've immediately set off alarms and alerted the CIA and CRC FININT staff. Besides, there was a very good chance that all that money would have been frozen while his estate was being wound up. Having no will and no family, that money would probably end up in government's coffers once Rex had been missing long enough to be declared dead. Seven years, he thought. On more than one occasion he wanted to kick himself for not making a last will and testament when he had the chance to do so.

Damn, I could've made it plain and simple; distribute my estate in equal shares to the families of those who were killed while on missions with me. That money could've gone to the families of Frank Millard, Trevor Madigan, and the others who were slaughtered in that ambush.

Well, the US government can shove that four million into a dark place. With Usama's thirty million at my disposal I'll rectify my mistake. I'd only have to figure out how to get the money to their relatives without blowing my own cover.

He'd heard about rich people's worries being different from ordinary people's—their biggest worry being how to best use and invest their money, to make more, and to safeguard it. With all this *acquired* money and not knowing what to do with it, he was beginning to understand what the 'unfortunate' rich people had to go through.

After a few days of going through all this stuff, Rex had made up his mind. For now, there was no need to move the money out of the secured accounts. He and Rehka were the only people on the planet who would be able to get access to it.

Mutaib's money would be transferred to different banks in India and held in trust for the seven escapees, to be distributed as needed by Rehka. Her share would be handed to her in a lump sum, so she could invest it as she chose. The rest would be divided equally between the trust accounts of the remaining six women who he rescued with Rehka. The money would keep them in adequate funds for the rest of their lives.

When it came to Usama's money, Rex would take out four million and transfer it to the various accounts he'd already set up in various banks in India. This sum represented the amount he, at last check, thought he had in his American and offshore accounts. The rest he intended to distribute among the teammates who'd perished in Usama's ambush, once he could figure out how to do it without drawing any attention to himself.

Four days of studying the financial wheeling and dealing of bad guys was utterly tiring. There were times during all of it when he would have been happy to be dropped off with a fifty-pound backpack and bottle of water in the Arizona desert thirty miles from base and told to walk back, rather than sit through this. Even a few skirmishes with a bunch of terrorists had more allure than this stuff.

How the hell can any person do this stuff day in and day out and remain sane?

But, finally, he was free to continue his history tour of the world. He had to admit, it was nice to be able to spend what he wanted and not worry about where the next dollar was coming from.

After saying goodbye to Rehka while having lunch at a street café, Rex looked down at Digger and said, "My friend, you and I are going to Peru. We're going to have a look at the land of the Incas."

Digger looked at him as if to say, "Where is that?"

"Yeah, I guess you didn't pay attention in dog school during the geography lesson. But don't you worry, I'll get us there. I can promise you it's going to be much better than what you went through the last two weeks. Well, to be honest, actually anything would be better than the last two weeks."

Digger took the last piece of chicken Rex offered him, sat down, and looked down the street and back at Rex while licking his lips as if to say, "Ready when you are, buddy."

Grab your copy...
www.vinci-books.com/french-girl

About the Author

JC Ryan is a bestselling author renowned for his intricate espionage, archaeological thrillers, and conspiracy mysteries. With over 30 acclaimed novels, including the popular Rex Dalton K9 Thrillers, Rossler Foundation Mysteries, and Carter Devereux Mystery Thrillers, Ryan has captivated readers around the globe.

Drawing from his diverse professional background—as a military officer, lawyer, and IT manager—Ryan creates compelling narratives that skillfully blend historical accuracy with thrilling adventure. He is celebrated as a master storyteller, known for crafting riveting plots, meticulous historical details, and engaging, multidimensional characters. Ryan's meticulous research lends authenticity and depth to each story, immersing readers in richly constructed worlds filled with intrigue, suspense, and adventure.

Fans of David Baldacci, Lee Child's Jack Reacher, Tom Clancy's Jack Ryan, Nelson DeMille's John Corey, Vince Flynn's Mitch Rapp, Mark Greaney's Gray Man, Gregg Hurwitz's Orphan X, Robert Ludlum's Jason Bourne, Daniel Silva's Gabriel Allon, Brad Taylor's Pike Logan, Brad Thor's Scot Harvath, James Rollins' Sigma Force, Steve Berry's Cotton Malone, and Dan Brown's Robert Langdon will find JC Ryan's novels equally compelling and unforgettable.

When not writing, Ryan enjoys spending time with his college sweetheart, whom he married in 1978. They are proud parents of two daughters, have two sons-in-law, and are grandparents to two grandchildren.